UNWANTED

BWWM Dark Bully Romance

THE BEN & LIBBY SERIES
BOOK IV

JAMILA JASPER

www.jamilajasperromance.com

I dedicate this book to my Patrons. Thank you for being here with me on this journey.

Join the Patreon Community.

Contents

BOOK #5

Description

This is a dark romance. You may find some of the content in this book disturbing or triggering. I cannot warn you about every possible trigger but there will be strong language, violence, graphic scenes and disturbing content ahead. Proceed with caution.

If there was any chance of melting Ben's heart, it's gone.
He's ice-cold and thirsty for revenge.
Rapetti's most terrifying tyrant rules the college once more.
Except now, he's ten times worse with no reason to toe the line.
Libby struggles to keep her head down.
When it comes to Ben Fox, she has a way of diving head-first into trouble.

British Bully Series

The completed 6 book series
The Ben & Libby Series

Unlovable
Unattainable
Undesirable
Unwanted
Unraveled
Unbroken

***

The spin-off series
The Crispin & Amina Series

Despicable
Damaged

King of the Freaks

The worst part of my day at Rapetti. I'd forgotten how horrible it could be to find a seat in the caf. I had a place once — a seat next to Ben Fox, the king of Rapetti. For the first couple days back, I skipped lunch, but now that classes were on and I had to fight for my place as valedictorian, I had to eat properly again. So here I was: standing in the Rapetti cafeteria and scanning for an empty table.

I thought Year 13 would be different. I thought I'd have Ben. I thought I'd have Theo. But Ben had unleashed his "gag order" and Theo hadn't spoken to me since Hope's party. I just had to make it to a small table in the back, a small table with a wobbly leg in the back where I was used to eating alone as a Year 12.

We always had the best food the first week back after a long break to ease our minds before the caf returned to serving slop like fish and chips or potatoes and gravy. The tables were roughly the same. The randoms. The art freaks. The rugby boys. The popular girls.

Bess graduated from art freak to one of Hope's subjects, and Hope took Jess's place as the queen of Rapetti.

When I walked into the caf, her entire table turned to look at me and then they burst into laughter and leaned over, whispering to themselves and laughing at me.

"Fat!" Millie yelled and the entire table laughed.

Hope smacked her.

"Stop," Hope said loudly enough for me to hear, "Ben didn't dump her because she's fat. He dumped her because she's horrible in bed."

Bess laughed loudly, snorting like a piglet as I walked past. Hope grabbed my skirt as I walked past. I froze, ready to empty my cup of cranberry juice all over her fresh twist-out.

"Yes?"

"Hey, Liberty. We had a question for you."

"No thanks. I want to eat lunch in peace."

"That's not an option."

I could feel his eyes on me. He always watched from a distance, but he never intervened. I couldn't tell if he wanted to or if he was just staring because he could. Because he was Ben Fox, and even if he let me go, a part of him would always want to own me.

"Where do poor people shop?" Hope asked, snickering afterward.

Millie smacked her sister on the arm.

"Stop! You're such a bitch."

"No, seriously. Yasmin's working on a creative writing essay and since you're poor, we want to know where poor people shop."

"I don't know. Walmart."

"Ew!" Yasmin shrieked, like I'd suggested her fictional character rob graves for clothing, "That's disgusting."

"Yeah, well. It's how most of the world lives."

"We have another question," Millie piped up.

I scowled.

"Why are you still alive?"

Amira and Charlotte snickered.

"Excuse me?"

"We think you ought to kill yourself. Your rich boyfriend dumped you, you're a garbage friend and really, you have no one. So end it. Kill yourself."

Millie snickered.

"Thanks for the advice."

"Sorry, Libby. But we had to ask. I mean, you could always become a slut."

"She's already a slut," Bess added.

"Good to see you again, Bess."

I stormed off when I felt a thud on the back of my head. In surprise, I dropped my tray. Fuck. The mean girls burst into laughter and I felt another apple hit my head again. Everyone was laughing. Including the table of rugby guys. I couldn't see Ben, but he was probably laughing too. I stood up and took one apple and I flung it at Hope's head. I missed. Which only made everyone laugh even more.

I ran out of the cafeteria. I didn't notice anyone follow me, but when I turned the corner. I felt a hand on my arm. A familiar grasp. I whipped around. Ben?

No. Not Ben. Barnaby Fox.

His uniform was crisp except for his tie, which he loosened. He had black liner smudged on his lower lid and unlike Ben, he never brushed or combed his long brown hair, which still had blond streaks from a wild summer. My ex-boyfriend's twin brother clamped his hand around my arm.

"Walk with me."

"Why?" I snapped.

"We need to talk."

"I have nothing to say to you."

I tried to pull free, but Arnie shared his brother's strength and he dragged me around another corner to an isolated hallway. I freed myself and got ready to kick him in the balls and make an escape when Arnie asked softly, "Are you okay?"

"What the hell do you care?"

Arnie clamped his hand over my mouth. Tight.

"Hush, Liberty. If my brother finds me talking to you, he'll have my bollocks. In case you haven't noticed, I'm not one of the elite at Rapetti and I don't intend to be. I came after you because you gave me a chance this summer. You forgave me for being a dick. And...

it pains me to say this, but you're a sweet girl. Too good for my brother. And too good for the bitches at this school."

He dropped his hand from my mouth and I snapped, "I should have bitten you."

"Kiss me instead."

"Shut up, Arnie."

He grinned.

"Fine. Sorry. It's been a while since I've had a woman's touch."

His smile sent a pang of pain rushing through my heart. It had been three weeks since I'd seen Ben's smile. Since I'd seen him at all.

"What even happened between you and Hope?" I asked him.

I had to distract myself from thinking about Ben. I had to.

"She dumped me for trying to fuck her sister. I thought it was obvious."

I rolled my eyes.

"You deserved that."

"Yes. I did. But you don't deserve torment."

"I'm a Year 13. I need to get over it and man up."

He laughed and shoved his hands into his pockets.

"I only wanted to make sure you were okay. If you're still hungry, you can come sit with the art freaks."

I raised an eyebrow.

"Are you sure?"

"My brother might be King of Rapetti, but I'm King of the Freaks. Come on."

I followed Arnie back into the caf. This time, there was silence as we re-entered. He pulled out a chair for me at the art freaks table and went to get me lunch. No one dared say a word to him. The rumors were wrong, but everyone at school believed he was responsible for Chloe's accidental death. Claire knew the truth, but I think she spread the rumors because that's what she did — she gossiped. No one knew what happened to Jess. No one except me, Ben, and Theo.

And I would not talk if they wouldn't. I still counted on Ben to keep my secret.

"Here's your lunch, Libs. I talked the staff into giving me an extra apple."

"Thanks."

Arnie's kindness was suspicious. I couldn't tell if he wanted to make Ben mad on purpose, or if he was just being nice.

"So, meet the gang."

"We already know each other," Eugenie Sutcliffe said.

She was my new roommate. We barely spoke. She wore heavy makeup and had long brown hair with blunt bangs cut into the front. Her wide, sorrel colored eyes fixed on Arnie, who raised a curious eyebrow.

"Oh?"

"We're roommates," Eugenie and I said simultaneously.

"Very well. There's Isla," Arnie continued, pointing to a red-headed girl with chubby cheeks and freckles splattered all over her face.

"Louisa."

"Aye," Louisa responded, shoving a chip into her mouth. She had platinum blond hair, fried straight, and an aquiline nose.

"Zack."

Zack didn't look up. He had heavy hooded lids and black circles under his eyes. He had a black in fineliner pressed to a napkin as he drew a morbid scene of the grim reaper having sex with a large-breasted woman.

"And Marty."

Marty, another dark-haired boy with black nail polish on his finger-nails, grunted.

"Hey. I'm Libby."

"We know who you are, princess," Marty said, in a thick Scottish brogue, "Ben Fox's latest slag."

The table snickered until Arnie settled them with a stern glare.

"Can we talk about the rave around her?" Isla whispered, as if I couldn't hear her.

Arnie nodded.

"She's fine. She's nothing like my brother."

"Excellent," Isla said, "So there's this drain pipe a mile off campus and if we hook up speakers, we can have a party."

"How much K can you get?" Louisa asked, nudging Zack in his side.

He shrugged.

"Fuck's sake, can you pour water on his head?" Louisa snapped, her sharp temper and sudden tone causing me to sit up straight.

Arnie snapped his fingers in front of Zack's face.

"He's totally out of it."

"Hold on," Zack mumbled, "I'm finishing the nips."

He drew large pepperoni-sized nipples on the woman and then set his pen down with a sigh.

"It's shit," he muttered.

"It's good," Isla said, "Now focus! We need enough to get everyone at this table high."

"What about my brother?" Arnie asked.

Louisa scowled.

"Your dick head jock brother isn't coming anywhere this."

"Got it."

"Holy fuck. She's coming towards our table," Isla whispered.

I craned my neck and observed Danny. I smiled and waved when I saw her. Arnie leaned back, observing. I didn't bother cast a glance at the rugby table to see if Ben was watching — if he knew I was sitting with his twin brother. If it bothered him.

"Um... Liberty? Can we talk?"

"Yeah. No problem. Uh... guys, I'm gonna go."

Arnie took my hand and pressed it to his lips.

"As you wish, Liberty."

I snatched my hand away as my heart raced. Did he know what Ben would do if he saw that?

"Party's after lights out tomorrow. I'll come get you from your dorm."

I'd never agreed to go to this party, so I slung my tote bag over my shoulder and followed Danny out of the cafeteria.

"What is it, Danny?"

"I wanted to talk to you about my sister."

"Yasmin?"

"Yeah. I… Oh… I didn't want to be the one to tell you…"

"Tell me what?"

"I heard a rumor that she's going out with Ben."

Competition For First

After lunch, I had advanced physics. I was so ready to meet for our first long lecture of the week. I didn't recognize any of the other Year 13s in my class, so I picked a seat towards the back on my own. More students piled in and I hardly recognized anyone except Edward Chapman, a rugby boy who naturally sat next to one of the blonde girls up front. I was spacing out, doodling in my notes as I waited for our teacher when the last student entered the class.

Barnaby. Arnie Fox sidled in next to me. Tears pricked my eyes. He smelled exactly like Ben. It was like Ben was sitting next to me. But it wasn't him. I would never be with him again. He's already moved on. To Yasmin. Bitchy, racist Yasmin, who called her black sister her slave. I guess it made sense. She had soft, caramel skin, puckered lips and hair the color of honey. She had a perfect hour-glass figure. Half-Argentinian, half-German, she was rich too. Another Jess.

Arnie elbowed me.

"Why so blue?" he whispered.

I yanked my notebook further onto my side of the table.

"None of your business," I snapped.

"It's a wonder my brother ever warmed up to you," he grumbled.

"I don't want to talk about your stupid fucking brother."

I could feel myself starting to cry. I didn't want to cry. I didn't want to let loose every emotion. I hadn't cried since we broke up. When Ben dropped me off in London, I'd been stone-faced and unreactive. I didn't want to give him the satisfaction of seeing me heartbroken. He convinced himself he was protecting me, and he didn't care what I thought. Screw Ben.

"Neither do I," Arnie said, "I'd rather talk to you about anything else."

Thankfully, our teacher walked into the room before Arnie could question me (or annoy me). My fortune wouldn't last. Science teachers have this nasty habit of assigning group work and Mr. Higgins announced, "Your partner will be your seat mate. Today's experiment, we'll go to the tallest buildings around campus and measure gravity with tennis balls. One person from each group come to the front and select your building from a hat. Come on."

Arnie walked up to the front of the class and selected our building, returning to his seat next to me.

"Hope you don't mind getting stuck with me."

I rolled my eyes. Great. If Arnie's attitude towards school was anything like his brother's, I'd get stuck doing most of the work while he smoked cigarettes or snorted lines of coke.

"Whatever," I snapped.

Arnie grabbed our tennis balls and Mr. Higgins demanded we meet back in class after forty-five minutes of experiments. We had to go to the top of the school chapel to make our measurements. We asked the chaplain for permission and he was well aware of the annual Year 13 physics project, so he didn't have a problem with us entering the old church building. We'd have to climb to the top of the bell tower behind the organ.

"Beware of the mice!" Reverend Row warned us.

"Mice?!" I hissed to Barnaby, "That was not part of the deal…"

"You aren't scared of mice," he said calmly.

"No."

He wasn't scared of anything.

"I can tell that you're lying. Don't worry. If we find any mice, I'll catch them."

"Shut the fuck up, Barnaby."

He stopped on the spiral staircase and turned to me.

"Don't call me that."

"It is your name."

"I go by Arnie now."

"Fine. Whatever."

"I'm not my brother, Liberty. I know we look alike. I know you have a lot of resentment towards him. But it's nothing to do with me."

"Nothing to do with you? It's your fault he dumped me."

"What?"

"Yeah."

"How is it my fault?"

"You kept fucking with me. He didn't think he could keep me safe from you. It's your fault."

Arnie stepped toward me. I pressed my back against the stone wall of the stairwell as he got close.

"He's a wanker for blaming me. And I'm sorry. I really am. I have awful habits. I do bad things. But I never meant to get between you and Ben. Not really."

"I don't care what you meant. The damage is done."

"Right. Lets get this project done then. How are your physics grades? I plan on becoming this school's valedictorian, so I can't have anyone screwing with my average."

I froze. What? Since when did a Fox care about becoming valedictorian. Or grades. They were set for life. Money. Connections. Oxford enrollment. Why did Arnie want this?

"Wait what?" I scampered up the stairs behind him as he began taking them two at a time.

When we got to the top, I was out of breath, but Arnie rushed to the edge to peer out at the bird's-eye view of campus.

"You know what a valedictorian is, yeah?"

"Duh. I'm the class valedictorian," I said.

"Competition, then."

"It won't be a competition. I have no intention of losing my spot."

"Good. It will be easy for us to get a proper grade then."

We finished our experiment, and I color coded the data before we returned to the classroom. We were the first students back, so Mr. Higgins gave us permission to work on our labs in the back of the class before the rest of the students returned.

"Party tomorrow then?" Arnie asked as I worked through the lab problems on our shared document.

"Huh?"

"Drain pipe rave?"

"Can't. I have homework."

He mocked my distress.

"Can't party and keep up your grades?"

"It's not about what I can't do. It's about what I should do."

"I want you to come."

I slammed my pen down and whispered, "Why?"

"Because. I like you."

"That's really fucking weird."

"Not like that," he said, turning red, "I want to be your friend. We got off on the wrong foot. I hate my brother. It blinded me. But now that you two aren't together, I'm understanding you have a mind of your own. You aren't just Ben Fox's trophy."

"I was never anyone's trophy."

Arnie grinned.

"Then you'll come to the party."

"Whatever. I could use friends."

"Great. What do you think of Eugenie?"

"She's cool. Better than my other roommates."

"Think she'd be great in the sack?"

I rolled my eyes.

"We aren't that close."

"If you won't fuck me, I have to find a girl who will. I can't go this long without having sex. It's nightmarish. In India, there were chicks willing to bang all the fucking time."

I shifted uncomfortably in my seat. It felt wrong to be talking about sex with Ben's brother.

"I don't get your obsession," I snapped, "Not everything's about sex."

"You're no virgin," he snapped, "I remember what you and my brother got up to at Blackmoor. Hearing your moans..."

I elbowed Arnie. Hard.

"Shut up."

"Fine. Fine. Tomorrow, then?"

"Whatever."

"Wear something sexy."

"I don't need your fashion advice."

We finished as much of our lab as we could during our class period. We'd have to meet in the library to finish the rest. I went back to my room to finish homework. Eugenie was at a music lesson. She was a musical genius with perfect pitch, and she took both violin and piano lessons. I nearly missed dinner when I heard a rock hitting my window. This year, my room was on the ground floor of the Year 13 dorms, on the back side of the dormitories, so it was easier to sneak out. Not like I had anywhere to sneak out to. Until the party, at least.

I flung my window shade open and there he was. Theo Hargreaves. We hadn't spoken since Hope's party.

"Theo? What the hell are you doing here?"

"Open your window. If Ben finds out I'm here, he'll lose it."

I flung my window open and Theo climbed in. He still had his rugby uniform on and he smelled like sweat.

"You could have showered," I snapped.

"Sorry. I had to come see you. What the fuck are you playing at?"

"I'm not playing at anything."

"We all saw you at lunch with Arnie."

"So that means you saw me getting bullied by Hope and her minions."

Theo rolled his eyes.

"It's like you're trying to throw it in Ben's face."

"What are you talking about?"

"He loves you, Liberty."

"He dumped me. And I'm allowed to have friends. After what I've been through, I deserve to have friends. I used to think you were one of them."

"That's not fair."

"Isn't it? You and Ben ignore me since we get back to campus. I have no one. And Benjamin Fox doesn't own me."

"He doesn't want you to get hurt."

"He doesn't want me to emasculate him. He doesn't care about me."

"Don't say that."

"Whatever. He's the one who moved on."

"Moved on? What on Earth are you talking about?"

"I'm talking about Yasmin. Yeah, I heard all about his new girlfriend."

Theo's cheeks turned red.

Wear Black... And Cover Your Drink

I didn't expect Theo to turn bright red and mumble. I was desperate for him to deny my allegations. Desperate to learn that I was wrong about Ben and he hadn't moved on at all. I was mistaken and this stupid boarding school gossip could slip behind us.

"It isn't what you think."

"It seems simple to me. Either Ben is dating another girl, or he isn't."

"Has Ben ever been that simple?"

"Stop the cryptic games, Theo. Tell me the truth."

"I can't."

"Great. He's totally dating her."

I flopped onto my bed and held my forehead. I didn't want to cry. And in front of Theo, I wouldn't.

"Don't tell Ben I said that," he snapped.

"What makes you think I still talk to Ben?"

Theo blushed.

"I ought to shut my mouth."

"What are you doing here, anyway?"

"I'm worried about you."

"Why?"

"I need not tell you that Arnie Fox is bad news."

"Is Ben jealous?"

"No. Fuck's sake, Libby. Arnie kidnapped you. He's a bloody maniac. He killed a girl. For fun. Remember that."

"Yeah, well, you know what I did this summer. So we aren't any different. We're both murderers."

Theo was one of the few people who knew. I could trust him with this. He offered a gentle smile. His eyes were bloodshot, so he'd probably had a spliff on the way over here.

"You don't really believe that," he said.

"You don't know what I believe."

"I know it isn't like you to hang out with the art freaks."

"It's not like I have a place at the rugby table. And Hope has it out for me ever since her party."

"You could apologize to her."

"You really need to lay off the weed, Theo. I did nothing worth apologizing over. She's the one who should apologize to me."

"Danny's a weird girl. Maybe there are two sides to the story."

"Unbelievable. If you're here to justify Hope's bullshit and Ben's stupid new girlfriend, you should just go."

"I don't want to go. Believe it or not, I'm your friend."

"I don't believe it. You're Ben's friend. Why else would you ignore me the way you have since the party? That's what Ben does... he becomes the center of your universe and when he's finished, he cuts you off. Better warn Yasmin."

"Okay. Fair. I've been a shitty friend. But don't forget my fucking parents kicked me out for being gay! That fucking matters. I have shit going on. And Ben's a piece of shit, but his brother is the man I love... and you think it's been easy? It hasn't!"

He stormed over to the window. I thought he'd climb out and leave me alone to be miserable on my own. This stupid school had too many memories of me and Ben. I wanted to get over him. But... as much as I hated to admit it, I still cared. He was moving on, though. That meant somehow, I'd have to move on too.

"Great. We're both assholes then."

"I care about you, Libby. I've cared about you for a long time now. I'm not giving up on our friendship."

"Great. Can you tell me what I should wear to a drainpipe rave?"

Theo groaned. "Please tell me you aren't going to that annual freak show."

"Arnie invited me."

"Are you sleeping with him?"

"No!"

"So what, you'll do ketamine with the art freaks?"

"You've been to the rave?"

Theo shook his head.

"Their freak fest is legendary. Every year it turns to a big orgy."

"I'll leave before it gets weird then. But I want to have fun. So I'm going."

"Wear black. And uh... cover your drink."

"Do you want to come?"

Theo groaned.

"Ben would kill me."

"Who cares?"

"I have practice. I'm not completely better. Sorry, Libs. Be careful."

"I will be. It will be fine."

Theo reaches into his pocket for a small bag of weed. I wouldn't have recognized it if I hadn't watched him roll up so many times. I couldn't have illegal drugs in my room, but Theo closed it in my hand.

"Here. You'll need this tomorrow."

"I don't smoke. And this stuff is illegal, remember?"

"To get into the pipe you have to give the Proctor grass or arse.

Trust me, we'll be much better off if you don't sleep with anyone else."

"Um. Okay. The Proctor? What is this, some kind of cult? I'm allowed to sleep with other people, by the way. Friendly reminder — Ben dumped me."

"Right. I've got to go. I wanted to make sure you were okay. And make sure you don't do anything stupid."

"Okay. Fine. Tell Ben I say hi."

Theo grimaced. Yeah. Like I thought, Ben forbade him from talking to me. It was bad enough he dumped me, now he wanted to control who I talked to. I was back to being at the bottom of the Rapetti totem pole and it sucked.

I did homework after Theo left, and then Eugenia came back. She smelled like weed and vinegar and she stumbled into the room laughing hysterically to herself.

"Hey, roomie," she slurred.

"Hey."

"You're doing course work? Wow. I have done no bloody course work yet. I've been too busy working on my ceramics project."

She giggled like laughing at a private joke.

"Too bad we don't have any classes together," I lamented.

Eugene shrugged.

"Wow. You're so sweet. Why didn't we hang out last year? Right. You were stuck with the bitches. No offense."

"None taken."

"Bess talked about you a lot."

"We didn't make good roommates," I replied, desperate to sound neutral. I wanted so badly to spend one semester with a roommate who didn't hate my guts. I'd been stuck with the worst of them for Year 12.

"No. You didn't. Wow. You're so honest. It's insane, Liberty. There are so many lights in my head. Fuck. I love MDMA."

"You do hard drugs?"

She snickered.

"Hard drugs? What are you, a narc?"

"No. I was just asking."

She didn't interpret my comments as defensive.

"Fine. Yeah. I do drugs… You look sad. Do you need a hug?"

Before I could answer, Eugenie hugged me. Unprovoked, she kissed the top of my forehead before pulling away.

"There? That better?"

Not really, but I felt bad turning down her gesture.

"Yeah. A bit."

"Sweetheart. It's about that rugby bastard, isn't it? He's such a dick. You need a rebound."

"A rebound?"

I'd never considered it.

"You fuck someone else. Make him jealous."

"I couldn't do that."

I only wanted to have sex with someone I liked. When I lost my virginity to Ben, I loved him. I wanted him more than anything. I thought we'd be together forever. I still had the ring he gave me, folded in tissue paper in the back of my desk. I wanted to believe he'd come back to me.

Eugenie snapped me back into reality.

"You haven't heard the rumors then? He's fucking that Year 12 slag, Yasmin. There are pictures of them all over her social media."

Social media? If it was official on social media, that meant it was real.

"Want to see?" Eugenie asked, whipping out her phone.

"No!" I said urgently. I didn't want to see, "I believe you."

"Sweetheart, is it okay if I leave you alone tonight? I want to meet a boy after check in and I need someone to cover for me."

Eugenie started stripping down and covered herself with her towel as she plopped her products into her shower caddy.

"Yeah. It's fine."

I wanted to ask who she was meeting up with, but it felt nosy.

"I've been sleeping with Isla," she blurted out, "Not sexually. She's just depressed. I'm scared she'll hurt herself. So I sleep in her bed with her to make sure she wakes up in the morning."

"That's sweet."

"Yeah. I hope she gets better. Anyway. Will you cover?"

"Yeah. If anyone comes in here, I'll tell them you're in the health center and then I'll text you."

"Great. See you at the rave tomorrow."

Eugenie showered and got into her pajamas. We met with the rest of the dorm for our evening check-in, and I worked on my homework until late after Eugenie snuck out the window to head over to the other Year 13 girls' dorm. Barnaby texted me about the physics lab and then sent me one last message.

Arnie: Bet you ten quid Higgins gives us a pop quiz tomorrow

Me: No way he gives us a pop quiz so soon

Arnie: ten quid.

I wanted to hold on to all the money I had, but it was worth a bet. No way Higgins gave us a quiz during our second lecture.

Me: Fine.

Arnie: Sleep well.

Me: Same.

The three typing dots showed up and then disappeared. I put my phone down and crawled under the covers. I woke up in the middle of the night to my window sliding open. I gasped and sat up straight in bed. When I saw the dark brown hair cresting over the windowsill, I recognized who it belonged to.

I Don't Want Sex... Not From You

I was wrong. Why was I so freaking obsessed with Ben? I saw him everywhere. Okay, I guess I couldn't blame myself for this. For seeing him in the face of his identical twin brother.

"How the fuck did you get up here?" I snapped.

"I climbed," he groaned, "What does it fucking look like?"

"You shouldn't be here," I snapped.

He leaned against my wall.

"You're so fucking full of yourself," he groaned, rubbing his shin, which he'd apparently injured on the way up, "I'm looking for Eugenie."

"She isn't here. She's in Isla's room."

"Bollocks."

"You can leave now. I'm like half-dressed."

"Get fully dressed," Arnie snapped.

I turned on my bedroom light and gasped.

"What the fuck happened to your face?"

He had a black eye. A serious one. The bruising traveled around the eye onto his cheekbone and down to his jaw.

"My fucking brother, what do you think?"

"Why? Ben wouldn't do that to you."

"I know you have some romantic version of him in your head, but he's a twat!"

"What happened?"

"He saw me talking to you. He got angry. He warned me to stay away from you."

"So you sneaked into my bedroom? Get the hell out of here!"

"I wasn't bloody looking for you!"

He rose and paced, groaning.

"Fuck!"

"Someone will hear you and I'll get in trouble for having a boy in my room."

"No one will hear me," he grumbled.

"I'm going back to bed then."

He approached my bed and watched me. I pulled the sheets over my head, but I could still feel Barnaby Fox's eyes wandering over me. He's insane, I thought to myself. But after five minutes, I heard no movement, and I could feel his eyes. Fixed. I flung my covers off and yelled, "WHAT?!"

He looked back at me like I had two heads.

"Are you mentally fit?"

"You're the creeper staring at me," I snapped.

"If I'm going to get a black eye every time I talk to you, we will have a horrid semester. We're lab partners. You talk to my brother and tell him there's nothing happening between us."

"Your brother doesn't want to talk to me."

"Fuck's sake... do you know how much it hurts?" Barnaby whinged.

"He's your brother. And do you know what he is to me? Nothing."

"You don't care about him, then?"

"I will always care about Ben Fox. But he's dating someone else. It's clear he's moved on."

Arnie snickered.

"You think he's dating someone?"

"Yasmin. Everyone says they're dating."

"She wishes," Arnie grumbled.

"They posted on social media together. I get it. She's got that sexy Latina thing going on."

Barnaby groaned dramatically.

"I did not come up here for girl talk, love."

"Don't call me that."

I hated hearing that word. Especially in Ben's voice. The voice he shared with his obnoxious twin brother.

"Do you want to make him jealous, then?" Arnie asked.

"Um... no. I want..."

"Tell me. Do you want sex?"

I bit my lower lip... It was hard to not feel some attraction to Barnaby Fox. He looked identical to his twin brother. Everything about them was the same. But their personalities made all the difference. Arnie was a straight-up psycho. That made him undesirable to me. He looked like Ben, but he was nothing like his brother.

"I don't want sex. Not from you."

"From Zack, then?"

"Zack Lewis?!"

I'd only just met him at lunch.

"Yeah. He's a diamond heir. Y'know, blood diamonds in Zambia? Total freak. He makes art out of his hook-up's blood."

"Why would I want that..."

"I dunno. Maybe you're kinky..."

"Okay. Arnie. This is going nowhere. Eugenie's not here. So leave."

"Ever heard of a rebound?"

"Yes," I snapped, "What is it with everyone and rebounds? I don't care about rebounds. I love Ben."

He stared at me again. I wanted to smack him in his stupid face.

"Sorry, Arnie. I've never liked you that way. I don't know if this is some trick, and I'm sure we'll get like 100% on the lab… but you and me will never happen."

"Right. I'd better go then."

"Please. I'm sick and tired of people climbing into this fucking window."

"Who else has been up here?"

"Theo came earlier. He was trying to tell me to stay away from you."

"Hm."

"Are we still on for our bet?"

"Huh?"

"The pop quiz, duh."

"Naturally. I'd better go."

He left and I triple checked the lock on my window. What the hell? I didn't notice Arnie and Eugenie have any chemistry between them. I guess I'd been wrong. In the morning, I picked out my rave outfit and hung it up in my closet before putting on my uniform and heading to the caf for breakfast.

I had breakfast early and then rushed off to my creative writing class. Theo limped into creative writing early and sat next to me, groaning.

"Thanks for that," he snapped.

"What?"

"He opened his blazer and peeled open his uniform shirt to reveal a bruised, bloody ribcage."

"What the fuck happened to you?" I snapped.

"Why the fuck did you tell Ben I came into your room?"

"I didn't!"

"Sorry, I'm imagining the fact that he kicked the ever living shit out of me!"

"Theo, I swear, I didn't tell Ben anything."

"We're supposed to trust each other. To mend our friendship!"

"I do trust you! I don't know what happened or how he found out."

"I do. You told him. What the fuck?"

"Theo, I swear, it wasn't me."

"Who was it, then? No one else knew. I'm going to the health center. I knew I'd find you here cowering away. But you know what, Libby? You aren't as fucking innocent as you act."

I wanted to run after him, but Mrs. Sainsbury entered the class and chided Theo for his undone uniform. I think she thought she caught us in the middle of a sexual encounter. Once she saw Theo's bruises, she promptly sent him to the health center. I spent all morning confused. Our physics lecture was in the afternoon, and I got ready to work on the project with Barnaby.

When I walked into class — a few minutes late because I'd eaten lunch in the bathroom again and got stuck in the stall as a Year 12 had horrible diarrhea — Barnaby waved at me. But he didn't have a bruise on his face anymore. There's no way in hell that black eyes heal that quickly.

Euphoria Set In

"What the hell? What did you do to your eye?"

"Nothing," Arnie smirked, "What? Do you like the green?"

He winked, and I wanted to slam my head in to the desk.

"You came by my room last night," I accused.

"Must've been a fantasy," Barnaby prodded.

No. This wasn't possible. I could tell them apart. I always knew when Barnaby pretended to be Ben. My stomach twisted into knots as it hit me: Ben was just a better actor than his brother.

"Fuck," I whispered.

"What's going on?"

"Your fucking brother. He tricked me."

Barnaby laughed.

"I've got to hear this."

"He had a black eye and everything. It looked real…"

"Oh, it's very much real. I punched him in the face yesterday."

"Why?"

"I'm asking the questions now. What did he want?"

"Nothing. He wanted nothing."

He wanted information. I should have figured it out.

"He's a much better actor than you are," I pointed out.

Barnaby calmly asserted, "I'm positive he is. Perhaps he can give me pointers next time we pull the old switcheroo.

"Did you know?"

"Of course not."

"How can I trust you?"

"No black eye. I'm not the one who lied."

"I fucked up. I betrayed Theo."

"Were you two sleeping together?"

"No! And you can tell your stupid brother than he doesn't have to punch Theo in the face for talking to me anymore."

"Ben and I didn't end on the best of terms yesterday."

I couldn't answer Arnie because class started and after a few stiff glares, we had to focus on our work. Our new lab project was an "independent study" where we had to come up with a way to show a mechanical property for the next three weeks.

Arnie gave all his attention to our project and for a while, I forgot what drama lay outside the classroom. I still didn't know why he'd hit his brother in the face and why the hell Ben snuck into my room when he gave me the cold shoulder at every turn. Did he want to talk to me? Or control me? Or confuse me? Then there was Theo. I owed him an apology.

Just when I thought I won my ten quid bet with Arnie, Higgins handed out a pop quiz during the last ten minutes of class. Fuck. I finished first and Arnie finished his quiz just after me. I suspected he was waiting for me to finish before he stuffed his notebook in his satchel and followed me out of the classroom.

"You owe me ten quid," he whispered.

I rolled my eyes.

"Whatever."

"A bet's a bet. I'll give you a week to pay me back."

I reached into my bag and fished out £10 — entirely in coins.

"Will I see you tonight?"

"I don't know if it's a good idea."

"You won't let my brother get in your head, are you?"

"Isn't that what you're trying to do?" I accused.

"It's called friendship, Liberty. Not everything has an ulterior motive."

"What do you know about friendship?"

He winked.

"Nothing at all, I suppose. But you could use a few friends right now. Friends who aren't bitches or arseholes."

"Why did you give Ben a black eye?"

"Tell you what… We'll talk about it tonight. That way, I make sure you show up."

"Fine. I'll be there."

"Good. And don't forget to do your part of the physics project."

We were still in the beginning of the semester, so choir auditions were still going on. After the party bus singing incident, the temptation to join the school choir grew and grew. As I passed the hall where I heard singing, I impulsively thrust the door open.

Eugenie stood on the other side. She waved me over.

"You're in the choir?"

"No. Isla's the violinist for today's audition. Are you trying out?"

"I didn't prepare anything."

"That's too bloody bad," the choir director's voice boomed across the hall, "You're here and there's no one else. What are you? Alto or soprano?"

"I… I don't really know."

"No matter. You look like the sort who can sing jazz. Name?"

"Liberty Jones."

"Year 13?"

I nodded.

I didn't have time to determine the potential racial motivations for his comment about jazz. The choir director, Mikhail Smith, pulled me in front of Isla.

"What songs do you know?"

"Church songs mostly."

"Can you sing Christmas carols?"

"Um… yeah."

"Once In Royal David's City?"

Isla exchanged glances with Mikhail (he was one of the few hip teachers who liked students to use his first name).

"Um… yes."

Isla cleared her throat, and he waved her off.

"From the top, Isla."

"You want me to start now?"

Isla lifted her violin, and Mikhail shrugged.

"Do you need time to warm up?"

I wouldn't have known how to warm up.

"No."

"From the top then."

Isla played the notes and my foot tapped involuntarily along with the beat.

"Once in royal David's city stood a lonely cattle-shed…"

I sang as much of the song as I could and stopped.

"Sorry, I forgot the lyrics."

Eugenie whistled from the back of the hall, and Isla set her violin down.

"That was perfect, Libby."

Mikhail whooped.

"Perfect?! That was bloody phenomenal! We've done it. We've bloody done it! We've found our soloist."

Isla cleared her throat, and Mikhail groaned.

"Isla, I don't give a shit what Yasmin thinks. The solo isn't guaranteed to anyone, even if their parents' last name is on the list of top donors. We have her… the perfect soprano."

"W-wait… You want me to be in the choir?"

"We want you to lead the Christmas show."

"Isn't that a few months off?"

"You have time to change your mind. Yasmin expected to get the lead," Isla said.

We exchanged knowing glances. Word traveled fast around Rapetti. I knew what Isla was getting at without her having to tell me.

"I'll think about it."

Eugenie clapped and Mikhail grabbed me by the shoulders.

"Honey, I would leave my husband if it meant you agreeing to join the choir. Don't think about it. Just say yes."

"Leave her alone, Mikhail," Isla sighed.

Mikhail, realizing he was coming on too strong, dropped my shoulders. Eugenie agreed to walk back to our room with me.

"Ready for tonight?"

"I guess."

"It'll be amazing. And congrats on the choir gig. I didn't know you could sing."

"I don't sing much."

"You have a lovely voice. Plus, you deserve the solo way more than Yasmin. She's such a bitch."

"You know her?"

"Everyone in our town knows her. Rumor has it, her grandfather was a Nazi — all their money comes from stolen Jewish gold."

"That's… creepy."

"Yeah. It is. I'd watch my back if I were you. Evil runs in her veins."

Eugenie changed the subject quickly and babbled on about her and Isla and then her clothes for the party and the drugs she planned to sneak into the drainpipe. She left the room early to get ready with Louisa. She invited me over to get dressed with them, but I wanted a chance to back out in case my better judgment finally kicked in and I decided not to go to a rave with a bunch of art freak druggies.

Me: I'm sorry for telling Ben. He tricked me. I thought he was Arnie.

Theo: Whatever.

Me: I'm going to the rave tonight.

Theo: I'm staying out of it. Be careful.

Me: Thanks.

Theo: You're forgiven.

I guess that was the best I could hope for. I slipped into black jeans, a black crop top and a black denim jacket over it. Nights at the Academy could be cold. I "checked in early" pretending that I wanted to get sleep before a big test, and our dorm leader noticed nothing odd about how clunky my body looked beneath my bathrobe. She probably knew that Rapetti kids were always up to something.

I snuck out around 11 p.m. and followed the directions to the drainpipe that Ben sent me. The illegal drugs Theo gave me burned a hole in my pocket. I couldn't wait to get rid of them. Zack Lewis leaned up against the entrance of the drainpipe. I could hear music deep within, but it was too dark to see anything.

"Grass or arse."

I handed him the baggie. Zack put his cigarette out on the wall of the pipe.

"Pity," he mumbled, "It would have been a stroke of luck to bang Ben Fox's girl."

"I'm not Ben Fox's girl," I snapped.

"Then you'd do it?"

He raised his eyebrows hopefully.

"I'll pass."

"Suit yourself. The party's down that way."

"Thanks."

I walked deeper into the dark pipe, following the intermittent light of glow sticks and a makeshift strobe. I felt a hand on my arm, sweaty and desperate. Eugenie.

"Welcome to the night shift," she said in a mock-scary voice, followed up by giggles.

"I've done enough shrooms to send me to the moon. Let's dance…"

She pulled me into the crowd: her, Isla, Louisa, and Marty Stuart, all dancing against each other, limbs flailing as their drug-induced euphoria set in.

My Idiot Brother

Arms wrapped around my waist. Possessive arms. Arms that reminded me of Ben's. I yearned to lean back into those arms. To let him take me. To forget our break up. To forget everything. He nearly felt like Ben, but this close, I could smell my ex-boyfriend's twin brother, holding me and dancing on me like he knew how to move.

Ben danced, and he partied, but not like this. For Ben, partying was a way to cut loose. For Arnie, partying had been his profession since his expulsion from the Fox household. He leaned forward and whispered, "Mind if we dance?"

I didn't mind. I wanted to feel something new. To do something new. To stop worrying about stupid Rapetti Academy bullies. Arnie moved his hips against mine and I moved back, responding to him, dancing with him and allowing myself to feel alive. To feel free. I didn't choose this… Ben dumped me…

Arnie turned me around, letting go of my waist and grinning. The music was too loud for me to hear him, but he mouthed something and I nodded mindlessly. Before I knew it, he pried my mouth open and slipped something between my teeth. Instinctively — and stupidly — I swallowed.

"What the fuck was that?" I yelled.

"WHAT?"

"WHAT THE FUCK WAS THAT?"

Arnie threw his head back, brown hair falling with his tilted head.

"Relax, lab partner. It's a rave. You need a little something to keep you going."

Arnie moved off into the crowd, pulling Eugenie away from her friends and dancing with her too. Within a few seconds, they were kissing and Arnie pressed her up against the wall. Isla grabbed my hand, giggling.

"Libby," she said, "Are you high?"

"No. I don't think so."

"Good girl. Don't do drugs. I'm so sad we didn't get to know each other last year. Like… you're so nice and Bess is such a bitch…"

She trailed off and with the music, I could hardly hear what she was saying. She dragged me into their circle and they switched up the music. I didn't notice the exact moment I slipped from sober to rolling on whatever pill Arnie stuffed into my mouth. Idiot. I should have known he would try to drug me up. But I didn't feel bad… not yet, at least.

Warmth spread through me and my heart opened, filling me with the deep yearning to let everyone in. Friends. These were my friends. At least they could be. Marty Stuart got between Isla and I, and the three of us danced together for a while. Eventually, all the invitees were in the drainpipe and Zack left his post at the entrance.

He danced with Louisa and then tried to dance with me, but honestly, I was a little scared of him, so I sidled through the crowd to a group of Year 12s — the new art freaks inducted into the cult of drainpipe raves, and drug-induced weekend comas. Arnie came back over to me and dragged on my sleeve.

"What?"

"Come. Let's get some air."

I followed him to the entrance of the pipe, and he handed me a bottle of water.

"It's not drugged. Promise. You need water."

"I'm fine."

"First time?"

"For what?"

"Drugs."

"Yeah. I didn't know what you were giving me!"

"You could have spat it out."

I'm an idiot. And he was right. Too late. I was definitely… something. But it wasn't how I expected to feel. I wasn't sleepy or 'out of it'. Maybe a little loopy, and everything made me want to laugh and make out and hold someone.

I drank Arnie's water.

"Mind if I smoke?"

"I'd prefer you didn't."

"Fine. I needed air. Y'know... I like Eugenie. But I'm fucked. Whenever I get close to a girl... I can't help it."

"Can't help what?"

"I want to kill them."

"Oh..."

My heart rate quickened.

"That doesn't apply to me, right?"

"First, we aren't close. Second, I can't kill my lab partner. That would totally fuck my grades up."

"Thanks," I grumbled sarcastically.

"I need to tell you why I hit Ben."

I'd forgotten about that. With some party drug in my system and the thudding bass from the speakers rumbling in my chest, Arnie and Ben's twin-problems were the least of my concerns. He scratched his head.

"He asked me not to tell you. But... we argued about you."

"About me? Why?"

"He told me I ought to stop talking to you. That it would confuse you and make it harder for you to let go. But you're my lab partner. And I don't do what my brother tells me to."

"Oh."

"I mean… It's not like you think of us as the same fucking person. He's being shitty and self-involved."

"Yeah. I guess."

I didn't know what to think.

"Why does he care so much? He has a new girlfriend."

"Yasmin?"

My cheeks burned. Yes. Yasmin. Danny's bitchy and racist sister. Some people never learn to pick a damn struggle.

"Yes, Yasmin."

"They're not dating."

"That's what Theo said."

"So you don't trust Ben's lap dog to be honest with you?"

"Theo's not his lap dog. Don't talk shit about him."

"Whatever. Point is, Ben isn't dating Yasmin. She wants him. Badly. But he's only interested in one girl. Don't you get it, Libby? My stupid brother's obsessed with you and he wants you to move on because he thinks it will force him out of it. He wants you to hook up with someone else. Anyone except me, that is. Not like I'd go there."

"I don't want to hook up with anyone else!"

"Then you two arseholes better talk it out with each other. Because other people keep getting hurt."

"Since when do you care about people getting hurt?"

"I have my shit going on. My own demons. I don't care — but I don't want to get involved in this mess either."

"Fine. I'll talk to him."

"Perfect. Now… you're still high and I'm pissed, so can we dance or are we going to talk about feelings until sunrise?"

"Dancing. Definitely."

"Good girl."

Drugs Are Bad

The sun crawled up the countryside. Orange light filtering through the clouds with hints of the perpetually overcast gray so familiar to the United Kingdom. I stopped feeling light and loopy after a few hours, but I desperately needed sleep. Thank goodness for the weekend. Eugenie and I left the party together and walked arm in arm back to our dorm.

She opened the door and shrieked.

"What the fuck are you doing here?"

Ben. Dressed in his Saturday morning best — a white button down and black trousers — staring ahead blankly and awkwardly. His cheeks flushed.

"I… um… I wanted to talk to Libby."

"Oh… um… Libs are you okay with that?"

"Yeah."

"I'll go over to the common room."

"Thanks."

Eugenie squeezed my hand and whispered, "If you need anything, come get me."

I appreciated the sentiment, but I could handle Ben Fox. Eugenie tiptoed off and shut the door behind her. And we were alone. For the first time in… I lost track of how long. But it felt like forever since we broke up.

"You look nice."

I looked like shit. I'd been partying all night. Sweaty clothes stuck to my torso and legs. I'd ripped my tights. And I had to fight the instinct to throw my clothes off in front of Ben. We didn't have that kind of relationship anymore. Right? He was the one who dumped me.

"Are you okay?"

"I could ask you the same question."

His eye was purplish black. Arnie hit him good. Whatever their fight had really been about (I wasn't sure I trusted Arnie to tell the truth) it had been a violent altercation.

"I'm fine."

"Good."

"Fuck… Libs… I stayed up all night worried about you."

"Well, I'm fine. There's no need for you to worry."

And there's no need for you to be here. Because this is confusing. I wanted to say these words, but it was too hard. My limbs tightened into my chest and my heart pumped hard and fast. I could feel the beating in my throat.

"Are you rolling?"

"What?"

Ben strode over to me and put his finger beneath my chin, tilting my head up so our eyes met.

"Your eyes," he whispered, "they look funny. Did you do MDMA?"

I dry swallowed. I wanted to scream. I wanted to cry. I wanted to hit him in his one good eye.

"I don't know."

"What did you take?" he demanded.

"I don't know. Arnie gave me something. I'm fine."

"Fucking hell," he growled, "I'll kill him."

I yanked my chin away from him and his mouth dropped open in slight surprise, as if it just registered that he'd touched me.

"You don't have to do anything to him. I'm fine."

"You're doing drugs now?"

"I'm not doing drugs. I accidentally took drugs once. There's a difference."

"Libs, this isn't you."

"How the fuck do you know?"

"What?"

"You dumped me. Now you're back to being the same old asshole, and I'm doing what I need to do to survive at Rapetti. Don't act like you give a shit."

His hands balled into fists and his cheeks darkened again as his brows knitted together in frustration.

"Stop it."

"Stop what? Telling the truth? You dumped me out of nowhere and now you're asking me about drugs, messing with my lab partner. What the fuck do you want, Ben?"

He grabbed my arm and pulled me close to him. Instinctively, my hands pressed to his chest. No. No… I had to stop this. I couldn't let myself fall into him so easily. I couldn't allow him to worm his way into my heart like this.

"I let you go to protect you."

"I don't need your protecting."

"Apparently, you do."

Then my stomach turned, and I couldn't help it. I drank too much. Or the drugs were affecting me. I don't know. I threw up. All over Ben Fox. Fuck. He didn't seem disgusted. He pulled a handful of my hair out of my face and rubbed his hand on my back. As he rubbed my back, tears pierced my eyes.

"Let it out," he whispered.

I couldn't take it. I dropped to my knees in front of my gross puddle of sick and sobbed.

"I can't do this."

"Have some water. You'll feel better if you have water."

"No... I don't want water. I... I need you to go."

"I will not leave you like this."

"Please... I can handle it."

"Libs. You're sick. And you're not used to party drugs. I can't leave you alone."

He walked out of the door to get paper towels and the dorm mop to clean up the sick. It was still early enough that none of the Year 13 girls in my hall were awake yet — except Eugenie, I guess. Ben cleaned up, and I sat on the floor as my head pounded. Once the sick was clean, he brought me a cup of water and sat next to me on the floor.

"That is so fucking embarrassing," I groaned.

"Drugs are bad, Libs."

"How can you joke right now?"

"Lightening the mood. Not typically my forte."

"Ben... You should go."

"What if I don't want to?"

"What do you want, then?"

In Big Trouble

Eugenie burst into the room.

"We have a problem. Dean Warren's on the way."

Our new Year 13 dean was nothing like Dean Chiswick. She was strict — super strict because she knew Year 13s hardly gave a shit about the rules and were wont to break them. Ben and I leapt up.

"Shit," I said, "What are we going to do?"

"I'd better go," Ben said, hoisting the window open and a brief wave of relief at the inconsequential ground floor drop.

Eugenie pushed him toward the window.

"I've got a boatload of drugs in here."

"I'll take them," Ben said from the other side of the window. Fuck. My head was still pounding, and I smelled like liquor and a night of partying. We both did. Eugenie tossed her plastic baggie of drugs at Ben and he disappeared behind the bushes.

"We smell horrible!" I hissed, "How far off is she?"

"Dunno. Let's get into bed. Our blankets will dull the smell."

I couldn't tell if this was a drunk idea, or a brilliant idea, but the heavy thud of Dean Warren's footsteps in the hallway left little time for debate. I dove beneath my covers and we snapped the lights off. Eugenie gave a little snore as Dean Warren thrust the door open. She peered around the room, standing there for what was (in my opinion) a little too long.

"Girls?" she called.

Eugenie mumbled some fake "sleep talk" under her breath.

"Hm," Dean Warren huffed and then after a few more minutes of close observation, she disappeared. Eugenie threw her blanket off.

"Fuck, that was close."

"We have to wait for her to check down the hall."

Eugenie nodded and rubbed her eyes, yawning.

"I guess we'd better get some sleep, anyway."

She was right. We'd been up all night, and I had to meet with Arnie later in the day to get our lab work done. Ugh. I stripped down to my undies and slid back into bed. I fell asleep easily and when I woke up around noon, the first thing on my mind was Ben. We hadn't finished our conversation.

Eugenie slipped into a black Juicy Couture tracksuit and I tossed on a pair of yoga pants and a sweatshirt to go to a late brunch. With Eugenie at my side, no one in the dining hall stared at me or made any sly digs. We made it past the popular girls' table with only a moderate amount of snickering. I heard Hope whisper, "They look so trashy…"

Considering what I was used to, her snarky comments barely made an impact. I sat next to Eugenie, who groaned.

"I feel awful."

"Yeah. I feel like shit."

Ugh. Arnie strode up to the table with a large glass of apple juice and a healthy brunch salad arranged on his plate.

"Rise and shine, everyone."

"How are you so bloody lively?" Zack groaned.

"New day. Lots to accomplish. Why not, eh?"

"What's got you all so tired?"

"Warren scouted the girls' dorm this morning," Eugenie said.

"Ah yes. Searching for drugs?" Arnie asked.

"We think."

"Or fornicators," Marty Stuart pointed out.

We all nodded and agreed that was just as likely.

"I take it you stayed out of trouble."

"Yeah. We did."

Before we could continue our banal conversation, a loud shriek pierced through the caf. We all looked over at the popular table. Standing in front of it — Danny. Drenched to the bone in milk. Yasmin stood up and poured more milk over her while the others laughed. Everyone laughed. Even Eugenie couldn't help but chuckle.

"It's in my hair!" Danny yelped.

"Who cares, dumps? Trying to impress someone?"

I couldn't stand back and watch. I leapt out of my seat and got between Yasmin and her adopted sister.

"Stop it. Right now."

"Or what?" Yasmin snapped, her lips fixed in a bee-stung pout.

"Or you'll find out what. Now back off."

"You back off," Hope said, standing next to Yasmin, "Don't you get it, Libby? We don't like you. Nobody at the bloody school likes you."

"Leave her alone."

"You don't get to tell me what to do. You're a dirty slag."

"I know what it is," Yasmin smirked, "She's jealous because I fucked her ex."

Hope and Yasmin laughed.

"Listen, I don't care what bitchy words you have to say to me. Danny, get out of here."

She didn't need me to tell her twice. Danny ran, but as I turned my back, I felt a cold liquid hit the top of my head. Fuck. I should have seen that coming. Yasmin poured her glass of milk over me after Hope did. My fists clenched. I couldn't risk my scholarship. I couldn't get into a fight and lose everything. But as rage coursed through me, I had to do something. My hands shot out against my will and I pushed Yasmin — hard. Unfortunately, Dean Warren entered the caf at that exact moment.

And all she saw was me pushing over a Year 12 girl.

"Liberty Jones!" she huffed, "Get over here this instant!"

Millie called after me, "Sayonara, fat whore."

The rest of popular girls laughed and the caf snickered as I stormed over to Dean Warren.

"Come here you little hooligan, we're going straight to my office."

She dragged me by the sleeves, apparently not noticing that they drenched me in gross cafeteria 2% milk. Once she shoved the door open to her office, she snapped, "Sit right here! I have a phone call and then I'll be out to deal with you."

I took the only seat open in the dean's office. A seat next to Ben Fox, who Dean Warren had apparently brought in too.

"Fancy seeing you here," he said, grinning from ear to ear, looking handsome even with a black eye.

"I'm fucked," I groaned.

Warren slammed the door to her private office and struck up a loud phone conversation. And once again, I was alone with Ben. But this time, we were both in big trouble.

"What are you in here for?" I asked him.

Narc

"I'm here because Yasmin's a narc and told Warren that I had drugs and liquor in my room."

Yasmin's name made me bristle. Her cruelty surpassed Jess's. My hair and weekend lounge clothes were still wet. Ben wrinkled his nose before I could make a smart-ass comment about his choice in friends.

"Why do you smell like milk?"

"It's a long story."

"I want to hear it."

"Maybe Yasmin can tell you," I snapped.

"Can you stop bringing her up?"

"I didn't bring her up. You brought her up."

"No, I didn't."

"Yes, you did. You just told me she was a narc."

"Yeah, but that doesn't count as bringing her up."

"Yes, it absolutely does."

"I don't want to sit here and argue with you."

"Fine. Don't."

"Fine."

We crossed our arms and stared straight ahead. Dean Warren's clock ticked. Her loud horse-like laugh emanated from her office. Was she planning on holding us here until the end of time? Her stupid phone call was taking forever.

"Yasmin and I are not together. Never will be. I've never even kissed her."

"Whatever. That's your business, not mine."

"Yeah. Right. I know you, Liberty. You're jealous."

"Jealous? Why the hell would I be jealous?"

"You can't lie to me."

"Listen, Ben. We're broken up. It's probably for the best if we left each other alone."

"Who threw milk all over you?"

"Are you listening to me at all?" I snapped.

"I'm listening well. But I asked a question."

"Hope, Yasmin, the rest of their stupid minions. They were bullying Danny again, and I played the hero and foolishly step in."

"Ah."

"Not like you care. I've seen you laughing as they torture people."

"I mean... it's a bit funny."

"To you, maybe. Sitting on your rugby high horse, knowing that no one dares cross the great Ben Fox."

"They'll pay for hurting you."

"I don't need you to step in and fight my battles for me."

I kicked my sneaker against the tiles and flinched as Ben's hand touched my thigh. He shouldn't do this.

"Warren should let you change first."

"Well, she didn't."

"I'm sorry."

"For what?"

"I made a mistake."

My throat tightened. Made a mistake about what? Before I could ask, Dean Warren thrust her door open.

"In here this instant, Mr. Fox."

"Yes, ma'am."

He winked at me before entering her office, and then Dean Warren shut the door. Their conversation never got loud, but it lasted at least twenty minutes. By then, I smelled of spoiled milk. When Dean Warren sent Ben on his way, she wrinkled her nose before inviting me into her office.

"Liberty, have a seat."

I sat perched uncomfortably.

"What on earth is that dreadful smell? Do you bathe?"

"Yes, I bathe," I said, holding onto my calm because in this situation, I had no power, and getting on the dean's unpleasant side was an awful idea, "Two of the girls poured milk on me before you found me."

"Why would they do such a thing? Were you aggressive?"

"No. I was standing up for a younger girl."

"When I saw you, you were pushing another girl. That doesn't look like stand up behavior where I'm sitting."

"I'm sorry, Dean Warren. I'll never do it again."

"Liberty, you're a star student and everyone speaks highly of you, so I'll make sure this issue proceeds no further. But you need to apologize to Yasmin and the other girls at their table. I'll ask them if they received an apology by next week. That's it."

"That's it?"

"I'm more than reasonable, Miss Jones."

"Thank you, Dean Warren. I'm sorry. I guess I lost control."

"Make sure you don't lose control again."

"Yes, Dean Warren."

"Good. You're dismissed. Please take a shower."

"Yes, Dean Warren. Right away."

Really, I'd got off light. Maybe Dean Warren's reputation for being strict had been overblown. I hurried out of the office and walked down the hallway towards the exit to the building, when an arm reached out and yanked me toward one of the more isolated hallways. I tried to scream when a hand clasped over my mouth.

I elbowed back hard when I heard Ben groan.

"Libby, what the fuck?"

I pried myself away from him.

"What the hell were you doing?"

"Trying to keep you quiet..." he uttered through more groaning.

Oops.

"Well, sorry," I whispered, "Who goes around dragging women from behind?"

"I thought you'd recognize me."

"What do you want, Ben?"

"To talk. That's all."

"Let's go into a classroom. 301A should be empty."

"How do you know?"

"I booked a study room to do homework with Arnie later today."

Ben grunted.

"My fucking arsehole brother."

"We're lab partners! Higgins assigned us."

He dragged me into a classroom and shut the door behind us. His eye still made me feel awful when I looked at it.

"What did Warren tell you?" he asked.

"Why do you care?"

"Answer the bloody question."

"She said that she wanted me to apologize to them. Whatever. It could have been worse."

"Good. Good."

"What about you?"

"I've got to go to drug and alcohol counseling. Again."

"I'm sorry. Eugenie and I didn't mean for you to get in trouble."

"It's fine."

"It's not. I'll tell her, and maybe we could make it up to you."

He raised an eyebrow.

"How?"

"I don't know," I said.

Ben grinned.

"I know exactly how."

A Lump In My Throat

"You know what... nevermind."

I rushed to the door, but Ben grabbed my hand. I wasn't fast enough to get away from him, and I totally should have been able to predict that Ben Fox would grab me the second he had a chance. I froze.

"I want you to kiss me."

"What?!"

"That's how you can make it up to me. Kiss me."

"Ben... We're broken up. Remember?"

"I know. But it's what I want. One kiss."

"Won't that confuse things?"

Okay. Maybe that black eye knocked a few brain cells loose because I couldn't think of any sane reason that Ben Fox would want me to kiss him in a school classroom on a weekend, after we'd come from the dean's office.

"No. It's a simple request, Liberty."

He let go of my arm. Giving me a choice. My heart pounded. Why the hell was I so nervous. It wasn't like I never kissed Ben before. Kissing him was old news. Something I was more than familiar with. Why did kissing him make my palms sweaty and my heart race? I was the old Libby again, permanently single, and desperately uncool. And Ben was… the same old Ben. Suave. Tricky. That perfect combination of dark and alluring.

I couldn't walk away from him. I wasn't strong enough. Wasn't that why he'd dumped me? He knew I'd never leave him. So he'd left me instead. For my safety. Given the chance, I'd dive headfirst into him again. So I did. I tiptoed and kissed him. I tried to make it a peck, but Ben wrapped his arms around my waist and kissed me back. Hard.

His tongue slipped into my mouth, and my fingers rushed to his hair. I raked them through his golden-brown locks, grabbing onto handfuls of his hair as our faces smashed together. Fuck. I had to stop this. I had to. He reached for my sweater, grabbing the zip and tugging until he exposed my white crop top beneath it, exposing my mahogany stomach and my low-rise yoga pants.

Ben ripped my sweatshirt off my shoulders and slid his hand over my stomach. His touch was firm. Commanding. And I wanted him. I wanted him so badly that I wasn't in control of my better senses. My body responded to him against my will, hurtling toward this train wreck decision.

He reached over my bra and flicked his fingers across my nipples. I let out a moan as Ben's tongue trailed to my neck and he sucked some of my flesh between his lips. He squeezed my hips as he held me close, pulling away for a moment to whisper, "I couldn't fuck another girl. Not after I've had you."

Our lips met again, and he hoisted me onto the teacher's desk at the front of the classroom. He positioned himself between my legs and my ankles hooked around him. His hand rushed to my cheek, and he pressed his forehead to mine, his green eyes locked with mine.

"I'm going to fuck you."

A lump formed in my throat.

"I know."

"It's a bad idea, isn't it?" he murmured, "It will fuck everything up."

"I don't care."

"I don't want to hurt you."

I bit my lower lip. How could I tell Ben that there was no way he could hurt me anymore than he already had? I hated our breakup. I hated not having him anymore. I hated feeling like I ought to be single. Like I ought to find someone else to love. I promised myself to him forever. And I meant that.

"I don't care."

"Fuck…"

He gripped the small of my back and I wriggled out of my pants, shaking them to the floor. He slipped his hand past my underwear and groaned.

"How are you so fucking wet?"

He buried his lips against my neck as I stroked his hair, my legs shaking in anticipation. I reached for his belt and undid it, sliding his slacks down as he reached for a condom in his back pocket.

"We have to be quick," I whispered.

"I want to take my time with you."

"Ben… we're in a classroom."

He smiled, that devilish smile of his, and whispered, "Moan softly then."

He rolled the condom onto his hardness and gripped the small of my back as he pressed the tip against my soaked entrance.

As Tight As I Remember

I cried out as Ben entered me. His veiny hardness slid between my legs all the way to the hilt. My fingers teased strands of his hair as his hips edged forward, driving his hardness into me. He carried me against the classroom wall and clamped one of his hands over my mouth as he worked his hips between my legs.

"Don't moan too loud," he murmured.

I couldn't believe this was happening. Me and Ben again. It should have felt wrong. I should have pushed him off. But I hooked my ankles around his lower back and drew him into me deeper. I moaned as my breasts bounced and his hips moved with an erotic rhythm. Ben Fox... I was having sex with Ben Fox again. And fuck. It felt good.

He plunged into me, harder. His urgent need for me present in his tensed muscles, his intently pinched brow, and the way he buried himself in me. I ran my fingers along his cheek, the sharp jawline and the prickle of stubble beneath my fingertips drove me wild. I wanted him. I wanted him so badly that this seemed inevitable. I couldn't stop myself from cumming. The tightness and swirling pleasure as Ben entered and withdrew from me drove me mad and I came hard. With his hand clamped over my mouth to stifle my moans, I didn't bother holding back my screams.

He bent his head down and swirled his tongue around my nipples again. His warm, wet mouth sent shivers of illicit pleasure surging through me. I came again, thinking about how we could get caught any time and I'd be here, legs spread as Ben's massive cock slid in and out of my tight entrance.

Ben pumped into me hard until he came. He groaned, his lips sucking on my neck as his cock throbbed and erupted between my legs. When my euphoria settled from the spontaneous and highly illicit weekend classroom quickie, I scrambled into my clothes.

"Holy shit," I whispered.

"You're tight as I remember, babe."

My cheeks burned. His dick was as big as I remembered. Maybe bigger. But whatever we just did shouldn't have happened. No way in hell.

"We should get out of here before someone catches us," I insisted.

"We should talk."

My heart pounded. Talk. What the hell was there to talk about? I had sex with my ex-boyfriend in a school classroom. I didn't think we'd talk to each other again. I didn't think we'd end up here. I didn't know what to say. I knew this was wrong and that sex wouldn't change anything. This was Ben Fox, the hottest guy in school. He could have sex no-strings-attached. I'd always known that about him. That sex didn't always mean love. Not for him.

But he was the guy I lost my virginity to. I'd always have feelings for him. I'd always remember him as my first everything. My first love. My first time. My first proper boyfriend. The first guy to promise me the world and then make it all come crashing down. He dumped me to protect me, but this... this fucked with my head. I didn't feel protected. I felt... confused.

I had to get out of there.

"Can't. I've got homework."

"Homework? Homework can't possibly be more important than what's happened here."

"I'm sorry, Ben. I've got to go."

"Liberty!"

I ran out of the classroom and sprinted away. He didn't care that I still stank like dining hall milk, I guess, but as I ran the gross smell of my earlier bullies' abuse overwhelmed me. My nostrils and throat burned, and as I left the schoolhouse, I threw up on the lawn. I wanted to keel over and cry right there, but I didn't want anyone to see me, so I ran back to the dorm, threw my clothes off and jumped in the shower. It took a long time and an overload of shampoo and conditioner to get the smell of milk out of my hair.

Sometimes I wonder why I even bother with my natural hair... It's long but sensitive and all this stupid shampoo won't help in the long run. I wrap my hair in a microfiber towel and walk back to my bedroom. Eugenie's off somewhere doing some art thing and I have some time before my homework meeting with Arnie. Even if he isn't Ben, I can't help but think of Ben when I see him, which means I'll think of the way Ben hoisted me up in the classroom and we had sex. Quick, thoughtless sex. An animal drive pushed us to bang, and I felt so stupid.

Am I a slut for having a quickie with a guy in the school class-room? Am I a slut for having sex with my ex? What if everyone found out?

Arnie: Changing meeting place. I'm in the library.

Me: Okay. Be right there.

Fuck. Time crept up on me and I had to meet Arnie. I threw on a pair of black jeans and a hoodie and trudged across the windy field from my dorm to the library. Arnie wasn't hard to find. He's picked a private glass study room on the bottom floor and he'd spread his physics books out over the table. He hunched over his work, fixated hard on the problems we had assigned outside of lab. I'd already finished them.

When I pushed the door open, he smiled and the lump in my chest did a little flip. Ben. Fuck. Seeing him made me think of Ben as I expected. Why had I just had sex with Ben?

"Have a seat," his twin brother said. An informal greeting as he chewed on his pen before finishing off the problem with a swish.

Deal With The Devil

"You have number six wrong," I pointed out.

Arnie scowled.

"No. I don't. You carry the 1."

"Yeah. And then you need to divide by g."

"Fuck."

"Told you."

Arnie glowered at my smugness.

"What's with you?"

"Nothing."

"You seem different... more... happy."

"I told you. Nothing."

"Did you talk to my brother?"

Talk… yeah. We talked. Well, not so much talking as tonsil hockey and sex. But we talked. Sort of.

"Yeah. Mhmm."

"You two totally banged."

"Shut up, Arnie!"

"Did it happen or not?"

"I will not talk about my sex life with Ben's twin. That's gross."

"So you admit you have a sex life?"

"Quiet, Arnie. We have work to do."

"We have plenty of time to work. I want to know how you and my brother worked things out."

"We haven't worked things out."

"But you had sex…"

"Arnie!"

"Sorry. This is good gossip. Could come in handy."

"Are you trying to get dirt on me?"

"I like having dirt on everyone. Keeps me informed."

"Keeps you in charge. God, you're so much like your brother."

"Don't insult me."

"How is that an insult?"

"If I were my brother, I never would have been stupid enough to dump you."

"Oh please. You're part of the reason... If you hadn't pulled that stupid hypnosis trick..."

Arnie laughed.

"What the hell is so funny?"

"You believed that?"

"Um... yes...?"

"Sweetheart. Sorry to confess now, but... it was drugs."

"What?"

"I quit once I figured Ben was getting close. Hypnosis is all bullshit. How did you fall for that?"

"But it worked... I swear..."

"Okay, fine. The power of suggestion has something to it but... I was only having a bit of fun."

"You ruined my relationship..."

"Are you upset?"

"No, Arnie. I'm fucking thrilled that you're a psychotic little twatwaffle."

"Where d'you learn language like that?"

"Do you even feel sorry?!"

"Not particularly."

"Ugh! You make me so angry."

"There's no point in being angry. It won't affect me."

"Screw you."

"Listen… We have to finish this course work. Why don't we take care of it and then I'll make it up to you?"

"How?!"

"A plan, obviously. To make sure Ben gets back together with you."

"Sounds like making a deal with the devil," I grumbled.

"I'm much, much worse than the devil."

"You wish," I snorted, "Deep down, Arnie… I think you're just an angry rich boy who does horrible shit to lash out. But I know your type. I know your twin. And I don't even think you're a real sociopath. I bet you wish you were. But somewhere beneath all your twisted games, there's someone with a heart of gold."

His ears turned bright red, and he flipped the pages of our lab assignment furiously.

"Believe what you want."

Yeah. I was right, wasn't I? Barnaby Fox might have been a piece of shit. He might have even been a murderer. But beneath all of that, there was somebody who could change. Maybe one day he'd become a good person. Most likely not today. We worked quietly for a while. I knew I ought to be angrier at Arnie, but how could I? I knew what to expect from him. He'd made it clear from the first time he met me. He was dangerous. Untrustworthy. He lied to get his way, and he'd do anything for attention.

When we finished our homework, he packed his things hurriedly, but I stepped in front of the door before he could escape. Nice try…

"So… what exactly were you drugging me with?"

"It doesn't matter."

"How am I supposed to trust you?"

"You shouldn't."

"What if I want to? We're working together on physics the entire year. We're friends with some same people. Can't we be friends? Like… proper friends?"

"I don't think my brother would like that."

"Is that what it is then? You don't want to share anything with Ben."

"Haven't we shared enough? We even shared a bloody womb."

"You're jealous of Ben?"

"I said nothing about being jealous. Now can you get out of my way?"

"Jeez. I didn't know you had such a sensitive side."

"You'll find out how sensitive I am if you don't move."

I stepped out of the way. It wasn't a big victory, but I was making progress. Arnie didn't push the door immediately.

"We have a deal, then? I'll help you and my brother get back together?"

"I don't know if I should believe you."

"Fine. We'll meet next weekend. Rapetti royalty are having a party, and Ben gave me an invitation. Plus one. I told him I was bringing Eugenie but… I'm sure she'll understand."

"Um… won't she take it the wrong way if you bring me instead?"

"Worry about what you will wear. This is Millie and Hope's party, so… you must dress up."

"Ugh. Everyone there hates me."

"I don't care. I'll work out a plan and you need to worry about looking absolutely fuckable."

"Arnie!"

"What? That sweatshirt get up is hideous."

"Thanks for the input."

Arnie didn't get my sarcasm, or he ignored it and he stormed off. I left the library for a while to get a late (and lonely) dinner. The cafeteria staff were cleaning up, but I made enough friends to get a late dinner. I returned to the library to get some homework done and grabbed the study room I'd been in with Arnie earlier.

After homework, I ran into Eugenie, and we chatted about everything. I guess Arnie hadn't told her I was his new plus one. Ugh. I climbed into bed kind of early, dreading Monday. Who doesn't dread Mondays when there's school to attend?

My phone buzzing woke me in the middle of the night. Who the hell was calling at midnight from an unknown number? I crawled out of bed and snuck into the hallway. Maybe it was Rita? It was only six p.m. her time.

"Hello?"

"Libs. It's me. Marley."

When Someone Has Your Sex Tape

"Marley? It's late? Where are you?"

"I'm in Scotland. Doing work for your dear boyfriend."

I bit down on my lower lip. Didn't Marley know we'd broken up?

"We aren't together anymore."

"Yeah. Right. Not based on what I found."

"What are you talking about?"

"Unless there's another dark-skinned girl at your school... there's a livestream of someone who looks exactly like dear Benjamin plowing into some girl in a classroom."

"What?"

"Yeah. The school has security cameras everywhere. Looks like someone hacked into it and clipped the livestream, uploaded it to the dark web."

"Are you serious?"

"I can send you the files but… be careful, Libby. I need to tell Ben about this, but I wanted you to watch your back."

"Sure. Fine. I'll watch my back."

"I'm serious. The caption was disturbing."

"What was it?"

"I'll send it to you. Not your school email. Give me the address."

I gave Marley an outside email address.

"Talk later. Your boyfriend's blowing up my phone."

"He's not my boyfriend…"

"Yeah. Right."

I hung up and felt sick. I walked to the bathroom and splashed water on my face. It was late, but there was only one person I could think of to message.

Me: Did you film me and Ben?

Arnie: So you had sex…

Me: Shut up…

Arnie: Sorry, love. Not that kinky.

Me: Love… ew.

Arnie: ;)

Me: I'm serious.

Arnie: So am I.

Me: So this isn't part of your grand plan to get us back together.

Arnie: It's late. Finishing history essay. England kicks ass.

Me: If you call colonizing most countries on the planet kicking ass…

Arnie: Cheers. Go to sleep.

Shit. My best hope was that somehow Arnie hacked into the cameras and posting the video to the dark web. He was dark. He was smart. That meant he knew about the dark web, right? And he was a liar. A known liar. But I believed him when he said he didn't know. He wasn't the sort to make your life a living hell unless he could gloat about it. He didn't have much of a motive for filming us. But who did? I closed one of the bathroom stalls and unlocked my phone to check my email.

From: celloboy01@benfox.net

Subject: video + screenshot of caption

Libby, check it out.

Attachment: sex_video.mov

Attachment 2: screenshot_241243.jpg

Marley

P.S.

Ben will kill me for sending you this. RIP.

We weren't exactly on good terms the last time we saw each other, but now that Marley was back in Scotland and apparently doing work for Ben that required him to be on Ben's private email servers, I couldn't help but appreciate him for this, even if it meant talking to Ben again, which I'd have to do. How could I have been so stupid? After all the incidents with Jess last year, after everything that happened… why didn't I think of cameras?

Caught up in the heat of the moment, wrapped under Benjamin Fox's spell, as usual, I'd plunged headfirst into danger. And what the hell was Marley's email address? www.benfox.net? Someone pushed open the bathroom door, and I lifted my feet up onto the toilet seat so no one could see me. It's not like there was a rule against the bathroom. Something about getting a video of your sex tape in your email inbox makes you a little paranoid, I guess.

A gross retching sound followed by the acrid scent of vomit wafted over the bathroom stall. I plugged my nose and waited for the mysterious midnight nausea queen to vacate the premises before I turned my sound off and watched the video. The guy in the video was obviously Ben. But it wasn't so obvious that the girl was me. Except… I'm the only person with skin as dark as mine at all of Rapetti. And just my luck, the video was in color.

"Fuck…"

I opened the screenshot. I gasped, nearly dropping my phone in the toilet when I saw it. No, no, no… This was bad. This was terrible.

Ebony school slut gets plowed by a white athlete. What will happen if Oxford University finds out their star scholarship girl is a total slut who takes every cock she can get?

My stomach turned. Another email pinged on my phone.

From: celloboy01@benfox.net

Subject: update

Video down. But someone still has that file. I have an audition tomorrow. Talk to Ben.

You ok?

Marley

No. I wasn't okay. I didn't know if I'd ever be okay after what I saw. The video was only one minute long, but there were... noises. My noises. My moaning. And my body pinned beneath Ben's as we had sex. We weren't even together. This wasn't fair. I wanted to cry. I wanted to delete the emails. But none of that would help. Marley was right. I had to find out whoever had the file, and I had to talk to Ben.

I snuck back into bed and tried to fall asleep. When you know someone has an illegally recorded sex tape of you they plan to release to your university, it makes it hard to think about anything else. In the morning, I waited for Eugenie to leave for breakfast so I could have one pocket of peace before my day started. A lump formed in my stomach with the realization that everyone at school could already have the tape. And they'd know it was me. And they'd call me a slut, even if Ben was the only guy I'd ever been with, no one would care. It would just be one more reason to bully me. One more reason to ruin my life.

I pulled on my plaid skirt, white button down, navy cardigan and hung my tie in a lazy, loose knot around my neck as I slid into white sneakers. Fuck it. I couldn't stay scared forever. For now, this was out of my hands. I had to stay on top of things. For once in my goddamned life, I couldn't let the Rapetti Academy bullies win.

The Reason My Best Friend's Dead

Nothing seemed out of place when I walked into the caf. Whoever the mystery hacker was, they hadn't sent the video to the entire school, so I was safe for now. I sat down at the regular art-freak table. Eugenie and Isla had an early morning class, so they left the table first.

Zack Lewis had giant dark circles under his eyes as he asked Arnie to review his essay.

"Your grammar's shit, mate."

"No, it isn't, you twat."

"There are commas everywhere. How bloody old are you?"

"Old enough to kick your arse."

"You wouldn't dare."

"Don't count on it."

Arnie scribbled on the essay in a red pen with a flourish.

"You have about an hour to get this fixed. And your conclusion's rather weak."

"Fuck's sake. Who decided we ought to learn this bloody language?"

"You mean English?" Marty says, "Mate, it's better than learning Gaelic.Way easier."

Marty smirked and turned to me.

"What's wrong with you?"

"Me?"

"Yeah. You okay?"

"She hooked up with Benjamin," Arnie blurted out.

"Arnie! Can you shut up!"

Marty snickered. Zack set his essay down, apparently giving up on his English grade to pursue boarding school breakfast gossip.

"So… does that mean you're back in with the cool kids?" Zack asked.

"No. I'm not in with anyone. And Arnie shouldn't have said anything."

I elbowed him… hard. But he only laughed.

"Why did you ask me if I filmed you?" Arnie said.

My cheeks burned.

"Are you trying to embarrass me?"

"Listen," Zack replied somberly, "We don't kink shame around here."

"Kink shame?! It's not a kink!"

"I wouldn't mind getting filmed," Marty trailed off, "Except my cock's not very big."

I guess they would not linger on the subject for long.

"What's the point of filming?" Arnie pointed out.

"Making your personal porno. Isn't it obvious?"

Louisa sat down with a small bowl of oatmeal and with another girl present, the boys finally stopped giving me the "one of the boys" breakfast treatment and packed away their porno talk. Arnie waited for me to leave for class before he raced to keep up with me.

"We aren't going to the same classroom," I said harshly.

"Upset?"

"No. Not really. I know what to expect from you."

"Ouch."

My harshness didn't deter him.

"Plan Benjamin's under way. But there's a problem."

"What?"

"He's bringing Yasmin as his plus one."

"Oh."

"Yeah… Don't worry. I'll take one for the team and distract her."

"I don't think I should have to steal Ben away from someone to get him back."

"Come off it, Libs. Yasmin and her little minions are bitchy slags. You need not worry about them. Ben would never choose Yasmin over a good girl. He likes… I dunno… corrupting you."

"That's your opinion. Not a fact."

"Well… we're at your classroom and I've got to run. Getting illegal liquor delivered to campus by the crate."

"You're nuts. Warren's been on the warpath, especially with the Year 13s."

"Unlike you and my idiot brother, I won't get caught. Especially not by Warren."

"How the hell are we even friends?"

"We're not, remember?" Arnie replied, "I have to prove myself to you first."

Ugh. He was right. I let him get away with being a total prick because of the promise he'll undo the damage he's done. He's Benjamin's twin brother, after all. If there's one person who knew Ben well enough to help sort things out, it would be Arnie. Even if he was annoying. Theo walked into class behind me with a scowl.

"Libs."

"Hey. Everything okay?"

"Yeah. Haven't seen you around much."

"You're only doing what your master commands."

"I realize you didn't snitch on me. I'm sorry for being a dick."

"It's okay. It's been hard. Getting used to the single life and everything."

Theo shrugged.

"Yeah. Charlie and I broke up."

"What?"

"He got a job in America. He's moving to New York next week."

"Shit. I'm sorry."

"We've been on and off for a while. It's not meant to be."

"Are you going to that party this weekend?"

"Are you?" Theo raised a curious dark eyebrow, raking his fingers through his messy blond hair.

"Yeah. I think."

"No offense, but… who invited you?"

"Arnie."

"Fuck."

Theo turned red.

"What?"

"I don't think I'm supposed to tell you this, but Ben's taking Yasmin to that."

"I know."

"And you don't have a problem?"

"Why would I have a problem?" I snapped, sounding super defensive, and like I definitely had a problem. If Theo noticed, he ignored me.

"I swear it means nothing."

"I'm sick of people telling me Ben and Yasmin mean nothing. If they mean nothing, why the hell does he keep hanging out with her?"

"I've said enough."

"Great. You know, I'm supposed to have friends who can give me a single straight answer."

"Sorry."

Class started, so I couldn't chew into Theo any more than I wanted to. My day was so busy, I didn't bother having lunch. After class, I went to the semester's first choir rehearsal for the big Christmas show. We had to wear choir robes even during rehearsal and I felt like an old weird priest as I got ready alone. As soon as I walked into the school chapel, the choir girls stopped dead.

Yasmin stood in the center of the group. I scanned the room for Mikhail, hoping there was someone to break the ice. Hope stood on Yasmin's left and Claire stood on her right. They snickered at me as I found my sheet music in the newly assigned choir lockers. I ignored them until Claire flicked her red hair out of her face and cleared her throat.

"Hey, Libby."

"Hi, Claire."

I shuffled the sheet music awkwardly, but eventually, I had to close my locker. The three girls surrounded me as the rest of the choir already filled the pews of the choir section. I was alone, cornered by the locker.

"So," Yasmin snickered, "This is why Benji can't get enough of me."

Claire giggled. Ben hates people calling him Benji.

"She's a slut," Hope said, "She slept with his twin brother over the summer too."

That wasn't even true. Claire grinned.

"Jess tried to warn us about her."

"Listen, bitch," Yasmin continued, "You may have Mikhail wrapped around your finger, but if you don't back off the Christmas solo, I will kick your arse."

"I'm not afraid of you. And warm up's about to start."

They closed me off from my one avenue of escape.

"After practice, you'd better run out of here. Or you'll regret it," Claire said, "It's your fault my best friend's dead."

Blood rushed past my ears. Did she know about Jess? No one knew except Theo, Charlie, and Ben. There's no way any of them would have told Claire, Hope, or any of the popular girls.

"I-I don't know what you're talking about."

Three Wicked Bullies

"Chloe died at your birthday party."

"Wow. That's fucked up," Yasmin said, popping her hip, "I'm not surprised. My parents warned me about her people. Thugs."

"Keep running your damn mouth and you'll see how much of a thug I am."

Yasmin turned her nose up as Mikhail came around the corner to ask what the holdup was. The three scattered and I stood in the soprano section as Mikhail led us through our warm-ups and our first song. On our break, he asked me to stay back after choir. Great. So much for blending into the crowd to avoid a confrontation with Yasmin, Hope and Claire.

I didn't have a choice, so I approached the organ once everyone left as Mikhail idly thumbed the keys, sounding like Count Dracula. He leaned back on the organ.

"Liberty, we ought to have a serious conversation."

"Am I in trouble?"

"Not at all. New girls on the choir have trouble fitting in and because of her background as a trained singer, I know Yasmin expected to have a bigger role. Unfortunately, Rapetti doesn't work like that. Training is nothing to talent."

"Oh. I don't want to cause any problems."

"Problems? I looked into your record with some faculty members. You're rarely in trouble, unless you keep the company of athletes. That doesn't seem to be a problem this year."

"No. It isn't."

"Good. I'll make sure the other girls leave you alone. But please, Liberty… don't quit the choir on their account. You have a beautiful voice. Oxford would be lucky to have you."

"Thanks."

"Here's some sheet music for the solo. If you can handle it, I'll consider adding you to another duet. I want to be fair to the other students, but I have a feeling you'll work harder than any of them. Take the music and we'll talk."

"Thanks, Mikhail."

"I know how lonely it can be up here with all these conservative Brits. I'm originally from London and well… let's just say it's easier to be gay down there than it is here."

"I bet."

"See you tomorrow. Practice, practice, practice!"

I stuffed the music into my bag and left chapel. I was hungry, so I turned toward the dining hall. I could see three girls in uniform leaning against the lamppost ahead. Ugh. I guess they determined to make good on their threats. I turned around. Dinner could wait. I didn't want trouble. I heard shoes hitting the pavement. Whatever. They could chase me, but I wouldn't show fear.

I heard a thud and felt something on the back of my head. Then I collapsed. When I woke up, I was naked. Yasmin snapped her fingers in front of my face. I moved my hands, but they'd dragged me somewhere and tied me up. Was I in the Year 12 dorm? Fuck, my head hurt.

"Take the fucking picture," Hope snapped.

Yasmin grabbed her phone and took pictures of me, naked. I moved and thrashed. Yasmin laughed.

"Ew. She's so ugly."

Claire laughed.

"Her nipples are huge. Hope, take the marker."

Hope uncorked the Sharpie, and the smell made me want to pass out again. They'd dragged me into Yasmin's room and tied me to the bed. She must have been one of the few Year 12s to have a single bedroom.

"What should I write?" Hope asked.

"Will marker show up on her skin?"

"It's silver you dumbass," Hope snapped.

"Write 'whore'," Claire said.

"Stop!" I screamed, "I'm going to report you to the Dean! Let me go!"

"No, you won't," Yasmin said, grinning, "Not once we're done with you."

Hope pressed the marker into my stomach. I thrashed again, but these three girls had tied me down well. With thick ropes and thick knots.

"I think we should put a dildo inside her," Yasmin said.

"That's disgusting," Hope countered, "I don't want to touch her pussy."

"I don't want to, but it'll be a funny picture. We can sell it online."

Claire laughed.

"That would be hilarious. God, I wish Jess were here. She'd love this."

"She's moving too much, Hope complained, "Look how bad it looks."

I couldn't see what she'd written on my stomach, but I could feel that she'd probably written exactly what Claire recommended. Whore.

"Put an arrow on her ass and write 'rape me'," Claire suggested.

"I'm going to call the police!" I yelled, "HELP!!! SOMEONE HELP!!!"

"Stick a sock in her mouth."

"I only have a dirty thong," Yasmin said.

Claire laughed and took the thong from Yasmin and stuffed it in my mouth. My eyes watered and I wanted to vomit. Oh, God... I couldn't move because I was just trying not to throw up. They'd probably let me choke to death on my vomit. I had to survive this. They were deranged. Wicked. And Hope... she used to be my friend. She shouldn't be helping these girls. She should be on my side.

"If we put the dildo in her, that's rape," Hope said, "We can't rape her."

Claire grabbed the marker and wrote on my thigh as my vision clouded from tears. She spread my ass cheeks apart and laughed.

"Look at her butthole."

"Ew!" Hope said, backing off.

Yasmin peered over and laughed.

"I can't believe Ben would choose her over me," Yasmin said.

"He won't want damaged goods," Claire said, "Trust me. He dated my best friend for like... ever. I know him."

"Do you think she'd tell?" Yasmin said.

"She never snitched before," Hope pointed out.

"I should call Benji," Yasmin said, "We can stick her in the closet and she can listen to us fuck."

Hope laughed.

"That's hilarious. She's a slut, she deserves it."

Claire snapped, "Can you two focus? We put the dildo in her ass, we get the pictures and we can drug her. She won't even remember."

"I'm calling Benji."

Hope tried to grab the phone, but Yasmin called anyway, scurrying to the other side of the bedroom. I would throw up now... for real... I retched and Claire slapped my ass with the dildo until I squealed. At least I didn't vomit.

Yasmin put on a fake Latina accent. I guess her family was Argentinian, so it made sense, but she played it up.

"Hey Benji. I'm sitting in my room and my pussy is so wet for you."

...

"Are you serious?"

...

"But you said we could have sex."

...

"Are you fucking gay?"

...

"We're still going to the party this weekend?"

...

"Love you, babe..."

Yasmin hung up.

"Ugh. He wouldn't come over."

Claire brandished an enormous dildo.

"So? Maybe he'll wish he had when he gets a picture of his ex with a dick up her ass."

"Seriously, this is too far," Hope interjected.

"Why are you being a bitch?" Yasmin snapped.

"I'm not being a bitch. I just don't think we should rape her."

"It's not rape. It's a joke," Claire snapped.

She spread my ass cheeks open again, ready to slide in her dildo. To complete my assault. To violate my body completely. The door to Yasmin's room thrust open. I guess they'd been too excited by making good on their threats to lock it properly. Either that or whoever walked in had a key…

"WHAT IN THE BLOODY HELL IS GOING ON IN THIS ROOM?"

You're Under Arrest

Dean Warren walked into the room. I wasn't sure whether I should be terrified or relieved. There's no way for Yasmin, Hope or Claire to hide what they'd done to me. Dean Warren rushed over to me as I lay on Yasmin's bed, naked and tied up while one of my bullies brandished a dildo and another waved a silver Sharpie and there was a thong in my mouth. That didn't even get into the words they'd written on my body.

I tried to scream but inadvertently got the thong lodged deeper in my mouth. I tried to yell and get her attention, but oh, I have it. Dean Warren grabbed the dildo and hollered.

"WHAT IS THIS PHALLUS DOING HERE?!"

Yasmin worked up crocodile tears. I guess this tactic worked for her before. Except, no one has ever caught her red-handed about to shove a dildo in another girl's orifices.

"They made me do it, Dean Warren!"

Hope put her hands up and Dean Warren yelled, "STAY COMPLETELY STILL."

She approached me and touched my cheek.

"Liberty, I'm calling the police. You stay right here…"

She pulled the thong out of my mouth at least, and I threw up. Cops. This is a crime. Some crazy bitch shoved a dirty thong in my mouth though, so I didn't register it right away. I threw up again, but Dean Warren didn't untie me. She wanted the cops to get here so they could see exactly what she found.

"What were you planning to do with that dildo?"

"It's consensual!" Claire yelled, "We're lesbians."

"Lesbians my fucking arse," Dean Warren yelled. She didn't ask the girls anymore questions. She paced back and forth, muttering to herself until the three British police officers entered the room. Dean Warren had to fight back a crowd of girls who heard the commotion and now wanted a peek. My humiliation was nowhere near its end.

The cops took pictures and untied me. The female cop crouched down and asked, "Were you penetrated, love?"

I thought I would die from embarrassment as I shook my head. The female detective pulled me aside and asked me questions about what happened. She couldn't seem to wrap her mind around it. Why would three girls attack one of their schoolmates and try to rape her? They got me clothes — not mine, but scrubs. And then they asked, "Is there anyone we can call?"

Theo, maybe. Or Ben. But I didn't want Ben to see me like this. We weren't even together.

"Theo. Theo Hargreaves."

The detective called Theo. After they interviewed everyone, they arrested Hope, Yasmin, and Claire. Dean Warren warned me that the girls probably wouldn't be there long — no longer than overnight. But it had to be enough for now. It was getting late by the time Theo arrived. He was concerned. Scowling. And Dean Warren asked if he'd take me to my dorm.

Theo helped me up, and we walked out of the room. I still hadn't washed the Sharpie off me yet. Once we were away from police and teachers, Theo asked, "What happened?"

"I don't want to talk about it."

"Warren told me it was a sexual assault."

Tears pierced my eyes. If I told Theo, I knew he'd tell Ben. And I was so embarrassed by everything. Yasmin called Ben. I'd screamed and heard his muffled voice on the other side of the phone as they abused me.

"Yes. It was."

Theo stopped.

"Tell Benjamin."

"No! I don't want to."

"Why not?"

"He's not my boyfriend anymore, in case you forgot."

"I didn't forget. But it's Ben. If he finds out what they did to you… He'll be furious."

"For once at this school, I don't need Ben fighting my battles. It's not like he cares. Yasmin was his date to the weekend party."

"That's exactly why you ought to tell him."

"What am I supposed to say? They humiliated me!"

Theo stopped uncomfortably at my outburst. I didn't mean to yell so loud, but I was freaking out. The weekend was only five days away, and it was becoming clear that whatever party they planned probably wouldn't happen.

"I don't want anyone to know."

"This bullying looks horrible for Rapetti. They'll try to cover it up. I don't think you should let them."

"What do you mean?'

"You've had an awful time at Rapetti Academy. I know it's your last year, but... no one involved should get away with this."

Rumors Spread

"With the police involved, there's not much more I can do."

"The police involved doesn't mean there will be justice."

Theo might have been right, but that didn't make me eager to invite Ben into the middle of a personal problem.

"I never thought they'd go this far."

"You still won't tell me what they did."

"I can't. Seriously. I'm still… in shock, I think."

"Fine. Go into your dorm and run a shower. I'll call you later."

We stopped in front of my dorm room, and I threw my arms around Theo. I couldn't wait to change into my pajamas and crawl into bed. Maybe Eugenie would tell me about her day and I could act like nothing happened. I already just wanted this to go away, even if cops entering a Year 12 dorm would inevitably spread around the school. Maybe I could keep my name out of it. Maybe for once, I could have a normal week at Rapetti Academy.

Theo hugged me back and left me with his last stern words for the night, "I still think you should tell Ben."

Yeah. Tell Ben that his new girlfriend planned to rape me by shoving a dildo into me. That she and her friends scratched words into me I hadn't even read yet. No thanks. I slunk into the shower near my room. Dean Warren called my dorm head so I wouldn't have to attend check in with the other girls. I could just shower and go straight to bed.

I went to sleep without seeing Eugenie or anyone else. In the morning, I woke up to Eugenie staring at me from her bed, eyes wide and black hair in a messy bush around her head as she raked her fingers through her blunt black bangs.

"Is it true?"

"Good morning," I mumbled.

"Did they really do that to you?"

"Huh?"

I yawned and sat up.

"I heard a rumor that Hope, Claire and Yasmin raped you."

Bile rose to my throat. I hadn't forgotten. I could never forget what they did to me. And no, it wasn't rape. But it was sexual assault. And I still didn't want to talk about it. If word spread to Eugenie in the middle of the night, that meant everyone knew. I checked my phone. Three missed calls from Theo. Fuck.

"They didn't rape me."

"So it's just a sick rumor, then?"

"Not... exactly."

Eugenie hopped out of bed and wrapped her arms around me.

"I am so sorry, Liberty. I don't know what happened or what they did but I am so sorry..."

"You have nothing to apologize for."

"Everyone's talking about it. They're saying that the three of them will go to prison."

"I don't know. The cops arrested them but I don't know."

"They fucked up. Are you going to class today?"

"Yeah. I don't see why not?"

Eugenie's lips curled downward.

"You are so strong," she said.

I didn't feel strong. I felt exposed. Like everyone in the school knew what happened, and they'd hold it over me. Public humiliation at Rapetti wasn't exactly new for me. The worst part was that this wasn't even my biggest worry. There was still the sex tape Marley found on some shitty website and the fact that anyone could have it and hundreds of people could have seen it by now. If not more.

"Why don't you get dressed and come to breakfast."

I got up to find one of my uniforms and my legs shook as I thought about changing in front of Eugenie. She wouldn't hurt me. She wouldn't do anything to me. I knew that. But the thought of changing in front of another girl made me weak at the knees.

"Um… Eugenie… do you mind waiting outside?"

She looked befuddled, but she didn't question my request, and she stood outside, waiting for me to get my clothes and get ready for the day. I quickly changed into my uniform, but instead of knee-high socks, I wore long black tights beneath my skirt so no one could see my skin. I didn't do much with my hair, two cornrows down the side of my head and a little moisture added to them. I packed my books for the day and Eugenie looked excited to walk me into the cafeteria.

"Do you think everyone knows what happened?"

"Yeah. But don't worry. If anyone talks to you, I'll kick their ass. Plus I told Arnie to take notes so we can make a hit list of anyone who messes with you."

"A hit list?"

"Not to kill them. But like… to get them back."

I groaned.

"Great. So Arnie knows."

"He didn't spread it around, don't worry."

"I wish no one knew."

"Yasmin was the one who told people. It's weird. I think her parents are getting her out of jail this morning."

I froze.

"So she'll be in the caf?"

She was just a Year 12. But I didn't think I'd have to face her, Claire or Hope so soon.

"I don't know. Trust me, Libs. We've got your back."

My phone buzzed again. Theo. I picked up the phone.

"Where are you?"

"On my way to breakfast. Why?"

"I'll meet up with you on the path. Wait up."

I told Eugenie, and she agreed to wait for Theo, even if she scowled when he got there. I couldn't blame her, but she didn't exactly trust any rugby boys. Including Theo.

"Did you prepare her?" he asked Eugenie.

"Yeah. I told her people knew."

"Good. Good. We've got to make sure no one says anything to her this morning, okay?"

"No offense," Eugenie snapped, "But I don't need you telling me how to handle protecting my friend."

"Yeah. I know. But… listen…" Theo stumbled over his words as he turned pink, "She's my friend too!"

I guess we were friends again. Even if Ben had definitely forbidden him to talk to me.

"Does Ben know?" I asked.

"Who cares what he thinks?" Eugenie asked.

Theo's answer brought me no comfort…

He Still Loves You

"Ben knows."

Naturally. Could anything happen to me or around me on this campus without my ex-boyfriend getting involved. But I didn't want him to know about this. I didn't want him to feel... responsible. It was over, wasn't it? And I could put the worst details of the attack behind me.

"I don't want to talk about him today."

"Give him a chance, Libby."

Eugenie snapped, "Don't tell her how to feel about her stupid ex!"

"Sorry, since when do you know Liberty better than I do?"

"We're roommates. So yeah, I'd say I know her well enough."

"Libby!"

"Can you two stop arguing?"

We stood in front of the caf, ready to go in.

"Deep breaths. If anyone says anything, we'll yell at them."

"We can find one of the loner tables in the back," Theo pointed out.

We entered the caf, and a low hush fell over the crowd. The popular table was noticeably deficient. The three most obvious missing members weren't there. Millie sat with a box of tissues as Amira and Bess Davenport comforted her. When she noticed me, she glared daggers, but there wasn't much else she could do about my presence.

Eugenie and Theo ushered me to a table in the back of the caf and Theo went to get me food while Eugenie sat with me.

"Don't worry, Libby. Everyone at this school has the attention span of a goldfish. They'll let go of this soon."

"I don't want anything else to happen."

Eugenie caught the eye of Arnie and the other 'art freaks'. Arnie appeared to be gesturing, asking permission to come over, but Eugenie shook her head.

"I know Arnie cares about you but… I think you need time alone, yeah?"

"Yeah. I do. What makes you think Arnie cares about me?"

"He talks about you all the time. Not creepily or anything. I think he's jealous. That you got so close to his brother and he never could."

I bit my tongue to avoid mentioning that maybe he should have stopped messing with Ben several years earlier. Eugenie was only trying to help. Theo returned from the long line and groaned.

"Eugenie, you'd better get something to eat. The vegan sausages are nearly gone."

Eugenie scurried off. Theo glanced over his shoulder at her and leaned in.

"So… is she hooking up with Arnie?"

"Why should I know?"

"She's your friend. And she's fit."

"You know, Theo… I'm not really in the mood to play matchmaker."

"Right. Has Dean Warren spoken to you about today yet?"

"No. She never mentioned."

"Expect her to stay in touch. I know we have first block together but after that… I'm only a phone call away."

I picked at my food, struggling to get any of it down. I focused on cutting a sausage up when Eugenie's chair slid out and I assumed she returned. I turned to see Benjamin sitting there. He didn't have his tie on and he was drunk. Very drunk.

"Libs."

I froze.

Theo put his hand on Ben's arm.

"Mate. I've got it, yeah?"

Ben wrested Theo's hand off his arm and scowled, raking his fingers through his golden-brown hair and fixating his attention on me. No surprise, Ben ignored Theo.

"We need to talk. Now."

"I… I have to go to class."

Tears pierced Ben's eyes, and he reached for his silver flask, which I suppose was his idea of 'breakfast' and took a giant swig.

"Liberty Jones. Please. Come talk to me. In private."

"I… I'm sorry. I need to go."

I got up and raced for the door. Theo ran after me. Ben stood up and yelled, "LIBBY!" Everyone turned to stare at him, but I'd already sprinted the hell out of there. Theo grabbed me by the arm and held me still.

"We ought to tell Eugenie we've gone…"

"Please… Theo. I can't face him right now. I just can't…"

"He still loves you."

"No… Please. Don't say that. Don't make this twenty-thousand times more confusing than it ever is. I don't want to think about him loving me. I don't want to think about him dumping me. I don't want to think about the fact that I always end up in the middle of some stupid mess! What is wrong with me!"

Theo tried to hold me still, but I pushed him. Hard.

"Why doesn't everyone at this damned school leave me alone!"

The Intervention

Ok, so I shouldn't have pushed Theo, but it's too late for regrets. I had to get to class and I wouldn't be able to avoid everyone forever. Theo didn't take my attack personally, and he still walked me to class. Afterward, I had a free period. Dean Warren found me before I could get to Physics class.

"Liberty, I need you to come to my office right away."

I knew realistically I wasn't in trouble, but talking about what she'd discovered the night before made me scared. Nervous. Uncomfortable. I didn't want to talk about what happened or relive any of it. I could still feel the eyes of fellow Rapetti students on me as I followed Dean Warren into her office.

She shut the door behind her and offered me a glass of water. I declined.

"How are you doing today?"

If I had to be honest, I would have told her not great. But I know how shit like this works. You say that you aren't doing well and next thing you know, teachers recommend you take the rest of the semester off. I wasn't even allowed in my home country anymore — something Rapetti teachers didn't need to know.

"Fine," I muttered.

Dean Warren pursed her lips.

"What I uncovered yesterday was very serious, Liberty. I know what I saw and I know that under no circumstances did you consent to such a thing, but we're facing a problem as an institution. The students involved in your attack come from wealthy and powerful families. Families that are accustomed to making horrible incidents disappear. Do you understand?"

I nodded.

"They don't want this to see a day in court and, my hands are tied, neither does the administration. But we recommend you seek legal counsel. The school will have a lawyer representing their best interests, as will each of the girls. Do you have any way of getting a lawyer?"

"I'm not sure."

"The court will provide one if you do not provide one for yourself. I'll send you the details on your school email."

"Thanks, Dean Warren."

"I want to let you know that we're doing what we can to settle this and that Rapetti has no intention of allowing the girls to continue their tenure here. However, we have no choice but to allow Yasmin to return to class. Based on the story she's told, she was the victim of bullying by the two older girls. Until the school investigates further, it's her word against theirs."

"So she'll be back on campus?"

"Yes."

"Oh..."

My hands went clammy instantly. I never considered that I'd have to run into any of them in the halls again. Claire and Hope were one thing. Hope had given up on our friendship and Claire had always been a mean girl, but at least I knew they had limits. Far from being the victim of other girls' bullying, Yasmin had been the orchestrator of the entire affair.

"It's not true, though," I said, "Yasmin wasn't a victim."

"I know. And your word helps. But they've tied my hands. We're dealing with powerful families, Liberty. I have your best interests at heart, but I'm not the one calling the shots. If you need anything, here's my private number."

Maybe Dean Warren wasn't as bad as everyone thought. She slid her private number across the table and I got the sense that she was looking out for me. That she genuinely cared.

"All I have to do is wait for this email?"

"And get yourself a talented lawyer, darling. This won't be easy, but you have access to the school counselor whenever you'd like. We've set up a mandatory appointment for you next Monday. That will be in your school email too."

"Thanks."

I felt numb. And I wasn't sure I was grateful. Counseling? Sure, Ben needed counseling because he drank. Lots. And he did drugs. But why did I need counseling? I had done nothing wrong. The whole thing confused me, but Dean Warren said "mandatory" and she was trying her best to help me out.

Dean Warren discussed more details with me, and then she let me go long after the rest of my classes ended. I guess she must have called my teachers ahead. I didn't get ten feet out of the office when Ben, Theo and Arnie formed a wall around me. I scowled.

"I'm going to scream."

"Told you we should have drugged her and run," Arnie muttered.

Theo elbowed him hard in the stomach.

"Since when are you three all talking?"

"I still think Theo and Arnie are pigs," Ben snapped, "But I needed help so you wouldn't run off."

Theo replied, "I'm here because you deserve it for pushing me this morning."

Arnie chimed in, "I'm here because you left me hanging and I need to make sure my physics partner doesn't go mental."

"Thanks," I replied sarcastically, "Can I go to my room now?"

"No," Ben said, "You're coming with us."

"Yeah, I've been through that before and it didn't exactly end well."

Ben's face fell. Theo turned red. Arnie rolled his eyes.

"Nice try. You might push those arseholes away with your shrewish tongue, but I don't care."

He grabbed me by the arm and dragged me down the hall.

"Arnie! Let go of me!"

Theo muttered, "At least his way works."

Ben scowled and shoved his hands in his pockets, walking ahead. Arnie dragged me outside where I finally wrested away my hand.

"My tongue is not shrewish you maniac!"

Students and teachers going from class cast awkward glances in my direction but otherwise ignored the yelling. I guess based on the rumors, they might have figured I was crazy or something and didn't bother to intervene. Ben scurried ahead, and I asked, "Where is he going?"

I hated being around him like this. A mess. Arnie rested his forearm on my head — he was that much taller than me, yes — and held me still.

"Wait young Padawan."

"You are so annoying."

Theo cleared his throat and clarified that he "didn't endorse kidnapping of any kind" and then Ben reappeared in the driver's seat of his Range Rover.

"Back seat or front seat?" Arnie asked.

"Put her in the bloody front, you twat."

"What if I don't want to sit in the front?"

Theo and Arnie exchanged glances. Before I knew it, they were carrying me. I shrieked.

"Can you imbeciles put me down! Put! Me! Down!"

So they did — right in the front seat of my ex-boyfriend's Range Rover.

I Never Stopped

Ben pealed out of the parking lot.

"Where the hell are you taking me?"

"Away from school."

"Is that allowed?!"

"Dad's calling the school," Arnie explained.

"You three planned this together? I thought you were all pissed at each other."

"We are," they chimed together.

This was so annoying.

"Where are we going? We have class tomorrow."

Theo leaned between the chairs and I fought the urge to elbow him in the damn face.

"You two need to talk."

He poked Ben with his index finger, causing Ben to shift uncomfortably. Talk? What the hell did I have to talk about with Ben Fox. I folded my arms and scowled.

"I want to listen to Spice Girls," Arnie said, "That sounds nice."

"Shut up, Arnie!" the three of us yelled.

He grumbled, "Do you three ever want to stop picking on me?"

"Shut up," Ben muttered.

We drove for another twenty minutes. I didn't realize Rapetti was so close to a coast, but I guess everywhere's relatively close to the coast when you're on an island. There was a little collection of trailer parks near the coast.

"Caravan for the night," Theo said, "Eugenie and the others will be over later."

I groaned.

"You told Eugenie?"

"She's taking my car. Poor lass. I don't think she knows how to drive well," Arnie said, sounding shockingly unconcerned about his car or his hookup/girlfriend.

We piled out of the Range Rover and I complained about how cold it was. Ben took his jacket off and threw it over my shoulders. We made brief eye contact that nearly made me forget how infuriated he made me. Arnie plucked the passcode in and the trailer door opened. The little house wasn't anything like how I expected. I guess over here they call them "caravans" and this one had beach house decor and two little bedrooms.

"Two bedrooms?"

"I'll sleep on the couch," Arnie blurted.

"What about Eugenie and the others?"

"They're camping outside in tents. They think it will be fun," Arnie said, half-mocking them.

Theo groaned.

"I'd better get the drinks then."

"D'you mind?" Ben grunted at his brother.

Arnie nodded, and Ben tossed Theo the keys to his Range Rover. When they closed the door behind them, it was silent except for the sound of the waves. Ben leaned against the wall and said, "I've fucked it, haven't I?"

"You did nothing wrong."

"I was on the phone with her that night. I pieced it together."

"You couldn't have known."

Ben blurted out, "I still love you."

My heart raced. I sank onto the couch. There was still so much distance between us. I wanted to keep it that way. This was the only way I could keep my head on straight. With Ben, it was so easy to confuse myself. To convince myself to jump headfirst into him without a second thought. We'd tried that once and look at where we ended up — broken up. Hurt.

"I promised I'd protect you. I thought I was doing the right thing."

"By dating Yasmin?"

"We were never dating. I talked to her. Sure. But… I… I thought if I hung out with her for a bit, she'd lose interest once she saw nothing was going to happen and you'd move on. I wanted you to move on... Damn it, Liberty! All I care about is you staying safe because this is exactly what happens when we're involved. Problems. Trouble. You get hurt."

"We weren't together when I got hurt. That was all me. How do you explain that?"

"I'm an idiot. I want to protect you, but I can't... ever."

"Stop thinking about protecting me then! You say you love me and you want to protect me, but I don't need protection. I need someone to stand with me, not in front of me or behind me. I need someone by my side."

"You deserve that."

"I know. And I thought you would be that person. But you abandoned me."

"I didn't want to. I kept an eye on you..."

"I know."

"What happened between us," he said, pacing now, getting closer to me with each step, "In the classroom. I didn't expect that."

"Neither did I."

"I thought I could stop feeling for you," he said, "I thought I could make myself get over you. But I can't. Damn it, Libs... From the moment I first saw you... I've wanted you. But I've never deserved you, properly."

"That isn't true."

"It is. Why do you even want me? Is it because of the money?"

"What?"

Now I was taken aback. I've loved Ben for so many reasons. But money?

"I don't know. I'm a piece of shit! Why do you want me around?"

"You're not like that at all. You're protective. You care about me. You... you're the first guy who realized I wasn't just some childish nerd."

"Fuck," Ben swore.

"Cigarette?" I asked.

"I don't smoke anymore."

"What?"

"Well... it's not been long. But I quit."

"Really?"

"I haven't smoked since we... had sex."

"Oh."

He sat next to me on the couch, spreading his legs open and leaning forward.

"Back and forth," he muttered, "Back and forth... but where does it get us?"

"I don't know."

"I want you back, Liberty."

He grabbed my cheek, holding my face so he could gaze into my eyes. I trembled as he touched me. I didn't know if I should kiss him or push him away.

"Ben, we need to talk this out. Not..."

"I know. I know. It's just... I always want to be so irresponsible with you."

"If we get back together, we can't fuck this up."

"So you're not saying no?"

"I'm not saying yes, either."

"Can I kiss you?" he asked.

Every fiber of me wanted to say 'yes' to him. But I knew where kissing led and the last time I'd been naked had been with the three bullies — Yasmin, Claire, and my ex-friend Hope. I didn't want to get naked again. I was ashamed. I was scared. This was worse than losing my virginity because they'd taken something from me I didn't know if I could get back.

"I... I'm not ready."

"For kissing or for sex?"

"For either of them."

"Theo didn't tell me what they did to you."

"I didn't tell him."

"Can you tell me?"

He pressed his forehead to mine, but he didn't kiss me. He held me there and whispered, "I'll wait. And whenever you're ready, you can tell me as much or as little as you want to. I love you, Liberty Jones. I've never stopped."

Caravan Party & Shoreline Kiss

I still trusted Ben. Even if we weren't together, that didn't change what I knew about him. He'd never hurt me on purpose. He wanted to help me, and even when he abandoned me, he thought he was doing the right thing. So I told him what they did to me. He turned red.

"I know what I need to do," he muttered.

"Cryptic…"

"You don't worry about it," he said, "We're here… away from it all."

"I can't outrun this, Ben. It happened. And once again, I was too weak to stop it."

"You're not weak. You've survived worse than I ever have. I lost a sister, but you lost a parent and your sister was a kid."

I bit down on my lip hard. I sometimes could forget that Ben knew everything about Niecy and daddy. And that even when we hated each other, it was one of the first things he knew about me. He didn't have to work hard to pry the secret out of me. Some part of me knew that I could trust Benjamin Fox. And I still could.

"That doesn't make me strong."

"I don't know why people pick on you… and I'm sorry for ever being one of those people. I'm sorry for letting a girl into my life who did this to you."

His voice trembled, and his fists clenched.

"I'm so angry with myself," he whispered, "All I ever wanted was to look after you."

"Theo and Arnie will be back soon."

"And the others."

"Can we go for a walk on the beach?"

"Yeah."

Ben, without cigarettes, without drugs, just Ben, slipped his hand through mine and led me out the door, popping the collar of his waxed jacket to protect his pale neck from the cold.

We walked along the sandy shore, fingers interlaced to protect our hands from the cold. The wind whipped up into a fury and despite our best efforts, my knuckles experienced a bone stiffening chill. Ben brought me to the shoreline.

"This summer would have been hard on anyone."

"Sometimes I wonder how we made it out alive."

"I don't want to pressure you."

"I know. But I also know that you won't wait forever."

"That's not true. For you, I would wait 10,000 lifetimes."

"I want to be sure we are making the right decision."

"Kiss me."

Saying yes to getting back together would have been so easy. There was no question, no doubt in my mind that I still loved Benjamin. But when we rushed into things, we both got hurt.

I wasn't perfect. I stopped on the beach and let the wind picked up my hair, blowing thick curls across my face. And I kissed him. Our lips parted in a deep, slow kiss that neither of us wanted to end. He pulled away and whispered, "I love you."

"We should go back to the house."

"I just want you to have a good time tonight."

I wanted to have a good time to. Now that I was over that kidnapping me and I realized why they had really done it, I didn't feel so angry. They were my friends. And then… I guess he was a little more than a friend. I wasn't ready to define what we were yet. I was just happy we were talking to each other. And that maybe someday soon, we could get back together and things could be like they were.

Except, I still had a nagging feeling that nothing could ever be quite the same again.

By the time we got back to the house, Theo and Arnie were piling bottles of drinks out of the Range Rover and into the caravan. They were arguing about rugby — philosophically, of course. Arnie insisted that it was a game for savages, and Theo criticized him for being the very savage he condemned.

Ben pushed the door open to allow them to bring in the last bit of food and drinks.

"Are you two sorted?" Arnie asked, pouring himself the largest vodka tonic I'd ever seen.

"Yeah," Ben said, "We're sorted."

"Thank fuck. So how are we getting back at the bitches?"

Theo rolled his eyes.

"You wanker, we weren't supposed to tell her."

"What? It's not like she can stop us."

Ben scowled.

"I swear you're half the reason I smoke," he grumbled at Arnie.

"You two act like you don't love me."

"We don't," Theo snapped, "We tolerate you."

"You're mad Charlie dumped you."

"This is why no one likes you, mate," Theo complained.

"Wankers. Bedroom."

Ben grabbed Theo and Charlie and they went into the bedroom. The door thrust open, and I asked, "Um… who are you?"

"We're the rest of the rugby lads. Here for the party. I'm Javier. This is Edward. Aren't you the girl they kidnapped?"

"Shut up, Jav. She knows who I am. She's a Year 13 too. It's Ben's ex," Edward Chapman said, pushing the awkward Year 12 into the caravan.

"Ben didn't mention you were coming."

"Yeah? Yo, Arnav!" Edward yelled, "Bring the MDMA."

Great. The last thing I wanted to do was anymore drugs. And I didn't know these new rugby boys. Before I could say anything, Ben opened the bedroom door from his secret conference with Theo and Arnie.

"You're early," he snapped.

"So? We got out of class and we're in our caravan. Heard you were inviting art freaks for us to bang."

"Eugenie used to be a slag in secondary," Javier "Jav" Fonseca chimed in with his heavy Iberian accent.

"Watch your mouth, mate," Arnie yelled.

"Or what?"

Theo pushed Jav back.

"Shut it."

The boy listened to Theo at least and ambled over to the table to pour himself a drink. I glanced at Ben and he shrugged.

"You don't mind if they're here? I told them not to come."

I shook my head.

"It's fine. It's better than being alone."

"Plus, you have me," Ben said, "I'll look after you tonight."

Unwelcome Party Guests Cause Trouble

Theo came up to me as I poured myself a drink — nothing with alcohol in it, just an orange juice and sparkling water.

"All well?"

"Maybe. If half the people in this room hadn't been bullying me before all this. I don't want people here because they feel like I'm some charity case."

"That's not it. The rugby guys don't hate you or anything. It's just... they do whatever Ben asks."

"And Ben asked them to treat me like shit and laugh at me while Yasmin and her minions bullied me in the caf?"

Poor Theo. I feel bad for him sometimes because he really is loyal to Ben and the rest of his crew. But he's a bit "thick" as my British peers might say. He stammers through an answer that doesn't make much sense and might have had some German words thrown in too.

"I get it. Ben feels bad. He wants to make it up to me. But it's going to take time."

"At least he apologizes," Theo grumbled, "Charlie never did."

"What the hell happened between you two?"

"Distance. You're lucky you have Ben here. He cares about you, Liberty."

I guess. It's hard for me to believe after everything that happened. But I had a good reason to talk to Ben. The sex tape and the link Marley sent me. Ben must have known about the tape already, but given everything that happened, he didn't want to bring it up. He stood in a circle refereeing a drinking contest between the tall, long-haired brunet, Nick Knight and Edward Chapman. Arnav elbowed Ben and said, "Mate, can my sister come with her girls."

Ben scowled, and Theo backed him up.

"You arsehole, did you tell her?" Theo snarled.

"What's the big deal, mate. She's my little sister. She's a Year 12."

"Think for one fucking second, you big lunk," Ben sneered, "She's best friends with Millie. Hope's little sister."

"Shit," Arnav muttered.

Arnie tapped on my shoulder before I could get involved. Millie and her friends coming would have been my worst nightmare.

"Libby. Eugenie's on the way. She's having trouble with the car. I want a smoke."

"I don't smoke."

"Outside. Come. Now."

"Okay…"

I followed Arnie outside, hearing the argument between Ben, Theo and Arnav escalating. We sat on the steps of the caravan while Arnie lit a cigarette. Two rugby boys were at their caravan and we could see them through the window.

"Wankers. I hate athletes."

"Hey. Your brother's an athlete," I reminded him.

Arnie shrugged and lit a cigarette.

"You don't happen to have your student ID?"

"Yeah. Why?"

I pulled the ID out of my pocket, and Arnie started crushing up some white pills with it.

"Arnie!"

I guess it was my fault. I should have seen it coming. I've never known him to spend a night without doing at least light party drugs. But why did he really ask me outside?

"Sorry. Libby, I have to ask you to do something for me."

"Um… okay…"

"I need to skip Physics in a week. Can you cover for me?"

"Why are you skipping?"

"Business."

"What kind of business?"

"Get a hint, yeah?"

"Okay. Fine. I guess I'm supposed to celebrate getting stuck with all the work."

"I'll make it up to you."

"Whatever."

"Thanks. And uh… don't tell Ben."

"Now I'm even more suspicious."

"Trust me."

"Why the hell would I do that?"

"Hey, I stopped drugging you!"

"My hero…"

"I'm trying to work things out with my brother. I don't want him all pissed at me."

"Got it."

Ben threw the caravan door open and pushed Arnav down the stairs. He stumbled over us and landed on his face.

"Wanker!" Ben yelled, "I should send you back to campus!"

"I'm sorry!"

"Get your arse out of here before I skin you alive!"

"Run up the beach," Theo added, "And don't come back until you've done three miles."

"Fuck's sake! I just had 'alf my weight in vodka."

"RUN!" Ben yelled, an angry vein popping out of his neck and forehead.

"Libs. Come."

He ignored Arnie and grabbed me by the hand, walking me around the back of the caravan, Theo dutifully following.

"I'm an idiot," Ben started.

Theo got straight to the point.

"Arnav told his sister Amira where we were and she's bringing her friends. Millie's her roommate, so she's coming, and then Emily Payne and Bess Davenport."

"I swear I'll chop his bollocks off," Ben muttered, spitting onto the grass behind the caravan.

"We can get out of here. Just the two of us."

"Oi!" Theo yelled, "I don't want to get stuck babysitting these bastards."

"We'll leave Arnie to babysit them. I'm sure he'll have a blast. It's up to you."

"I'm not scared of Millie and her minions."

"Atta girl," Theo said.

Ben cast a sharp glance in his direction.

"Are you sure?"

"Millie might be a bitch, but she didn't attack me. I don't want people to think I'm too scared to show my face."

"So you're ready to party then?" Theo asked.

I nodded and joined everyone inside. What usually happens when you have a rugby party throw down is half the guys end up with their shirts off only an hour in. Tonight was no different. Nick Knight stood on a table with his shirt off. Arnie argued football loudly with Edward Chapman. Theo and Arnav took tequila shots and soon Eugenie's car arrived.

I was glad she got here first before Millie and the band of bitches. Eugenie wore a cute little crop top and rushed to give me an enormous hug. I didn't want to drink alcohol with her, so I had little shots of orange juice as she got started on the tequila.

The party was ridiculously fun, especially when Nick Knight started telling hysterical stories about his year at an American boarding school (he got kicked out for flashing a teacher his genitals). I didn't know if our fun would last when a pair of headlights pulled into the caravan lot. It could be no one else but Millie and her minions.

You Don't Want Me To Love You

❦

Millie stepped out of her car and into a puddle of mud. I felt like the shore was on my side. She squealed as her six inch strappy sandal sank into the muck and she stuck there, ankle deep in mud. Amira Seth, Arnav's sister scremaed too late, yelling, "Watch it Millie!"

She kneeled in the muck to pull her Queen B's shoe out of the mud. I might be the victim of Rapetti bullying, but one thing's for sure, I will never get on my knees to pull another girl's foot out of mud, getting my own knees dirty. Millie flicked her honey blonde curls out of her face and squealed as she used Amira to pull her foot out of the mud and out of her sandal.

"Don't stand there watching!" she whined, "Theo, help me!"

Theo bounded over to help her like an obedient lap dog. I get that the popular girls at Rapetti and the rugby boys fit together like wine and cheese, but I felt weird watching Theo bound to her defense without a second thought. He helped her out and Arnav helped his sister

Amira up. They're both insanely beautiful with long dark hair and round brown eyes. You couldn't miss the fact that they're siblings.

"Stupid," Arnav bellowed at her, "Why would you get into the mud?"

"I was helping."

Millie barked at Arnav, "Can you shut up? Keep yelling at my friend and I'll stop shagging you."

"You shagged my brother?" Amira gasped.

"Oh, quiet," Millie snapped, "I need a drink."

She hobbled into the caravan, ignoring me, Arnie and Ben as she walked past, as if we were invisible. I supposed it could be worse. Maybe her sister getting into trouble with the Rapetti administration affected her. Once Millie entered the caravan and her crew followed, Arnie laughed.

"Guess I'd better go babysit," he said with a wink.

"I owe you one, mate."

"Yeah."

Arnie pulled the door open and Eugenie fell out, tipsy and losing her balance, right into Arnie's arms. He picked her up and carried her back in.

"Nights like this, I miss smoking," Ben admitted.

"We'd better go inside and party."

"Yeah. Can I confess something to you?"

"Keeping up with our party tradition?"

"I suppose."

Ben scratched his head and sighed.

"I'm freaking out about the sex tape."

"It's not a sex tape! That makes it sound like I was trying to be some kind of porn star or something."

"It is a tape of us having sex…"

"Ugh. Fine. Call it whatever you want. Do you think we can talk about it here? I don't want someone to hear us…"

"Listen, Libs. It's too weird how Marley found it. Too perfect."

"I didn't realize you still had him skulking around stalking me on the internet."

"Not stalking. Monitoring."

"I think the law would still call that stalking."

"Whatever you call it. I didn't break up with you to hurt you. I still cared about you. I care about you now."

"Ben… I don't want to do this here."

"Fine. But I want you to be careful. Someone set us up. And it's been hard to find out who it is. I don't trust anyone. Not even Theo."

"Theo? Come on, Ben. He's your best friend."

"I get that. But… you can never be too sure."

"You're getting paranoid."

"I'd be paranoid, crazy, whatever I had to be to keep you safe."

"Ben…"

"I get it. I fucked up. It's my fault Yasmin attacked you. But I didn't know she'd get… crazy like that."

"I guess you like them crazy."

Ben scowled.

"What's that supposed to mean?" he snapped.

Oops. That was one of those thoughts that I probably should have kept to myself.

"Nothing."

"What other crazy girls have I liked?"

"Um… Jess?"

"Really, Liberty…"

"I mean Jess, Yasmin… I wonder what I have in common with the girls you go for sometimes!"

"Wow. It's like you've been sitting for that one a while," he muttered bitterly.

"Maybe I have."

"What the fuck does it matter who I've gone for in the past?"

"I'm not like those girls. I'm not popular. The only reason any of your friends talk to me is because you make them or you let them. Let's be real, Ben. I never fit in with your people. I know tonight's supposed to be chill, but rugby guys can't get together without the big bad bitches of Rapetti. I fit in better with the art freaks than I've ever fit in with your friends."

"That's not true. Liam and Jezza might have been wankers, but we got along for a time. And Theo."

"Theo's your friend. Not mine."

"He doesn't see it that way."

"He sees it whichever way you tell him, which proves my point."

I can't stop myself from talking, even if I should. Ben was trying to help me, but I didn't want help. I wanted to spill all my pent-up feelings that built since the breakup. I wanted to spill my guts out. I wanted to scream.

"I mean... I don't have a single popular girl friend. The ones I thought were my friends all fucked with me! Even Bess turned into a total bitch. No one at this fucking school gets me and the only people weird enough to accept me are the so-called 'art freaks'. We don't fit together!"

"Stop it, Libs."

"What? It's true. You know it. That's probably the real reason you dumped me."

Ben yelled, "STOP IT!"

He stunned me silent. I'd never heard Ben raise his voice like that with me. With pure, blind rage behind it.

"I LOVE YOU!" he yelled, "I DON'T CARE IF YOU THINK WE FIT TOGETHER. I DON'T CARE! I MADE A MISTAKE AND I KNOW THAT NOW, BUT DAMN IT, LIBERTY. WE FIT TOGETHER AND WE WERE GOOD. WE WERE MAGICAL. I KNEW THE MOMENT, I WALKED AWAY FROM YOU, I'D NEVER LOVE ANYONE THE SAME. AND YOU DON'T BLOODY GET IT."

My mouth was dry. Two rugby boys peered out the caravan window. Great. We were being "that" couple. The ones who get into fights at parties while everyone's trying to have a good time. I couldn't leave Ben hanging. I had to say something. His hand trembled and his green eyes flickered back and forth across my face as if he could stare an answer out of me.

"I'm sorry," I squeaked, a pathetic response to all he'd said.

"I. LOVE. YOU. I will never stop. I hate when you're like this! I never say this to you, but I hate it! You find every bloody reason to push me away and even when you succeed, you aren't happy. It's like you don't want me to love you."

Ben Sticks It To Me

Ben's never spoken to me like that. He's never shown his anger like this toward me.

"That's not true."

"Fuck's sake, Libs! Don't bloody deny it."

"Stop yelling."

"Stop yelling? You want me to stop yelling? Well it's too fucking bad! Yelling's the only way I can get you to listen to me. Otherwise... Otherwise... BOLLOCKS!"

"Ben!" I yelled sharply.

Now, I was angry. But I wasn't precisely sure why. Ben was pissing me off. But that was only part of it. Deep down, I knew he was right. I acted like I didn't know what I wanted. I was always letting life pull me in random directions. I had it together with coursework, but aside from that, it was like I had a deep, paralyzing fear of getting close to people.

"I love you too, Ben."

"I know."

"What?"

"I know. You love me because you and I are more similar than we'd like to admit. We fall hard. We love hard. And we don't know what to do with ourselves once we have. But I think you're right. We can't move too fast. I'm going for a walk along the shore."

"I can come with you," I offered.

"No. I need to think," Ben responded before disappearing into the night. Theo opened the caravan door once Ben was gone. I sat on the steps, numb. I could hear Millie causing a scene inside and Arnie yelling at her and the other popular girls, desperate to get the scene under control.

"You okay?"

"Ben's pissed at me. This attempt to make me feel better is a total failure."

"Not total. Maybe you'd do better if you had a drink."

"I didn't want to drink tonight."

"Liberty, you're 19. Are you going to say 'fuck it' anytime soon?"

"It's not exactly a winning life philosophy," I countered.

Theo shrugged.

"Fuck it."

He took the spliff he'd rolled from behind his ear.

"Marijuana?"

"I don't do that stuff."

"Take a walk on the wild side. Or do I have to have Benjamin Fox's face for me to get you to have fun."

Right. A dig at the fact that Marley successfully coerced me into doing drugs. Maybe Theo was right. It was time for me to say 'fuck it' and stop worrying. Look where worrying got me. Nowhere. I put the spliff between my teeth and Theo pulled out a lighter.

"Atta girl."

I drew in and coughed. Hard. I nearly spat the damn thing out of my mouth.

"Theo! Ew! It tastes disgusting."

He laughed and then grumbled in frustration as he wiped dirt off his precious spliff, "It's not that bad, although now it's covered in dust it might be."

"How do you smoke that stuff?"

"Dunno. It's relaxing. Oh. There he is."

Ben came back from up the beach, and he was calmer. A lot less red.

"Libs. Behind the caravan."

He exchanged nods with Theo, who took his cue to go back outside. Ben held my hand behind the caravan, the tight possessive hold I knew him for.

"I'm sorry," he said hoarsely, "I'm an arse. I've lost many people in my life. But so have you. And you've done me worse. You've lost a parent. I can't possibly understand what that's like. And I can't understand how it hurts. I'll give you all the time in the world. But before I do…"

He grabbed my cheeks and kissed me. Hard. His lips spread mine open, and I allowed his tongue into my mouth. Like Theo said… Fuck it. I grabbed his face back, and we kissed. Ben pressed me up behind the caravan wall and raised one of my legs to his hips so he could stroke my thigh as he pushed his hips into me.

When he pulled away from me, he uttered hoarsely, "I'm hard…"

"Fuck me…"

Not quite 'fuck it' but close enough.

"Out here?"

"Please…" I whispered, "Don't give me time to come to my senses."

Too much time had passed since we last touched each other. And hey, out here, against the wall of our rented caravan, at least I could have reasonable certainty that there were no cameras. His tongue grazed my neck, and I pushed my hand beneath Ben's shirt, touching his bare chest and pulling him close to me.

"I want you," he murmured, "I want you so badly…"

"Take me…"

I undid his belt, dropping his trousers to the ground and snaking his thick, hard cock out of his pants. We could be quick and then no one would catch us. Ben surprised me by flipping me around, pressing me face first against the wall of the caravan and stripping me down. But instead of driving his rock hard cock between my legs, Ben Fox dropped to his knees.

Where He Put His Tongue

Ben's tongue spread my lips apart, and he drove his tongue between my legs. He wrapped his tongue around my clit and I couldn't stop myself from screaming. I relented to his tongue between my legs, allowing him to slide his tongue deeper inside me, taking every inch of me as I spread my legs further apart. My chest slammed against the side of the caravan as I moan louder. I didn't even care if anyone heard my loud, hot moans. Ben's tongue between my legs robbed me of all common sense.

I became fixated on one thing: climaxing. My thighs clamped around Ben's head and my fingers raked through his golden-brown hair as he held me up and buried his nose and lips between my legs. I couldn't stop myself from cumming. My legs trembled and the apex of my thighs dampened. I got wetter and wetter. Ben's eager tongue lapped every drop of my juices up.

He spread my ass cheeks and licked from my clit to my ass crack with full hungry strokes, unbothered by grazing his tongue against my tightly puckered hole. He pushed his tongue into my butt and ate my pussy and ass as I leaned against the caravan. Ben removed his face from my pussy and slid his entire cock into me urgently.

I cried out as Ben's monster dick slammed into me with one eager stroke. My walls stretched around his perfect dick and he wrapped his arm around me, grabbing my hips and pressing his body close to mine as he entered me deep. His tongue grazed my earlobes, and he nibbled on the soft lobes with his lips before his tongue slid down to the length of my neck.

"Your cunt's still perfect," he groaned, easing his hips against me and forcing his cock deeper. I cried out and Ben whispered, "Shh… I love you… I fucking love you…"

I came after his next thrust. I couldn't control myself. His cock was enormous and spreading me wide with how thick it was. I braced myself and pushed my hips back against him so Ben spread me wider and I took him deeper between my thighs. He groaned and grabbed onto a handful of my hair, craning my neck back as he kissed my neck and murmured to me as he fucked me.

"I'm never letting you go again," he whispered.

I came loudly, and he fucked me harder.

"You're mine, Liberty Jones…"

"Yes…" I whimpered, losing control of my legs as another intense climax overwhelmed my senses.

"Say it," he whispered, "Say what you love about my cock…"

"It's… big…"

"What else…"

I moaned again, unable to answer him as I screamed.

"I love… I love your big white cock…"

Ben groaned and pressed his body against mine, and he came. Hard. I squeezed my thighs together around his gigantic cock and Ben pulls out of me. He turns me around to face him and pins my hands over my head.

"What was that?"

"What?"

"Big… white… cock."

"Heat of the moment."

He pressed his fingers between my legs, splitting my wet pussy lips apart and rubbing my clit.

"Interesting…"

I wanted to ask what was so interesting about it, but his fingers rubbing around my sensitive engorged clit made me cum.

"W-what," I moaned out. Not exactly a complete question.

"It's hard to believe you were a virgin when we met… you're a very dirty girl."

"I am not!" I protested.

Ben kept my hands pinned with one of his hands.

"Yes you are," he whispered, "And I like it…"

He kissed my neck while fingering my pussy and I moaned again. He kissed me on the lips and then pulled his mouth away.

"It's good to fuck you again," he murmured, "And I plan on doing it more."

"Ben… I'm supposed to… have time to think."

"I'll give you time to think," he whispered, "But that doesn't mean we can't have sex until you decide."

"Won't that cloud my judgment?"

He grinned like a Cheshire cat.

"Am I that good, love?"

"Stop it," I whispered, "I'm trying to be serious."

"So am I…"

"So what? We're fuck buddies now?"

"Until you come to your senses and take me back."

I rolled my eyes.

"Is this you being apologetic?"

"I'll get on my knees and apologize more. I just plan on doing it by using my lips on your cunt."

"Does that count as apologizing?"

Ben dropped to his knees and gazed up at me.

"We can find out."

"Haven't we been out here long enough?" I whispered, "Someone might come out and find us."

"Do you really think they'll leave the MDMA and the drinks to see what we're up to?"

"I guess not."

"Spread your legs," Ben commanded, "I need to taste your cunt again."

Our Little Secret

I always knew Ben was crazy. I mean… that's kind of what I love about him. Let's be honest here. He's dark. Mysterious. And he makes no fucking sense. But isn't that half the fun? Still, as crazy as my rich British ex-boyfriend is, there's a reason he's my ex-boyfriend. He dumped me. And suddenly he wanted me to come to my senses and take him back.

To make matters worse, right when I had to make this critical decision, he kneeled in front of me, after giving me a good hard fucking behind the caravan, and he spread my legs again. Ben's tongue found my clit, and he nibbled my outer pussy lips before slipping and sliding his tongue around my engorged clit. Ben ate my pussy until I came harder. And harder. I couldn't stop myself from cumming when he finally moved his tongue away from me.

My legs wobbled as he rose to his knees again.

"Your cunt's delicious."

"B-Ben…"

Was he going to eat my pussy every time I tried to say something serious tonight?

"Shh," he whispered, "Don't say anything sensible."

"Why not?"

"Because. I've realized that thinking gets the better of both of us. It's better when we're like this."

"You're crazy."

He pressed his forearm against the caravan wall, leaning close to me.

"Yes. But you're the one with your cunt exposed outside a college party."

I scrambled to get dressed again as Ben chuckled, closing the distance between himself and the wall, pressing me closer there.

"Here's what I think the problem is," he whispered, "I've fucked it up by failing to show you how much I want you. So until you come to your senses, I'll do my best to show you."

"Why do I feel like this means trouble?"

"Because it does. And anyway, time apart is good for us right now. Someone has it out for us."

"How is time apart good?! Shouldn't we talk things through. You know… conversation!?"

"We need to find out who took that video and put it online. Plus, there's the whole Yasmin, Hope and Claire thing. We can handle that together, I know. But with the video, Marley will help, bless his soul, and once we find out who did it, I'll take care of them. Just like I plan on taking care of Yasmin and her band of bitches."

"You're scaring me again."

Ben kissed my forehead.

"Good."

"Ben…"

"Listen, Libs. We're going to go back inside and act like it's all neutral between us. I know you don't want us to be properly together again… yet."

"I love you… I just need time to think things through. I promise, I'll figure it out."

"Fine. But while you're figuring it out, and while everyone's asleep, I'm going to climb into bed and taste your cunt one more time before tomorrow."

"That sounds like a crazy plan."

"Yes. Probably. But you're right. We need time to figure us out. And we can't figure it out while someone's fucking with us. So whatever this is, whatever's happening between us, we can be… low-key."

"So a secret."

He shrugged.

"Sure. If you want to call it that."

"Don't you think Theo or your twin brother will figure it out?"

"Not if we're smart. Not if we're careful."

"If I'm with you, even kind-of-with-you, I don't want it to be a secret."

"Trust me, neither do I. But I've failed to protect you so many fucking times, I don't know if I can trust myself again. Plus, we can work together to find out who's fucking with us. It will be like… a secret mission."

"So your grand plan is for us to work together secretly while having sex until we figure out who's messing with us and then we get back together once it's sorted out."

"Exactly," Ben said, nodding and super proud of himself.

I hated to admit it, but his plan didn't sound too bad.

"You get space. You get time. We get to work together. And best of all, you still get to have my big white cock."

He lewdly grabbed at his dick through his boxer briefs and my cheeks grew hot.

"Don't make fun of me!"

"I'm not. I rather like it. My big white cock… It fits nicely inside your tight black cunt."

Before I could protest his word choice, Ben pushed me against the wall, kissing me hard again.

"A kiss to seal the deal?" I whispered, my hands rushing to his cheeks. I could hold those cheeks forever. I wanted to be cautious, but Ben was right. I could never quit him for good. My body didn't want me to. Not after so many orgasms.

"Yes," he responded.

"And… while we're figuring this out… no dating other people, right?"

Ben chuckled.

"There could never be other people. I think it's about time the two of us admit that to ourselves."

I nodded and kissed him again. He pulled away from me and murmured, "It's taking everything in my power not to fuck you again."

"We'd better go before someone figures out we're having sex. I mean, whoever's messing with us could be at this party."

"You're right."

"Should we go in separately?"

"Yes. I'll stand outside and pretend to have a cigarette. Fuck, I miss smoking."

I kissed his cheek.

"I'm proud of you for quitting."

He grinned.

"It's hard."

"I know. But I'm still proud. I never wanted you to dump me, Ben."

"I fucked up."

"I'm sorry I can't just leap into your arms again."

He shrugged.

"It's my fault. Like I said, I'll show you just how much I love you. But please, can you do me one favor, Libs?"

"What?"

"Don't push me away. I'm trying. I'm trying to be the guy you want me to be. But I can't do that if you force me away."

I nodded.

"Head inside 007," he teased, "I'll be there in a minute."

"Got it. And as far as anyone knows, there's nothing going on between us."

Ben nodded.

"Our little secret."

Millie: Punished

We walked back into the party separately. Theo and Arnie exchanged glances, and tried to get us to reveal what happened between us. I had no intention of spilling the beans. Ben was right, maybe this was smarter. Theo came up to me with a drink.

"It's only juice. What happened out there?"

"Nothing crazy."

"So… are you two back together?"

"No," I said, trying my best to sound sad, "I don't know if that will ever happen."

Theo scratched his head.

"I'm surprised you two spent that much time around each other without having sex."

I buried my guilty expression in a cup of juice.

"Uh oh, incoming," Theo whispered.

I glanced up to see Millie stomping up to me. Arnie watched from the corner of the room and Theo puffed out his chest as he stood next to me.

"What, Millie?" Theo snapped before she could say anything.

Millie gasped and tousled honey blond curls out of her face.

"Why are you talking to me like that?"

"You're coming over here to bother Libby, aye? Then get to fuck, because I'm not having it."

"Since when do you care?"

"Whatever you have to say to Libby, you can say to me."

"Fine. I think she's a stupid fat ugly cunt who's jealous of Yasmin because Yasmin fucked Ben. There. I said it."

Except. I know the truth. Yasmin never had sex with Ben.

"Sorry you feel that way," I said to Millie, smiling sweetly.

"I'm sorry that they didn't rip your gash you stupid slut. Everyone knows you fucked Arnie after pretending to be friends with my sister. Man stealing bitch."

"Are you done, Millie?"

"No, I'm not done. I'm saying what everyone else thinks."

"You know what, Millie?"

"What?"

Yeah. I lost control. I took an open bowl of punch and threw it all over her. Oops. I stormed off to the bedroom in the back of the caravan and slammed the door shut. Millie was screaming. Obviously. But I had to get away from there to cool off. Dean Warren was already keeping a close eye on me because of the incident. And I'd have to fight the "incident" once I got back to campus — in court. I couldn't risk fucking with Millie and having that used against me. But I couldn't stand there and listen to her mouth off at me. A fucking Year 12?

Hell no.

But, I'd just made a scene, so naturally, Arnie and Theo came into the room to check on me. Arnie laughed and high-fived me.

"That was fucking hilarious. She's a cunt."

"Whatever. I'm over it. I just want to chill and go to bed."

"Sure?" Theo asked, "I'll sit in front the door and guard it."

"You two should have fun."

"I'll tell Ben."

"Don't bother. I swear, I'm okay."

And I was. But I'd had enough partying and wanted to chill for the rest of the night. Alone."

Arnie and Theo eventually gave up and went outside. I could see Theo's shadow under the door and he was standing guard like he promised. I got under the covers and woke up a couple hours later. The last men standing at the party were the only ones left in the caravan. I climbed out of bed and pushed the door open, rousing Theo, who'd fallen asleep against the door.

He jumped up once he saw me.

"You're up?"

"Who's still partying?"

"Nick Knight, Ben, and Arnie. Crazy wankers."

Nick Knight stood on the table shirtless, performing a Boris Johnson impression while Arnie and Ben drank. It was like Ben could only quit one substance at once… Once they saw me, they set their drinks down. Arnie and Ben were getting along better than I'd ever seen.

"LIBBBYYYY!"

Nick Knight followed their lead and cheered my name too.

"Hey," I muttered sleepily.

Arnie brought a bottle of vodka to me. The smell made me sick, and I wrinkled my nose and waved him off.

"No thanks."

"Feeling better?" Arnie asked.

"Yeah."

"Good. We've taken care of Millie," Nick Knight said, jumping off the table and putting his shirt on.

"What? How?"

Ben shrugged.

"Don't worry about it."

"What the hell did you guys do…"

Nick Knight pressed his finger to his lips.

"Shhh…"

He pointed to the caravan bathroom. I could hear a light pounding of fists against the door once the boys fell silent. I swore I heard Millie say, "Let me out of here you wankers!"

"Did you lock her in there?!"

"Worse. She's in there with the biggest dump I've ever taken in my life," Nick Knight laughed.

"Nick's known for legendary dumps," Theo said.

"I don't even want to know why you know that…"

"Seriously, we fight on rugby trips so we don't have to share a loo with him."

"Dude, don't expose me to a girl."

"Okay. You guys are gross. Can't she just flush!?"

"I turned the toilet off outside," Arnie said.

"You guys are wicked."

"I don't like anyone fucking with you," Ben said.

We exchanged glances and glanced away from each other.

"LET ME OUT!" I could hear Millie yelling louder now. She probably figured she should pick up the pace now that it was quiet.

"Well… I guess she'd better learn her lesson."

"We'll let her out in the morning," Theo said.

"We should get back to school in the morning."

"Aye, aye," Arnie said, pouring more vodka right down his throat.

"Let's play a drinking game," Nick said.

"Like what?"

"I don't... I'm so fucking pissed... I don't even know."

"Get his arse to bed," Ben said, "We ought to call it a night."

Theo nodded and dragged Nick Knight's drunk ass back to his caravan. Arnie went into the bedroom he was sharing with Theo while Ben climbed onto the couch in the messy caravan living room.

"I'd better get back to bed. Thanks for cheering me up, guys. It's been... distracting. That's for sure."

I climbed into bed again after saying goodnight and thanks. The morning mess would be hell, and if we needed to get back to school, it made sense for me to go straight to sleep. I fell asleep quickly but woke up to a dark figure creeping into bed with me. I gasped and felt a hand clasp down over my mouth.

"It's me. Shhhh," he whispered.

Ben. He snuck into bed next to me and put his arm around me. He didn't get my clothes off, he just pulled me close and kissed my cheek.

"Tonight wasn't perfect... but I know we'll make it through, love."

"Yeah. So do I."

"And what happened with those girls... we'll fight this."

"How? Dean Warren hasn't even mentioned what's really going to happen."

"Do you have a lawyer?"

I groaned.

"Now you do," Ben whispered, "Trust me… I'll handle this. And we'll make sure those girls pay."

"Millie's paying," I whispered.

"Yes. I'm glad you didn't stop us… I'd hate to have her stinking up the party, smelling of shite."

"Ew! Ben!"

"Come here… I miss you falling asleep in my arms."

"I miss you too, Ben…"

A New Lawyer, An Enemy Returns, A Proposition

In the morning, Ben's back on the couch. Arnie and Theo cleaned up the entire place before I could wake up as Ben grumbled at them to let him sleep in peace. Once they finished, Arnie inched toward the bathroom where Millie had presumably slept with the potent stench of Nick Knight's mega-dookie. He flung the door open and my eyes watered from the smell. Holy fuck. They weren't kidding around about that. Millie shrieked, but she didn't stop to make a bitchy comment or even to hit her kidnapper in the face. Getting locked in the bathroom had humbled her, I guess. I couldn't help but smirk as she tearfully burst out of the caravan back to her friends. After that, it was time for us to leave.

Arnie drove his car home with Eugenie in the front seat half asleep. The rugby boys and Millie took their respective cars, but we left before they did. It wasn't long before we returned to campus. By the time we got to campus, Theo walked me back to my dorm.

"So... you and Ben... still not happening?"

"Nope."

"Hm."

"What?"

"Not sure if I believe you."

"Believe me. Ben and I are… too messed up right now."

"If you insist. Guess I'll see you later, then?"

"Yeah. Dean Warren will probably want to talk to me."

"Right. Okay. Well, I'm off."

"Thanks for trying. I have to admit… it was nice to get off campus."

"Good. Let us know if Dean Warren chats to you."

"Yup."

Eugenie bounded toward the door and Theo tipped his head before he walked off, sticking a spliff into his mouth before leaving.

"He's going to get expelled if he's caught smoking that stuff," Eugenie commented.

I shrugged.

"Theo Hargreaves is… complicated."

"He's cute. Do you have a crush on him?"

"No!"

Eugenie smirked as we entered our bedroom together.

"I know. You still like Ben, don't you?"

Eugenie leaned forward and wrinkled her nose, mock gasping.

"I knew it! You're turning red."

"I don't know if you've noticed, but I don't turn red."

"Are you sure? You seem a little red to me. Maybe it's purple."

"I don't like Ben!"

"Ha! A confession!"

"How was that a confession?"

"I know you, Liberty. Anywho. We'd better get to sleep."

She was right. Our caravan night wasn't enough sleep, so we passed out for a while. By the time I woke up, my phone was vibrating off my bed. I groaned and answered it.

"What?"

"Liberty."

"Who the hell is this?"

I didn't look at the number before I picked up.

"It's your fucking lab partner. Where are you!"

"Hm?"

"We're supposed to meet at dinner tonight to discuss the lab."

"Shit. I didn't remember."

"I didn't tell you."

"Arnie!" I hissed.

"Hurry!" he hissed back and hung up.

It was almost like I enjoyed having those stupid boys torture me. I changed quickly and hustled to dinner where Arnie sat alone with his physics text books spread out. A lonely-looking Year 12 approached his table and Arnie loudly exclaimed, "Beat it, Year 12! Unless you have an understand of mechanics, this seat is taken... Libby!"

"You are evil."

"I've had a breakthrough for our final project."

"Ever heard of texting? I'm exhausted."

Arnie ignored me, and we worked through our project for a while. I'll give him credit, his idea wasn't half bad, and we got ahead on our assignment and triple checked the problems. I couldn't stay long to hang out with the rest of the art freaks because Dean Warren sent me a message on my school email, ordering me to report to her office. The incident reared its ugly head again.

I got to Dean Warren's office, and she solemnly invited me in. I mentally went over whether I'd missed anything. My mandatory counseling appointment hadn't come up yet. Maybe it was the lawyer thing. Fuck. I had to check on that. Seriously.

"Liberty, have a seat."

I obeyed her instructions, pulling up a seat across from her desk as Dean Warren fidgeted with a rubber band ball until I sat down.

"Your lawyer contacted the school. We're going to use the chapel to conduct an unofficial proceeding and negotiation. I would consider pressing criminal charges... except... I think you ought to hear what they're offering first."

I raised an eyebrow suspiciously. I knew boarding school administrations well enough to understand that they often did what was convenient to them and what kept their prestigious name out of the press, rather than what was best for their students. I had friends behind me who'd help me fight this.

"Dean Warren, I'm sorry if this is speaking out of turn, but what they did to me was awful. What could they possibly offer that would be worth that?"

"You must discuss it with your lawyer. She's on the way here right now. Oh, and we got in touch with your mother. She's on the way."

"What?!"

"Yes, she called the office and said she wanted it to be a surprise, but... who likes surprises?"

"M-my mother?!" I squeaked.

"Don't worry dear, you don't have to tell her all the details of what happened. She'll be with your lawyers, making sure it all works out. She sounded very concerned about you."

"Dean Warren, I'm not in touch with my mother. I... My mother has nothing to do with this!"

"I understand these situations can be awkward to contend with. Lord knows, I'm a parent. But every mother would want to help her daughter through something like this."

Yeah, every other mother. Not mine. Fuck. Fuck. Fuck. Just my luck. Rapetti Academy couldn't put their expert detective work to use anywhere else, huh? I whipped my phone out, intending to send Ben, Arnie, Eugenie and Theo a quick 'S.O.S.' text. Eugenie didn't know about the drama with my mother, but she was a good friend now. Frankly, she was the best roommate I'd had since entering Rapetti.

Before I could get the message sent out, the door thrust open and a tall, blonde woman with familiar blue eyes strode into the room. My first impression was she looked like someone I knew.

"H-hello. I'm Liberty Jones," I said, sticking my hand out and shaking it.

She grasped my hand with a firm lawyer's handshake.

"Wow. You're stunning. He told me you would be. Gorgeous!"

She continued, setting down her briefcase on Dean Warren's desk.

"I'm Leonora Hargreaves. Theodore's half sister."

£10,000,000

Surprise! My lawyer's Theo's sister. She has some of his mannerisms, but she's polished and coiffed. Dean Warren gives us a room so we can talk alone. I feel so embarrassed that Theo's sister knows the details of my case. I guess she has good instincts because detecting my worry she smiles and says, "Don't worry. We have client confidentiality. I know you and my little brother are good friends."

"Yeah. We are. Sorry… It's just… I didn't expect you to be here. I didn't know Theo had a half-sister."

"We're not close. It surprised me to hear from my little brother but your case… I'm sorry to be forward, but I've wanted to work in racial discrimination for a long time."

"Racial discrimination?"

Was she sure she had the right case?

"Yes. This case won't be before a jury. We'll hash it out with a judge and I believe that what happened to you was both motivated by race and gender. We have a strong case and I know the families we're dealing with. We're going to aim high and ask for a settlement of £25,000,000."

"Twenty-five million pounds!?" I squeak.

"They'll lowball us, probably. Maybe they'll settle for ten to fifteen million."

"So… they wouldn't go to jail or anything?"

"Dean Warren never mentioned you wanted a criminal trial."

"Do I have a choice?"

"I'm getting paid very well, love. Whatever you want to do, I'll do it. But we're more likely to get money than harsh prison sentences, I'll be honest."

"Then we'll do it."

"Sure? This is up to you, Liberty."

"If you think we can win."

Leonora smiles.

"Love, I don't know if they told you but I've never lost a case. I don't plan for this to be the first."

"Thank you."

"No problem. Now… let's review what happened."

She took notes dutifully as I told her all I remembered. I was getting used to rehashing my trauma for people. This wasn't the first time something awful happened to me and once I finished, Leonora looked concerned.

"Please, Liberty. After what you've gone through, go see the counselor. Rapetti has great counseling."

"Leonora? I have a question."

"Yes?"

"Dean Warren said my mother's on the way but... I don't want to see her. Can you help?"

"I'll handle it."

"Thanks."

"Counseling. Take my advice."

I'd take her advice if I could. After the meeting, Leonora promised she'd stay in touch and when I exited the Dean's office, Theo leaned against the wall. Leonora stayed behind to talk to Dean Warren and review my case.

"How was it?"

"Don't you have rugby practice right now?"

"I asked our dear captain if I could come late today. Want to walk me to the fields? You can watch practice."

"Sure."

It wasn't like I had anything better to do. Whenever I thought about the incident with Yasmin and the other girls, I felt sick to my stomach. I didn't want to be alone, and going to watch Ben and Theo on the rugby field was as good an idea as any.

"We're doing shirtless practice today. If you get lucky, you can glimpse my fit guns."

"Ew."

"Oi! I'm not half bad."

"Whatever. Let's go."

We walked to the rugby fields and Theo thankfully didn't ask me about the case or his sister. When I got there, I was in for a visual feast. Every single rugby guy had his shirt off and Theo set his bag down on the stands. Luckily, I wasn't there alone. There was someone else sitting and watching the game. Someone I didn't expect to see.

"Danny?"

"Hey!" she waved.

I walked over to sit next to her.

"What are you doing here?"

"The boys are soooo hot. I watch every practice."

"Um... all of them?"

Didn't she have homework? Even when Ben and I were properly together, I never watched every single one of their practices.

"Yes. I love rugby. Plus, they're so dreamy. Look at Theo..."

I glanced over at Theo.

"His tattoos are so sexy."

I giggled. Danny was... blunt, to say the least.

"Girl, you crazy."

"I have a crush on Edward Chapman. He's so fit. I love blonds."

Ben waved at us as he passed the ball to Nick Knight. I waved back and Danny gasped.

"Are you two back together?"

"No! Why would you ask that?"

"Don't know. I heard you were a cute couple."

"Who said that?"

"Okay, don't tell anyone, but a couple weekends ago, I snuck into a rugby party and the boys were gossiping about it."

"The boys?!"

"Don't let them fool you. They're such gossips. And they're not mean all the time… only to impress the popular girls."

"I know what you mean."

"My sister's been so pissed off ever since…"

She trailed off.

"Ever since what?"

"I don't think I'm supposed to say."

"Now I'm curious!"

"I should be loyal to my sister."

"I get it. She's family."

Danny bit down on her lower lip like she could hold the words back.

"Yasmin's been talking about getting revenge once she gets back to campus. I don't think she'll come back so... you probably don't have to worry."

Right. I didn't have to worry. But not for the reason Danny thought. I'd been doing some thinking. I'd been the nice girl for so damn long. I only acted up once in a while. And when I saw the way Ben and Theo and everyone else defended themselves, I felt like I could never do that. But maybe there was a bad bitch in me deep down. Instead of waiting for Yasmin and her crew to get revenge... maybe it was time for me to act first. But I'd have to be patient.

I changed the subject and after rugby practice I walked with Danny to the caf and we had dinner together. I met Arnie in the evening to do physics homework and then Eugenie joined us and told me she'd be sneaking out to sleep in Arnie's room that night, so I shouldn't worry. As far as I was concerned, that was none of my business. I was happy to get some time alone before bed.

But before I could fall asleep, pebbles flew at my window, rattling the glass and waking me up. I put my hands up to the glass to peek outside. Benjamin. I threw my window open, and he approached.

"Good evening, fair maiden. I know your roommate's out."

"Arnie planned that with you, didn't he?"

"Yes, milady. Now... may I enter your humble abode?"

Enticing Ben

I reminded Ben that we could get in huge trouble for this as he thrust my window open and climbed in, taking my stern reminder as a tacit agreement that he was allowed to enter. I didn't mind. Ben left the window open and leaned against the sill, stuffing his hands in his pockets.

"Missed you."

"I missed you too."

"Unfortunately, I'm not here just for a chance to see you naked."

"Who said you had a chance to see me naked?"

"Dreaming, Libby. As I always am about you."

"Why did you come?"

"I got something in the mail today."

He set a small envelope on the windowsill next to him. I grabbed the opened envelope and pulled out the sheet of paper with pasted magazine letters, like something out of a movie.

"It's blackmail."

"Yes."

"Any idea who it's from?"

"I had Marley trace the server of whoever uploaded the video, but he thinks it's a VPN since the server came in as from Belarus."

"Shit."

"All we have to work with is this letter and anyone who may have it out for me."

"Why you?"

"Read it."

Dear Ben,

You cannot get away with murder.

Who was that girl in the video?

Does she know you're a killer?

I will end your life.

What can you do about it?

Nothing.

No signature.

"This message is weird. Maybe they're trying to throw us off the trail."

"Maybe. But it came from outside Rapetti. Definitely. Look at the postage mark."

"It's from Scotland."

"Yeah."

"Do you know anyone who has it out for you in Scotland?"

"Malcolm. But he's not the type. He prefers to handle his problems more directly."

"So all we have is this note… It's not much of a clue."

"I know. I guess we have to wait until they send something else."

"That last line is creepy as hell."

"You know what I've done."

"That doesn't make you a killer," I say.

Ben presses his finger beneath my chin, tilting my head up so I can see him.

"You're right," he whispers, "It doesn't."

"Aren't you scared?"

Ben's green eyes met mine and he shook his head.

"No."

"They threatened to end your life."

"Idle threats. I won't allow them to intimidate me."

"Should we go to the police?"

"I don't know what we'd tell them. The best option we have is a private investigator but… Marley will do."

"You trust Marley with this?"

"We have an agreement together. It works out."

"I'll never understand boys."

Ben grinned.

"How was Leo?"

"She was great. But… My mom's in town."

"Shit."

"I told Leo to fend her off."

"Good. I had no idea she was here."

"Neither did I."

"Do you want me to handle it?"

"No. I'm hoping a lawyer will scare her off. She doesn't like dealing with the law."

"Aye."

Ben stroked the soft stubble that was coming in on his cheeks and chin.

"We've discussed business. I think it's time I see you naked, eh?"

"Ben…"

He squeezed my cheeks and pulled my face close to his so our lips were inches away from each other.

"Don't deny me your cunt, princess. We're risking life and limb for our secret mission."

"Kiss me," I murmured.

Ben kissed me, his perfect lips meeting mine and distracting me from the pressing issues surrounding me: my mother's pending arrival, Ben's blackmail note, and my school grades. Hey, I still wanted to be valedictorian, despite all our shenanigans.

"Clothes off," Ben murmured, "I'll be quick."

"You don't have to be quick," I blurted out.

He grabbed me by the hips and lifted me onto my bed, sliding his torso between my legs and squeezing my thighs.

"Is that so? Do you want me to fuck you slowly?"

I wrapped my arm around his shoulders and hooked my ankles together around his torso.

"I want… I want you to stay the night."

"Ah, you'll condemn me to the walk of shame in the morning. Naughty girl."

"Only for you."

"I love it when you talk dirty."

His fingers scuttled up my thighs and Ben slipped a probing finger past my underwear, sliding it deep inside me. I cried out as his finger plunged into my depths and I bucked my hips forward across the bed so his finger could enter my pussy deeper. He massaged my inner walls with his finger until I moaned. He clamped his free hand around my mouth and whispered, "Shhh…"

"I'm trying," I gasped as he pressed another finger inside me, causing me to feel ridiculously full.

"Good girl," he murmured, "Keep trying. It'll get harder once my lips are against your cunt."

"Ben..." I whimpered.

Keeping two fingers buried inside my pussy, Ben crouched and slipped my panties to the side as he bent his head to my pussy and flattened his tongue along the length of my soaked slit. I squeezed my thighs around Ben's head and his tongue drove inside me deeper. Ben ate my pussy until I came and when I finished, he pulled my underwear off and spread my thighs, lying me back on the bed as he crawled between my thighs and pressed his head between my legs again.

"I love it," he whispered, "Tasting your beautiful black pussy."

Hearing Ben talk dirty made me horny. Super horny. His tongue flicked across my clit and I couldn't control myself again. I came. Hard. Ben kissed my inner thighs, and licked up my juices before he used his tongue on my outer lips, massaging me to a near climax before he returned to my clit. When I came again, he pulled away from my pussy and kissed my lips, pressing his warm, muscular body into mine as we made out. I could feel his hardness straining in his pants, yearning to get out of his pants, but Ben didn't make a move to enter me right away.

He pushed hair out of my face and murmured, "I love you."

"I love you too."

"I don't want you to take more time."

"Ben... please... I have a lot going on right now."

"Okay. I get it."

"Are we going to fuck now?"

He chuckled and kissed my forehead.

"Love… I can't have sex with you again until you decide?"

"Are you serious?"

Ben was a nineteen-year-old boy. I couldn't imagine a world where he'd have me in bed with my panties off and restrain himself.

"Gravely so. It's clouding our judgment, innit? And it's not withholding, because I ate your cunt until you came. It's… abstinence."

I laughed.

"Abstinence?"

"Temporary abstinence."

"This is torture?"

"Oi, you're the one who climaxed several times tonight."

"True."

"Lie with me, Liberty Jones. I miss falling asleep with you."

I snuggled up next to Ben. Maybe he was right about the temporary "abstinence". But this was… torture. I wanted to fuck him. I mean, women are like that, right? You get your pussy eaten and the last thing you want is to roll over and drop to sleep. I curled up as the little spoon and then poked my butt back so I could find Ben's cock through his pants. He kissed my shoulder and wrapped his arm around me, ignoring my wriggling butt rubbing against his package.

I started methodically grinding my hips back and Ben whispered, "Nice try, Libs. It won't work."

"You won't fall asleep hard!"

"Hm," he murmured, "I might. I like your little bum on my cock. But I won't fuck you tonight. Or at all until we get back together."

"Now this is blackmail."

"No. It's keeping our heads clear. We'll sort everything out. I know we will."

I poked my butt back a little more to entice Ben, but he pinned me beneath the weight of his muscular arms and murmured one last time, "Move your arse again and I'll spank your little bum."

I quieted down and let him hold me as we fell asleep. In the morning, I noted Ben's absence in my bed. He'd taken the blackmail letter with him but he left another letter on my desk. I picked it up to read Ben's shockingly neat script.

I Swung Hard At Her Head

*D*ear Liberty,

I ducked out before either of us could get in trouble. I want to see you again tonight. And kiss you. And stroke your hair. I'm going to do everything in my power to win you back properly. Until then, we wait. Whoever messaged me will probably send another. Come to rugby practice again today after school. When I watch you in the stands it makes me want to work harder.

Love,

Benjamin

His note was sweet, and I folded it before slipping it in my bag as I dress in my uniform for school. Eugenie snuck back into the room right as I was about to leave. She was sniffling and looked a bit upset.

"Everything okay?"

"Yeah. I'm fine. Arnie and I… We decided to stop hooking up."

"Aw. I'm sorry. Did something happen?"

She shook her head.

"I knew he didn't want anything serious, but I guess a part of me hoped that he would change his mind or something."

I hugged Eugenie tightly.

"Boys are weirdos."

"I know. I shouldn't let it bother me."

"There's got to be someone else you can have a crush on. You know, distract yourself."

Eugenie smiled.

"I wish."

"What about Vandy?"

"Him?"

"He's blond. He's American. That's exotic."

"Not more exotic than Arnav."

"Arnav?"

I thought her problem might have been with the fact that Vandy played rugby. But Arnav played rugby too, and he was as much of a jock as Vandy.

"Is it weird that he's Indian?"

"No. It's not weird that you like him either."

"Ok, I have a confession to make," Eugenie said.

"What?"

"It's not that I like Arnav. I like Arnie. But I think Arnav's fit. And after the party… I wanted to talk to him. But… my parents are racist. Like they're racist. I feel like if I go after him and they find out. I dunno. It's stupid."

"They'd really have a problem with you dating outside your race in 2020?"

"Big time."

"Shit."

"I know. Maybe I'll try talking to him today."

"It can't hurt. Don't let haters tell you who to date. All that race stuff, it's all imaginary in a way, you know? We're all just people. We love who the hell we love."

"Thanks, Libby. You know how to make me feel better."

I planned to make it to the dining hall early. I wanted to talk to Theo some more about his sister and get some homework done before classes. Dean Warren had other plans. She intercepted me and insisted I come right with her to the Dean's office. And there she was when she entered. My mother.

Dean Warren ushered me into her office and said, "I'll leave you two to talk. I need to meet with Miss Hargreaves and the other lawyers."

"Mom."

"Libby!" My mom squealed and wrapped her arms around me. I didn't hug her back. What the hell was she doing here?

Hadn't she put me through enough this summer? Hadn't she

messed with my life plenty? Why did she have to keep doing this? I wrested myself away from her.

"Seriously, mom. What are you doing here?"

"I brought your sister."

"Mom…"

"And listen, I know you are deeply involved with that Ben boy but stay away. Their family's dangerous. His father faked everything. Faked the paternity results. 'Proved' it wasn't his baby. Nonsense. The baby has his eyes! Whose baby could it be? I know it ain't Ben's. Well, *you'd* better hope not!"

I folded my arms.

"You should leave. I don't care if you have my so-called sister with you. I don't care if you brought the Queen of Fucking England. Whatever's going on here, I don't want you involved."

"They raped you. I get it. You blame me. Like you blame me for every damn thing."

"Why the hell did you come here?"

"Don't talk to me like that, Liberty. I'm here because my daughter is a rape victim. And those girls will pay for everything they did to you. You can't put a price on my daughter's virginity."

"Virginity? What the hell do you think happened?"

"I don't know what happened! All I know is they raped your dumb ass and now… well, I heard you and Mister Fox are no longer together. It's no surprise. He wouldn't want a pass-around hoe with all that money he's got."

"Mom. I'm not a fucking virgin."

Chilling and awkward silence descended between us. But I'd started and I couldn't make myself stop.

"I'm not a virgin because I fucked Ben. I've fucked Ben… oh, over a hundred times by now, probably. And he's not even the only guy I've kissed!"

"You're a slut. I knew it."

"Did you, mom? What else do you know about me? I mean, you're probably the worst fucking mother on the planet, so enlighten me. What the fuck do you know?"

"Liberty, watch your damn mouth," she huffed.

Her fake-nice façade that she always put on when we hadn't seen each other in a while was falling faster these days. Whatever. I couldn't deny that I enjoyed wiping the smile right off her face. She had no right to do this — to show up here after everything that happened and act like we were friends. She didn't even know what I'd been through. She didn't even know what happened at the end of the summer. She didn't know that I took a gun, and I shot…

"Why are you staring into space like a dumb goldfish?" she snapped, "No wonder that white boy got tired of you with that ghetto ass mouth of yours."

"Shut up."

"What did you say to me?"

"I said… SHUT. UP."

"You shut your mouth little girl or I'll box your fucking head?"

"Drinking again, mom? Or are you here to pretend to be a half-decent mother so you can get some settlement money? Aren't you tired of using your family member's trauma for money?"

"Liberty Jones, I swear your ugly black ass looks more like your dead daddy every day."

My hands clenched into fists.

"What the fuck did you say?"

My body shook. I could feel myself losing control. My neck tightened and blood flowed to my head too fast. My fists clenched.

"Your ugly black ass daddy made himself an ugly black ass kid. I learned my lesson with you two girls and with those ain't shit black men."

"Don't talk about dad like that," I answered, my voice falling to an unsettling whisper.

"Oh, you real quiet now, huh? Done looking like a hoe ass fish with your mouth hanging open."

She imitated my mouth and crossed her eyes before laughing.

"Say sorry," I said.

"For what?"

"Say sorry."

"The only thing I'm sorry about is that I didn't make that daddy of yours bust a nut in a condom. I mean, look at you talking about how you ain't a virgin. Fast ass hoe. That's what you are. A dirty little hoe."

"Say. Sorry."

"Or what?"

"Fuck you, mom."

She raised her hand and slapped me across the face. That was all I needed. I hit back. Hard. I lost my goddamned mind. There was nothing in this world that could ever get me that mad except talking shit about not just daddy, but Niecy. Those were the only family I had and while my mom scammed fundraisers after their death, I was a lonely little nerd who didn't fit in with the other St Louis girls. All I had was a dream. And while I made that dream happen, all she could do was fuck with me. And shit on me. And tell me I would never be good enough.

I swung on my own goddamn mama, but she wouldn't let that slide. She put her hands around my neck and she squeezed, slamming my back against the wall as she choked me out in Dean Warren's office.

I Lost My Mind

I struggled to pry my mother's hands from around my neck. But I get it. Someone like her doesn't get that involved with the Russian mafia without learning how to fight. Plus, my mom could fight back in St Louis. I took after my dad. I liked people who got into trouble, but I kept to myself, not looking for problems with people as much as I could. All the good that did me. Her thumb clamped down around my neck and I freaked.

My legs shot out and my feet hit her right in the crotch. She didn't let go of me at first, but then I kicked again. Harder. She couldn't hold on to me anymore and her hands left my neck. I raced for the door. She grabbed my hair and yanked back. I screamed and elbowed her in the stomach. She swiped forward, throwing me off balance. I nearly hit my head on the side of the desk, but I grabbed onto the side and pull a stapler off Dean Warren's desk. I hit her shoulder. Then her head. Then her shoulder. I pushed my mom hard against the wall and screamed, "GET OUT. GET. OUT."

Her eyes widened in terror, and she fumbled with the door handle before running. Naturally, Dean Warren came scuttling back. She didn't hear everything, but she heard a lot.

"What is going on here, Miss Jones? Are you okay? Fix your uniform!"

I adjusted my skirt. My heart pounding.

"Sh-She attacked me. I'm fine."

Dean Warren glanced around the corner down the hall where my mom took off running.

"She attacked you? Oh my word, child. You look battered."

"I'm fine."

"We've got to get you to the health center. And what about that counseling appointment?"

Shit. I'd forgotten about counseling. I didn't want to go to counseling. I wanted to go sit and watch Ben play rugby with his shirt off. I wanted to sit next to Danny and feel like I had a friend. I wanted to hang out with Eugenie and gossip about boys.

"Yeah. I'll go after class."

"Good. Now what about the health center?"

"I'm fine, Dean Warren."

"If you insist, Libby. I have to let you know. The hearing is in three weeks. You'll have a meeting with Miss Hargreaves a few times beforehand to review the case, but other than that, it's in her capable hands."

"Thank you, Dean Warren."

She handed me a sheet of paper.

"This is the time, date and location of the hearing."

"It's going to be on campus?"

"In a private meeting room. You can have friends wait outside for support."

"Okay. Cool."

"I'll check in with the counselor to make sure you show up."

I was shaking and nervous when I left Warren's office. The last thing I wanted to do was run into my mom again. I had to assume she left. My throat hurt and I was so angry, I could scream. Or hit someone. I had an apple at breakfast, but I didn't have time to sit and eat it. And I didn't want to go to class either. Fuck it.

I wandered the hall of the schoolhouse until I saw Theo in one of the student lounges, scratching his head as he tried to solve some math problem. Poor Theo, math wasn't his strongest subject. He smiled and looked up when he saw me.

"Libs! Leonora talked to me about the hearing. She thinks you're going to win. Wait… are you okay?"

"What class does Ben have?" I snapped.

"Um… I dunno."

"You're his best friend."

"Why do you want to know what class Ben has?" Theo asked suspiciously.

"Tell me. Now."

"He's got Latin seminar with Dr. Perez."

"Classroom?"

"A2 in the basement."

I walked off without saying goodbye and ignored Theo as he said, "Where are you going?"

I paused in the basement student lounge near the mailroom to rip out a sheet of paper where I imitated Dean Warren's handwriting.

"Dr. Perez, I need to see Benjamin Fox urgently — Warren."

I folded the paper neatly and knocked on the classroom door, interrupting the lecture and putting on my best innocent voice.

"Um, excuse me, Dr. Perez, I have a note from Dean Warren."

I was a top student who never seemed to be the one perpetrating trouble. Dr. Perez had no reason to doubt me and he pointed at Ben.

"Mr. Fox, this young lady requests your presence in Dean Warren's office. Run along so I may continue the lecture."

If Dr. Perez had been any more hip to student gossip, he might have found it suspicious that Ben's ex-girlfriend was the one signing him out of class, but he was older and blissfully oblivious. Ben followed me out of his classroom with his book bag but he wasn't suspicious either.

"What's wrong?"

I grabbed his hand and walked two doors down to the "family" restroom in the basement. I pushed the door open and dragged Ben inside, kicking the door shut and locking it.

"Are you on one?"

I slammed my hand over his mouth and locked the door behind him. I needed to talk without Ben interrupting or questioning me.

"Ben. My mom came to Dean Warren's today. Things got heated. She choked me out. I pushed her and kicked her and it was a mess. I don't know why she's here but, she's back. And I don't want to talk about it."

I removed my hand from Ben's mouth and he uttered, "Are you serious?", before I clamped my hand over his mouth again.

"I don't want to talk about it. Pants off. Now."

I removed my hand from his mouth again and Ben stared back at me, dumbfounded.

"Have you lost it?" he gasped.

"Pants off."

"Liberty… Think… Someone could hear us."

I undid Ben's belt buckle myself. He loosened his tie and undid the buttons of his shirt as I pulled his pants down. Ben was hard. I unzipped my skirt and let it fall. Ben grabbed my waist and kissed me hard, pressing me against the wall of the bathroom and lifting me off the ground.

"Condom," Ben whispered.

"No. I don't care."

"Libby."

"Fine. Whatever."

Ben fumbled around for a condom and slid it on his cock before he pressed the tip of his cock against my entrance and he pushed his hips forward, sliding the full length of his cock at the apex of my thighs. Fuck. I ran my fingers through Ben's golden brown hair and moaned, "Fuck me. Fuck me, Ben…"

Danny's Secret

Ben eased his hips forward, plunging into me deeper.

"You've lost your mind," he whispered.

"Harder…"

Ben kissed me, pumping into me deep as I moaned.

"Harder, Ben…"

"Libs… What's gotten into you."

I dug my nails into his shoulder and gasped, "Harder."

I was close. So close. Ben thrust his hips forward, and I came. Hard. Ben ushered his dick into me deeper until he came. When he pulled out of me, he tossed the condom in the bin and set me on the ground, clutching my hips, staring madly into my eyes for answers. Had I lost my mind? What came over me?

I grabbed his cheeks and kissed him.

"You'd better get dressed."

"I'm not leaving this loo until you tell me what the hell that was for?"

I shrugged.

"I wanted sex. You wanted sex. We had sex. It doesn't need explaining."

"Liberty… Is it because of your mum?"

"I don't know."

"I told her to leave us alone. I told her not to bother you. If she's back, I'll handle it."

"I don't need you to handle it. I got her ass pretty good earlier."

Ben stared at me a few seconds again, his mouth hanging open.

"Stop looking at me like that."

"What, like you've gone completely mental?"

"I'm fine. I had a lot of energy and we worked it out. It's all fine."

I pulled my skirt up and zipped the sides. Ben grabbed my wrist and squeezed, drawing me into him.

"I wouldn't be a good boyfriend if I didn't worry."

"Good thing you're not my boyfriend."

His grasp tightened.

"I want to change that. You know it."

I pulled my arm away from him.

"Put your clothes on, Ben. You'd better get back to class."

I left the bathroom and Ben in it. He probably thought I was cuckoo crazy, but it was too late for me to worry about that. Fuck. I probably should I have told Ben that I couldn't make it to his rugby practice because of counseling. Whatever. I could tell him later. And so much for holding back from sex… We couldn't even last a day. Sigh. Maybe I am going crazy. I mean, I practically pounced on him.

After classes, I made my way to the counselor's office. I knocked tentatively on the office door and it swung open. A short, bearded man with a red bowtie opened the door.

"Liberty!"

"Hi. I… um… I have an appointment."

"Yes, come on in."

I sat on the patient chair as the counselor asked me boring questions about school. And then he leaned forward and adjusted his glasses and I knew something serious was coming.

"We need to talk about the reason you're here."

Why couldn't these people come out and say it? We both knew exactly why I was here. What was the point of beating around the bush?

"I… I don't know what there is to say, honestly. I mean, it happened. And it sucked, don't get me wrong. But the hearing is right around the corner. I'm staying positive!"

Isn't that what counselors wanted to hear? That you're staying positive?

"It's easy to act like everything is okay when it isn't, right? But sometimes these events have a way of coming back to us in unexpected ways. Have you had any trouble sleeping?"

"No."

"Have you noticed any behavior in yourself that's out of the ordinary?"

I averted my gaze. Okay. I had spontaneous sex with my ex-boyfriend in a school bathroom and I hit my mom. Hard. I was here anyway. I might as well talk about that.

"My mom came to campus earlier. We have a terrible relationship. I… I may have hit her. Kicked her. She's gone now but… I guess that's unusual."

"You kicked her? Tell me everything that happened."

I couldn't explain the entire sordid history of Keri, but I could at least give the rundown of what happened earlier. The counselor listened closely, ears pricked and when I finished, he nodded.

"I see. Does your mother normally choke you or anything of that nature?"

"No. I mean, she's slapped me when she's mad but… you know… she wasn't really around enough when I was a kid to give me a good whooping."

"I see."

"I mean, that's not why we don't get along."

The counselor nodded.

"Does she normally call you names too?"

"Names?"

"You used the phrase 'fast ass hoe'."

"Oh. Yeah. My mom says stuff like that all the time. Mostly when she's been drinking."

"She drinks?"

"She's an alcoholic. I think. By my definition at least."

He didn't give me that annoying "I feel sorry for you" look that a lot of people gave. He just nodded. And I felt at ease.

"Do you have anyone you can rely on for support?"

"Benjamin."

"A boy? Is he your boyfriend?"

"No. A little bit. He's my ex… but… it's complicated."

"Teenage relationships can be complicated."

And then we talked about Ben. By the time counseling was done, I didn't feel that different like I had a major breakthrough or anything, but I felt better. And I checked my phone to find out that I still had a few minutes to catch the end of rugby practice.

I hurried to the rugby field and Danny waved me over in the stands. I plopped down next to her and she offered me a chocolate covered raisin.

"You're late!"

"I know. I was in counseling."

"Oh. Was it brutal?"

"Not as bad as I thought."

"Cool. They've been playing like shit today. Coach is losing his mind. He called them a bunch of fucking lemmings."

"Lemmings?"

Danny giggled. We talked for a bit and as practice ended, I asked if she wanted to go to the caf for dinner.

"No thanks," she said and she leaned in to whisper, "I'm going to meet a boy."

"What? Who?!"

"It's a secret. But… he's so fit. I'm going to ask him to take my virginity."

"Danny!"

"What? I want to lose it. Does it hurt?"

"No. Not a lot. I mean… it feels weird but you get used to it."

Danny grinned.

"Awesome. Once I lose it, I can work out my secret plan."

"Your plan?"

"I want to get popular. And I know how I'm going to do it."

"Um… how!?"

"I'm going to become a slag."

"Danny!"

"I'm serious… It works. Girls hate you but boys love you. That's what I want."

I assumed she was at least half-kidding.

"You're crazy, I'll see you at practice tomorrow."

"Tata, girlie!"

Danny bustled off and I walked to the caf alone. I grabbed some food and tried to walk past the rugby table to the table with Lousia, Isla and Arnie. Ben grabbed my arm.

"Sit," he commanded.

I stopped and stared at him, then looking at all the boys sitting at his table. Seriously?

"Um... I'm going to sit with Louisa and Isla."

Ben's gaze sharpened.

"I said sit down, Liberty."

Liberty. Shit. He was serious. And I was in big trouble now.

A Long Walk With Ben Fox

I sat. Not like I had much of a choice. I'd gotten into it with Ben in the caf before and we both knew this could end badly. I sat between Ben and Theo. The other boys at the table bent their heads and obediently spooned food into their mouth.

"How's it going, Libs," Theo said politely.

"Good. I'm fine."

"How's working with my brother?" Ben asked, "He giving you any trouble?"

Here he was, acting like everything was normal between us when it was far from it.

"Not at all."

Nick Knight interrupted with a thought that appeared to have entered his head out of nowhere.

"Does anyone think Dean Warren would let our dorm get a dog?"

"Why would she let us get a dog."

"I dunno. It's character building, innit?"

"What would happen to the dog after this year?" I asked.

Nick shrugged and stroked his five o'clock shadow.

"Dunno," he answered after far too long lost to consider, "The next boys could have it."

"Wouldn't it be traumatic to bond to a dog and have to leave it behind?" Theo asked.

"Nah, mate. Character building," Nick Knight insisted.

Then the rugby boys started up a riveting conversation about the ethics and morality of bringing a dog into the dorm. As they discussed what breed of dog they could convince the Deans to allow, Bess Davenport walked in with the remainder of the mean-girl-table. Millie walked abreast of her, followed by Amira. It was hard to ignore the notable absences: Claire, Hope, and Yasmin, all gone.

Nick blurted out, "I'd give my bollocks to have a wank on Amira's tits."

Arnav pushed him. Hard.

"Mate, that's my bloody sister."

"Her tits are mint. Are they real? Do you have pictures?"

"No, I don't have pictures of my fucking sister's tits."

"Think you could get some?"

"Oi!" Ben yelled, "Can you stop talking about tits for five seconds."

"What mate? Jealous that you aren't getting any."

"Yeah, mate. That's my problem."

Ben cast a sidelong glance in my direction. We finished dinner with the boys talking about random things and everyone left except me. And Ben.

"C'mon. Let's go for a walk."

"Ben, I —

"Don't argue."

Ben squeezed my hand as we walked out of the caf. It would have been romantic if it weren't for his death grip that let me know he was definitely pissed off and 100% done with my shit. Uh oh. Maybe I should have known better than to play with Ben Fox of all people.

"Where are we going?"

"My car."

We got to his car, which he had hidden a little way off campus, parked in a clearing. Ben let go of me and held my shoulders.

"Libs. I told you we shouldn't have sex anymore."

"I know."

"You didn't listen, and you clouded my judgment and I'm a fucking idiot so I let you have your way with me, but this isn't like you. Recklessly fucking me in a school loo. What the hell were you thinking?"

"I wasn't thinking. I wanted to have sex."

"Whoever's blackmailing us has eyes on school cameras."

"They don't put cameras in washrooms."

"I don't care. We have to be careful."

"Then why hold my hand all the way here."

"I'm worried about you!"

"I'm fine."

"Why do I have trouble believing that?"

"You're too obsessed with looking after me."

"Would you rather I leave you alone?"

He stared at me with this pained expression on his face. Sigh. I couldn't keep this up for long. I couldn't act like I hated Ben when every part of me loved him.

"No. I don't want that."

"Be careful, Liberty."

"I know. I'm sorry."

"I'm not. Latin's boring. Getting inside you was the best thing to happen to me all day."

"Ben!"

He leaned against the car, pushing me into the door of the Range Rover.

"If you want to walk on the wild side, we can do it here too."

"In this clearing? What if we get caught?"

"Now you care about getting caught, eh? Turn around..."

"Ben."

He pressed his forehead to mine, olive eyes boring into mine.

"Don't make me ask you again."

I turned around and squeezed my eyes shut as Ben reached his hand beneath my skirt and fondled my panties, rubbing his hand on my mound through my uniform. Oh, God. He was really going to do this... lift my skirt and fuck me against his Range Rover in the middle of a public clearing. Ben slipped his fingers past my panties and I moaned as he plunged two fingers inside me.

Ben worked his fingers inside me until I came, and he pressed me against the Range Rover as he undid his belt with one hand.

"No more games, Libs," he muttered, running his tongue roughly along my ears and neck, sending a surge of desire riveting through me.

"I'm not playing games."

He reached beneath my skirt and squeezed my butt until I moaned.

"Yes you are," Ben groaned, "And you're playing with the wrong man. Now spread your legs and let me have your cunt."

I opened my legs slightly but Ben forcefully pried them apart, rolling a condom onto his dick before he slid inside me. I moaned as Ben filled me, thrusting his perfect enormous cock into me as I leaned against his Range Rover. I moaned as the tip of his cock touched me deep and the thick girth of his member stretched me wide. I shuddered as juices spilled from my pussy, dripping down my thighs as Ben eased his dick out of me and slammed into me again.

Once he had me pinned against the car again he pulled my hair away from my ears and whispered, "You've been such a naughty girl, Liberty Jones. I don't know what I'm going to do with you…"

"B-Ben… We could get caught," I choked out, my thighs trembling as my pussy soaked with pure euphoria from his dick driving between my legs.

"I don't care," he murmured, "Let them catch me with your skirt up and with my cock between your legs. That's the risk you took earlier."

I moaned as he thrust into me deeply again.

"I know. I was reckless…"

"Yes, you were. Very reckless, love."

I moaned as Ben grabbed my hands and pinned them behind my back. I came hard as he thrust into me again. And again. Fuck. I came again as Ben pinned me against the car, dominating me completely as I gave him full control. I'd been a naughty girl and fuck, it felt good for him to punish me. At least I wasn't thinking of anything else. I didn't worry about anything. All I needed was Ben's gigantic cock. I climaxed again and as juices ran down my thighs, Ben's cock stiffened between my legs. He spilled his seed and pulled out of me.

I adjusted my skirt as juices ran down my legs. My knees wobbled together and Ben turned me around, kissing me on the lips. He leaned against the car, sandwiching me between his toned rugby body and his car.

"Kiss me…"

I grabbed Ben's cheeks and kissed him.

"Good girl."

Fuck. More juices gushed out from between my legs as he said 'good girl'.

"We should go."

"No, love. I'm headed for a drive. You walk back to campus with your juices spilling down your legs and think long and hard next time before you pull another move like that."

"Where are you going?"

"Don't trouble yourself."

"I worry about you."

"Don't. I'm a big lad. I can handle myself."

"I have to meet Arnie tonight for homework."

"Tell the lad I said hello."

"So you two are cool now?"

"As cool as we can be."

Ben stroked my cheek and pressed his forehead to mine.

"Once we find out who is doing this to us, I'll do anything it takes to get you back."

"Ben…"

"Shh. Go back to campus, love. I'll find you tomorrow."

Ben kissed my forehead and unlocked his car as he put his clothes back on. I walked back to campus, heat flushing over my face. We weren't far off campus. Anyone could have seen us. But Ben was right. Someone could have caught us on the school campus too, especially since we knew someone was watching us. I made it back to my room fine, but Eugenie looked worried.

"What happened? I heard Ben Fox carted you off."

"I'm fine."

"Are you sure? You look like someone's tossed you about. Did he hit you?"

The corners of my mouth tugged upwards. Ben? Hit me... Not exactly. "Hitting it from the back" doesn't exactly count.

"I'm fine. I swear."

"You two didn't fight, did you?"

"No. We didn't. We're getting close to getting back to normal."

"What is normal for you two?"

I smirked.

"Okay. Fine. We had sex."

I waited for Eugenie to make fun of me, but she squealed with joy.

"No. Way."

"Yeah. We did. It was intense. Up against his Range Rover..."

She gasped and wriggled her legs with delight.

"Oh, my goodness. You two are getting back together!"

"I don't know about that."

"Oh, you have to! I have a bet going with Arnie."

"With Arnie?"

"We both think you'll get back together. I bet in the next few weeks. Arnie thinks you're already together, but you're hiding it. He says he knows his twin brother."

"Arnie's crazy."

I neither confirmed nor denied her suspicions. Ben and I were getting better. At least that part was true. I gossiped with Eugenie a little longer and then I had to go to the library to meet Arnie. I took a shower first — much needed. When I went back to my bedroom to change into my study clothes, Eugenie left and there was someone sitting on my bed. The last person I expected to see there.

A Startling Confession From A Surprising Source

"Danny? How'd you get in here?"

"Your door was open. Sorry…"

"It's fine. You just scared me."

"I have a confession to make. Is your roommate coming back?"

"Um… no. What confession?"

"You can't tell anyone I told you. I promised not to tell."

"Seriously, Danny. What is it? You're scared the crap out of me."

"Okay. Fine. I'll work up the courage."

"Mind turning around? I need to change."

Danny didn't mind obliging. I changed into sweatpants and a cropped hoodie before I told her she could turn around.

"Now. What is it?"

"I hooked up with Barnaby."

I didn't know what to say.

"What?"

"I know. It was stupid. But… we talked, and then he asked me to meet him in one of the school classrooms. I didn't know what would happen but… we kissed and then… we didn't have sex but then… someone sent him blackmail."

"What?"

"Someone posted the video online and sent him a message."

"But you didn't have sex?"

"No… But I was still… loud. Oh, Libby, I've been losing my mind. I haven't been able to sleep since it happened."

My arms prickled with goosebumps. The video Marley found… Could it have been a video of Arnie and Danny? It wasn't like it was high definition footage or anything. Maybe we'd confused ourselves for Danny and Arnie. But what kind of weirdo twin brain connection makes brothers go have sex in the same place… ew.

I wrinkled my nose.

"Who do you think is blackmailing you?"

"I don't know. Barnaby told me not to tell anyone. He's looking into it."

"So he hasn't told anyone? Not even Ben?"

She shook her head. Shit. Boys could be so clueless sometimes. Naturally, they hadn't even communicated with each other.

"This may be weird, Danny, but... do you have a copy of the video?"

She nodded and pulled out her phone.

"You can't tell anyone. If this gets out... my parents are going to ship me off to Argentina! I don't want to go back there. Granddad's a Nazi!"

I cast a sidelong glance at Danny. I'd heard rumors about her adopted sister Yasmin's family, but I thought it rude to ask.

"I won't tell anyone. I just... trust me, Danny."

"I trust you. Don't worry."

She opened her cellphone's video app and showed me the video. Holy shit. It was the same one. Someone was using this video of Arnie and Danny to blackmail both of us... but that meant...

"Were you sleeping with Arnie before he broke up with Eugenie?"

Danny shut her phone off.

"Yes... I know. I'm a horrible person. It's just... Barnaby has a way of making you do things you never thought you'd do. Plus, they weren't ever more than friends with benefits."

"Danny!"

"I feel awful about it. But I couldn't tell anyone. Barnaby made me promise not to tell."

"Don't worry. I can try to help."

I didn't think it was smart to tell Danny that someone was using the same video to blackmail me and Ben. I just needed her to relax, and I needed to find some way of bringing this up with Arnie without letting him know Danny broke her vow of silence.

"Don't tell Barnaby I told you… Please. He doesn't want anyone to know about us."

I folded my arms and rolled my eyes. I was used to the Fox brothers commitment issues before but Barnaby was a whole new level of crazy… especially since he claimed to be a diagnosed sociopath.

"Danny. For the record, you deserve some guy that isn't afraid to claim you publicly."

"Easy for you to say. You're the prettiest girl at this school."

I scoffed.

"Trust me, when I first got here everyone including Ben deemed me 'unfuckable'. I'm far from the prettiest girl here."

"That's not true. To me, you're the prettiest. You make me feel more confident in being a black girl. Maybe it's stupid, but… My parents only raised me around white girls like my sister all my life. They bullied me. They called me ugly. And I know you've gone through the same thing, but you hold your head high no matter what happens. You might fall, but you always get back up."

"Danny… That's so sweet."

"Thanks for being a good friend."

"I'll find a way to talk to Arnie without telling him you told me. Trust me, I'm good with the Fox brothers."

"Thanks. I'd better go."

"Yeah. And Danny… Don't tell Eugenie, okay? I don't want her to get hurt."

"Got it."

"I've gotta go. I'm meeting Arnie to do physics homework."

"K. I'll walk you to the library."

Danny walked to the library with me and then peeled off to the Year 12 girls' dorms. I met Arnie at our usual physics table. He leaned back, sticking spit covered wads of paper into a straw and shooting them at goth Year 12 girls who giggled hysterically as he hit them. He winked and blew them a kiss as I put my bag down with a disgusted look on my face.

"Ugh. Can you not?"

"You're late, babe."

"Barnaby Fox. Do not call me babe."

"You're testy."

"I'm not."

"You are. Maybe my theory's wrong. But… I don't think it is."

He set his gross straw on the table and leaned forward.

"Be honest, babe. Is my brother fucking you right?"

"Arnie!"

I smacked his arm hard and the Year 12 girls giggled louder. I rolled my eyes.

"Don't you ever get tired of flirting with everything that walks?" I accused.

"Never."

"We'd better get our work done," I grumbled.

We'd have time to gossip later. Just as I pulled up our assignment, I got an email from the choir director. Shit. He still wanted me to sing. I'd skipped the last few practices. After the drama and the attack, I couldn't bring myself to go back. But he still wanted me to have the part.

"Earth to Libby?" Arnie questioned, raising his straw like he'd shoot a spit wad at my face.

"Don't you dare."

"You're distracted."

"It's about choir. They still want me to sing the solo."

"Busy girl."

"Yeah. I don't know if I should do it."

"Maybe we can discuss after we ensure our A+ in physics."

Arnie was right. We spent a couple hours getting our homework done and only had one argument over the correct way to solve the electricity and magnetism problem. It nearly came to blows, but that was the nature of our tense lab partnership. At least we got good grades. Once we'd finished, Arnie folded his arms and leaned back.

"So. Choir. Here's what you do. Take the role. Kill it. Make those bitches regret messing with you. And for revenge, I can procure you a fine specimen of human shit."

"Arnie, you're disgusting."

"I didn't say it was mine."

"How the hell would that help? They aren't even on campus."

"Whatever. I'm only trying to help.

"Fine. Barnaby. I need to talk to you about something."

"Barnaby? Is that what you're doing now?"

I rolled my eyes.

"This is serious."

"It's almost like you consider us friends."

"Can you shut up and listen?"

"I'm all ears."

"Ben hasn't told you about the blackmail, has he?"

"Blackmail?"

"Talk to him. Ask him about the blackmail. Don't say I told you. Say it's some twin connection. Trust me."

"You're a weirdo. I don't get my brother's jungle fever."

"Arnie! That is so racist."

"How is it racist?"

"Read a damn book. You're a straight-A student, and if it weren't for me, maybe you'd have a shot at getting valedictorian."

I grabbed my book bag and stalked off. There. I set the twins on a collision course without exposing Danny. I just had to hope this would work out. I emailed my choir director back and agreed to the role, just as Leonora Hargreaves rang my phone.

Twins Working Together

Leonora had nothing but good news. She'd prepared for the hearing, and she'd spoken to Dean Warren about keeping my mom off campus and away from the conference room on the big day. She told me to wear a white dress that covered my knees.

"Trust me," she said, when she heard the hint of questioning in my voice. I couldn't question Theo's half-sister.

That night, Ben didn't come back to campus. He texted me to warn me, and then Arnie texted me later to remind me he'd asked me to cover for him.

"What's such a big deal that you can't tell me?"

He didn't respond to me, and I didn't trouble myself further with worrying about the Fox twins. They fit their last name so well: sly, sneaky and ultimately, both independent. Eugenie came back late from hanging out with Isla and I felt guilty for not telling her what Danny told me. Still, the last thing Danny needed was to end up on someone's shit list. She was already having trouble fitting in.

But Arnie? He never mentioned her. He never acted like he was interested in her in public. What the hell was that about?

I woke up early the next day and went to the choir practice before classes. The choir wanted me back, and I'd earned my audition. I couldn't let Yasmin and her cronies take that from me. I had to stop letting the horrible shit that happened to me run my life. Everyone treated me fine in rehearsal. No one was super friendly, but they weren't outright mean. After choir practice, our director stayed with me to go over the parts I had to learn from the solo.

"Can you read music?" he asked.

I shook my head bashfully. I was self-taught in singing. I could read music a little, but not well.

"I'll talk to Dean Warren about setting you up with private lessons. Would you like that?"

I nodded. I had a crazy busy schedule, but it couldn't hurt. I loved singing. And I'd kept it bottled away for so long…

After choir, I had breakfast alone and then an early morning class with Theo. He looked like he'd seen hell. Apparently he stayed up all night studying for a test later that day. I went to my other classes and then had an afternoon Physics lecture with Arnie.

I had to walk past Dean Warren's office to get to Physics, and I couldn't help thinking of my pending hearing. I was super distracted when Arnie elbowed me as we were about to walk into class.

"Hey," I grumbled.

As I looked toward Arnie, another elbow jabbed into my other side. Ben. The twins sandwiched me before I could get in the door.

"What do you two want?"

I was instantly suspicious. Ben and Arnie working together? Yeah… that didn't exactly happen without one or the other kicking and screaming. Maybe they'd finally figured out our blackmail situation.

"We're being blackmailed," Arnie said.

"The four of us."

"Yeah. I already knew that."

"We compared notes. We think we know who did it."

"Um… okay? We have like five minutes until physics starts. Will this take less than five minutes?"

"Absolutely not. But we need your help. After class, rugby field before practice."

"Okay. Fine."

"Cheers, mate. Bye, love."

Ben glanced over his shoulder at me as he stalked down the hall to his next class. Arnie smirked and leaned down to whisper in my ear, "You two are definitely still fucking."

"We are not!"

Then I realized he saw the video. But we hadn't been the ones in the video. So Arnie had no proof.

"One time," I admitted, "Just once. But… we're broken up."

"You're a worse liar than my brother."

"I'm not lying."

Our physics teacher interrupted our disagreement by handing us a pop quiz. Shit. I hadn't studied hard at all, and I hardly understood any of the problems. I glanced over at Arnie and he was whizzing through the problems. I bit my lower lip. I couldn't let Arnie do better than me in this class. I answered the problems I could and gave my best efforts to the others, handing in my paper last.

When I returned to my seat, Arnie kept smirking.

"Struggled?"

"No."

"If it makes you feel better, I think I failed it."

"When you pretend to be humble, it's ridiculously unnatural."

We split off from the class to work on our experiments and as usual, Arnie kept things strictly business once we got into it in class. After physics, I had one more class before I wandered down to the rugby field. Arnie caught up with me on the way down there and when we arrived, Ben was there early, doing pushups shirtless on the field as he waited for us to arrive.

Ben jogged over to us, covered in sweat and smoking hot. My heart still fluttered when I saw him, even if we weren't together. And while I wasn't as shy talking to him as when we first met, I could still get those tightening knots in my stomach when he gazed at me with intriguing green eyes.

"So. Let's talk blackmail."

"We think it's Danny," Arnie and Ben blurted out together.

It was weird hearing them do that twin thing, where unplanned they say the same words at the same time. But it happened, and that was somehow the least stunning thing to come out of their mouth.

"No way. Danny wouldn't do that. She's my friend."

Arnie gave Ben a "get your girl in line" look, which made me want to elbow him in the stomach.

"We aren't saying this out of nowhere. We have reason to think that."

"I don't care. You don't know what it's like to get bullied by people for your race. Everyone bullies Danny. They call her Dumps! She's the victim here. She's not the type of person who would go around blackmailing people. And why the hell would she blackmail Arnie? She has a crush on him!"

"Listen, Liberty. We can explain."

"I don't want you to explain. This is stupid! I thought you two got me down here for a good reason, not just to rag on a black girl like everyone else at this stupid school. I'm leaving."

"Libs!" Ben called after me.

"Let her go," Arnie said, "She'll come 'round."

No. I wouldn't come around. I couldn't figure out why, but Ben and Arnie had to be lying. They just had to.

The Proof Is In The Manila Folder

It's official. I hated it when the twins worked together. Ben and Arnie waited outside the chapel for me after my next day's choir practice. They leaned up against the chapel walls, Ben in a long-sleeved navy and white rugby polo and olive pants, Arnie wearing skinny black jeans and an orange paisley silk shirt. Arnie had his nails painted black, and he nodded at me and muttered, "There she is," as I left.

I tried to ignore them and walk ahead on the path. I still didn't have that many friends in choir. Some people were content to have me. Some people feared the fact that I'd upturned Rapetti's social structure. Some didn't like me. I heard whispers. They didn't believe Yasmin could do what I accused her of. Forget the fact that I never accused her. Dean Warren walked in. And she saw what she saw... I couldn't stop it. But I had to deal with the consequences. Anyway, the last people I wanted to deal with were Ben and Arnie.

"Libby! We need to talk," Arnie called.

"I'm busy!"

"Leave it, mate," Ben grumbled, "She's still upset."

"Oi! Libby!"

"Go away, Arnie!" I called back at him.

"LIBERTY JONES TURN AROUND THIS INSTANT OR I'LL TACKLE YOU!"

I turned around and stomped my foot.

"What is wrong with you two?!"

"Libs, please. Listen to us."

"I won't listen to you unless you apologize. I won't have you two targeting Danny like everyone else on this campus."

"We aren't targeting her. And we'll prove it to you," Arnie said, "Although, if I were Ben, I'd question why you still refuse to trust him, especially since you two are secretly sleeping together."

Ben and I screamed at once, "We are not sleeping together!"

Arnie smirked like he'd lured us into a trap. Shit. We didn't exactly sound innocent. Arnie snaked his arms over our shoulders and drew us together.

"Listen. Liberty, you're going to come to my Range Rover. We're going to drive to a coffee shop off campus and we'll explain what we found. Got it?"

"You're insufferable," I grumbled.

"Yes. I am. But so are you. Don't you agree, Benjamin?"

"Don't drag me into this," Ben grumbled.

Arnie clamped his hand around my shoulders and led us to his "secret spot" where he parked his car. Arnie's hiding spot wasn't particularly hidden, at least not compared to Ben's.

"Seriously? This is where you keep your car?"

"Hiding in plain sight works, miss."

"Why don't I ever get tired of having you two kidnap me?"

Ben and Arnie smirked, their faces looking more identical when they smiled. I rolled my eyes.

"You're powerless to this face, babe," Arnie said.

Ben elbowed him, "Watch it."

Arnie shrugged.

"What? Can't steal her if she isn't your girl."

"Shut up, Arnie!" Ben and I said.

Ben sat in the front, I sat in the backseat, and Arnie drove us to a café. I didn't know what the hell they could say to me that would make me think Danny filmed herself and Arnie and then black-mailed the twin brothers. What could her motive be? She was my friend…

We sat and Arnie rudely ordered espressos for all of us instead of waiting for Ben and me to say what we wanted. Then Ben pulled out a manila folder, sliding it across the table to his brother Barnaby.

"We have our evidence right here."

"I still don't believe you."

"You will once you see this," Ben said.

"Before you show me anything, I want you to answer this simple question. Why the hell would Danny do something like this? She's not like the other girls at Rapetti."

Arnie and Ben exchanged glances. Arnie tapped Ben's forearm as if to say, "I'll handle this one."

"Libby. I know you're both African and you think it makes you the same person. But Danny's not like you. Yasmin's her sister. She's more like Yasmin than you'd imagine."

"African? Really, Arnie?"

"Well you were African at one point."

"You two shut it," Ben grumbled, "Let's show her what we have and stop wasting time."

"Thank you, Ben," I responded smugly.

When Arnie emptied his manila folder, the smug look left my face. A magazine. The subscription tag on the front said exactly who the magazine had been sent to. Daniella Friedrich. Holy shit. Arnie flipped through the magazine, flashing before missing letters.

"Anyone could have had that magazine."

"We had Marley trace the upload. He hit a VPN — at least we thought it was a VPN — it wasn't. She sent the video to someone else to upload, someone who lived in Argentina."

"We all know Yasmin's Nazi scum grandparents live in Argentina," Arnie blurted out.

The waitress who came to collect our empty coffee mugs cast suspicious glances in our direction. The word "Nazi" isn't exactly one you come to hear in public often.

"We couldn't find the exact IP, but Marley believed it to come from somewhere in one of the wealthy areas of Buenos Aires."

"Doesn't this point to Yasmin? I mean, she'd have access to her sister's magazine and Argentina. And she had it out for me. She was the one going after Ben."

Ben groaned.

"We're idiots," he grumbled.

"They were playing us. And here's how I know."

He pulled a phone out of the manila envelope.

"What the hell is that?"

"Danny's phone."

"What?!"

"Nicked it off her last night and added my thumb to the passcode while she was in the loo. I read through the conversations and… you should too. We have our proof, Libs. I know it's not what you wanted to hear, but… Danny's involved in this."

"Holy shit."

Arnie snapped his fingers at the waitress.

"Is it too early for a pint?"

She rolled her eyes until Arnie pulled out a £50 note.

"We'll have three."

"I don't day drink anymore, mate!" Ben complained.

Arnie rolled his eyes, "Make that six pints!"

UNWANTED

Question The Motive

S ix pints showed up at our table and Arnie slid four of them over to his side. I took one and Ben reluctantly took the other one. Sobriety became a lot more difficult with a twin brother like Barnaby Fox. Arnie unlocked the phone for me and the conversations I skimmed made my body stiffen. They were right. Arnie and Ben were right.

She played us all against each other. Including Yasmin.

Danny: Yaz. I know he wants you. You're beautiful. Blonde. What's not to love?

Yasmin: Whatever, Dumps.

Danny: I'm serious. Go. After. Him. He's not gonna choose her over you. Let's be real.

Danny: She's fat too. Fatter than me, lol.

Yasmin: I don't think he's over her tbh.

Danny: So? Once he fucks you, it's over between them. Trust me. I know her.

Yasmin: Whatever, loser.

Danny: Love you.

Yasmin: Why are u being nice to me?

Danny: Because. U scare me.

Yasmin: Haha

Yasmin: I just don't think he likes me that way. IDK. I fucking hate her.

Danny: Then do something about it.

Danny: Punish her.

"I'm going to be sick," I muttered.

"Drink, love," Arnie said.

Ben took a reluctant sip of his beer, and I chugged half of mine, prematurely eyeing one of the pints Arnie had spread out in front of him.

"This is crazy," I said, "I just… I don't want to believe this. Danny and I are friends. We were getting close."

"Keep reading," Benjamin grumbled.

I flipped to the conversation between Danny and Barnaby.

Danny: It has to be tonight. In 301A.

Arnie: Babes. I have to meet Eugenie later.

Danny: Fuck her. She's a bitch.

Arnie: Watch it.

Danny: What? It's true…

Arnie: Danny. Maybe we ought to slow down.

Danny: You weren't saying that last time.

Arnie: I wasn't sure last time should have happened.

Danny: 301A. You don't have a choice.

Arnie: I'll talk to Eugenie.

Danny: Good. I need sex. I need it from you.

Arnie: Naughty girl.

Danny: I'll show you how naughty big boy…

The text messages got more graphic than that, and I scrolled past.

"You're gross," I snapped at Barnaby.

"Me? So you've never had sex?"

"Whatever. You know that's not what I mean."

"Keep reading, love."

I read more text messages. All concerning the same things. But it became clear. Danny planned this. She played everyone, including Yasmin. And she blackmailed the twin brothers. But why? That was the one part I couldn't get from her messages or from the mountain of evidence suggesting she'd filmed a sexual encounter and used it to blackmail Barnaby and Benjamin Fox.

"I don't get it," I said, having finished my pint and the rest of Ben's.

"What don't you get love?" Barnaby replied, "Let's discuss."

"Why would she do this? Why would she pretend to be my friend?"

"That's what we need you for," Ben answered, leaning forward onto his elbows, "We're going to find out the old-fashioned way. Espionage. Sending in a man undercover."

"Let me guess. I'm that person."

"Bingo."

"What am I going to do? Confront her and explain that you idiots stole her cellphone?"

"Exactly."

"How will I tell her I knew?"

"Tell her you went to a voodoo priest," Arnie said.

"Arnie… Can you go thirteen minutes without being racist?"

"What? I've seen one."

"Okay, disturbing… but do either of you have a suggestion that won't sound like horse shit?"

Arnie leaned over to Ben and whispered, "Is she this difficult to please in bed?"

"Arnie! I can hear you!"

"I was only asking," Arnie grumbled.

"It's easy, Ben said. Get her to confess. And tape it."

"How the hell am I supposed to bring that up?"

"Trick her."

"Great. Thanks, Ben. That'll be simple."

"Sorry, but… you'll have to figure it out, Libs."

"I… What if she denies it?"

"Make her confess. Come on, Libs. If you can hit your own mum, you can do this."

Arnie laughed.

"What? You hit your own mum?"

"It's a long story and thanks for telling him, Ben," I snapped.

"Sorry," Ben apologized again.

"You know, I have enough on my plate without running around doing stupid errands for you two doofuses. Why don't you handle this yourself?"

"Liberty," Arnie said, "I promise you, this will go much better if you make her confess. Seriously. If we do it, she'll manipulate the situation. And anyway, Ben's right. You're tougher than you give yourself credit for."

"She's got more to worry about than you do," Ben answered.

"Fine. I'll do it. But we need to get back to campus. I have other shit to do aside from choir practice."

"Same."

"Does Theo know about this?" I asked Ben.

"We're keeping it to ourselves."

I folded my arms and glowered at Arnie, "What about Eugenie?"

He raked his fingers through his hair and rolled his eyes.

"I haven't told her. Don't want to."

"If I have to talk to Danny, talk to Eugenie. And Arnie, you are way too drunk to drive. Ben? You only had half a pint. Take the keys."

"Yes, ma'am."

I didn't know what to expect when we got back to campus. I didn't want to run into Danny right away, and luckily I didn't. Eugenie seemed over her crush on Arnie and had been trying her best to talk to Arnav since I encouraged her crush. Louisa and Isla were doing well, and my meeting with Dean Warren about the pending hearing went well too.

Later in the evening, when I was about to go to bed, Ben sent me a text message. Tomorrow. That was all it said. Great. I had less than 24 hours to come up with a way to get Daniella to confess to blackmail. And I didn't want her to confess. I didn't want any of this to be real. I'd trusted her. And now, I had to figure out why she did this. This was the problem with being a minority student on campus, I thought morosely. I wanted so badly to have just one other black girl to be friends with… but it was so hard to find someone normal. Someone I got along with.

Maybe after Rapetti, things would get better. Maybe at Oxford, I'd find my people…

Until then, I had to get Daniella Friedrich to confess to making a sex tape and blackmailing the Fox brothers. No easy task…

Confrontation & Entrapment

Luring Danny was easy. Well, it was easy for me to get her to agree. The pit in my stomach knotted more tightly as the time arrived. Arnie and Ben attempted to send "encouraging" text messages.

Arnie: If she gets mad at you… y'know… stab her.

Me: That is horrible advice…

Arnie: Doesn't always work

Me: Let me know when stabbing has ever worked for you…

Ben's texts were slightly better.

Ben: don't panic. And if she does anything… I'll stab her.

Me: How are you two the same?!

Ben: Wot?

Me: You and Arnie…

Ben:...

Great. I guess I'd have to figure everything out on my own since Arnie and Ben were giving me terrible advice. My instinct was telling me that Danny would deny all their claims. And without proof, I'd have to go through hell to get her to confess.

Danny came into my room with an open pack of gummy worms.

"Want some candy?"

"Sure."

I took one, and she sat on my bed.

"Danny, we need to talk."

"Uh oh. It's never good when people say that."

"No. It isn't. And um... this isn't exactly comfortable for me to say."

"Tell me. I can handle it."

I glanced up at her and questioned whether she could. Even if I saw the evidence, I didn't want to believe that Daniella could be so... two faced.

I sighed and continued, "I need to know why you filmed yourself having sex with Arnie and then used that footage to blackmail the twins."

She sucked the gummy worm back into her mouth with a loud slurp, but otherwise her face didn't change. There was no recognition of what I said. No emotions exposed.

"Oh," she answered once she finished chewing the worm.

I folded my arms and waited for her to say something else.

"Danny? You did it, didn't you. Filmed yourself and Arnie. Black-mailed Ben… But why? It doesn't make any sense. We're supposed to be friends."

Danny glanced up and me and rolled her eyes.

"Oh, please. Don't do that nice girl act. I know you can be a bitch when you want to be."

"Danny? Seriously?"

She folded her arms and hopped off my bed.

"Yeah. I did it. But what are you going to do about it?"

"Why? I don't get it. Why would you want to do something like that? We're supposed to be friends. You broke up Arnie and Euge-nie. We've hung out every day at rugby games for the past few days. I've been nothing but kind to you."

"Oh please. Does that stupid nice girl act work on anyone? This is a boarding school. It's kill or be killed around here. I already started off as Dumps and I have no intention of ending that way. It's clear you're willing to be the school punching bag. You're dating a guy who bullied you. My sister almost shoved a giant dildo up your ass. People walk all over you and you don't care. Well, not all black girls want to be treated that way. I did it because I want to be legendary. I want people to know that they can't fuck with Daniella Friedrich the way everyone fucks with you. And we aren't friends, Libby. You're pathetic. And everyone at this school except those desperate twin losers think so."

"Wow."

Danny smirked and put another gummy worm into her mouth.

"You look shocked. Guess what, Libby. I know you won't do anything about it. So, you caught me. I blackmailed Ben. I blackmailed Arnie. And I don't regret anything. I still have the footage. I could still ruin all three of you. And you're too much of a nice girl to do anything about it."

"Get out of my room."

Danny laughed.

"Yasmin was right about you."

"Maybe she was right about you two… Dumps," I snapped.

For a moment, I saw a flicker of sadness in her eyes, quickly replaced by a steely coldness.

"Nice try, Liberty. Names don't hurt me. I'm not built like you. I'm not weak."

"We're the only two fully black girls at this school. It's stupid for us to fight like this."

"I don't feel some dumb allegiance to you based on skin color. Like I said, I'm not weak. Bye, Libby. Don't even think about trying it with me because I will send that footage to every cellphone on this campus. People can hardly tell us apart. They'll think you're the school slut. Everyone already knows you nearly took a big fat dildo from three girls."

"I said to get out," I whispered.

"Ta-ta!"

I let Danny leave my room before I snapped. She hadn't seen what I did to my mother. She didn't know what I did to Jess. Danny didn't know what I was capable of. And you know what? She was right about something. I never went too far. I never tried to play by the Rapetti kill or be killed rules. But she was wrong about everything else. And she was wrong to threaten me.

I had a lot of bullshit on my plate. I was about to explode from the pressure. The last thing I needed was some bitchy Year 12 blackmailing me.

I texted the recording of our conversation to Ben and Arnie. And then I sent them both another text.

Me: No more Mr. Nice Guy from me.

I'd let so much slide, but this was the last straw. I'd trusted Danny. I wanted to look after her. I didn't want her to become another victim. But she'd taken my kindness and thrown it in my face. Danny's words stayed with me as I sat on my bed and waited on a response from Benjamin and Barnaby.

Too much of a nice girl to do anything about it? Ha. Maybe she was right, but I was just about done being the nice girl. Kill or be killed? I'd killed before — in real life — and I didn't want to get involved with Rapetti bullshit because I wanted to end up at Oxford. But maybe Danny was right. I'd survived here long enough by playing the nice girl route. I tried to be kind… and I was fucking sick of it. The bitches of Rapetti Academy would have another thing coming.

An Unlikely Alliance

When Eugenie got back from her evening hang out with Louisa, I was pacing our dorm room.

"Everything okay?"

"I'm fine. But I need to tell you something."

"What's going on?"

"It's about Arnie and Danny."

"What about them?"

"Danny slept with Arnie. While you two were still together. I've known for a couple days, but I didn't know how to tell you or if I should. But... I'm telling you now."

"Holy. Shit."

"Are you mad?"

"Yes, I'm mad. But not at you. I'm mad at Arnie. He lied to me."

"I know. I don't want to mess with your friendship… but we're roommates. I had to say something."

"Did he tell you?"

"No. Danny did."

"She wanted to do the right thing," Eugenie whispered, her eyes softening. The last thing I wanted was her softening to Danny Friedrich. Not after what I discovered.

"Don't feel sorry for Danny. She's not as innocent as she seems."

Eugenie plopped onto her bed.

"What do you mean?"

I explained everything to Eugenie. She jumped off the bed.

"Wow. This is bullshit."

"I know," I said.

"We have to do something."

"I'm going to do something. But I don't know what."

"I have an idea…"

Eugenie was good at this. Before I could respond to her idea, she patted me on the shoulder.

"Think about it. I'm going to go talk to Arnie."

"Uh oh. Should I worry?"

"No. But we ended on a weird note."

Eugenie left, and I did some of my homework before bed. Eugenie snuck out after evening check-in and in the morning, she hadn't come back yet. I put my uniform on to get ready for breakfast when Eugenie burst through the door, dressed in her uniform, but with messy hair.

"Should I worry about where you were last night?"

"No. But you've got to go to the caf. Now. Ben and Arnie are waiting."

"Waiting for what?"

"Ben bribed the dining hall staff to keep everyone out until they're ready, but they can only hold them off for so long."

"I'm coming!"

I stuffed the rest of my books in their bag and raced to the caf past a throng of students waiting to get in. The staff let us in and I found Arnie and Ben leaning against one table.

"What the hell is going on in here?"

"Stage one."

"Of what? I see nothing."

"Don't drink the lemonade."

"What?"

"We spiked the lemonade with absinthe. And we bought the absinthe with Millie's credit card."

"How the hell did you get Millie's credit card?"

"Don't worry about it," Ben said, "Point is... it's time we shake things up at Rapetti. The rugby boys are planting the evidence in her room right now. She's sleeping with Arnav now, so she'll be none the wiser. And in about three minutes, everyone's going to come in and the rest of the day will be a party."

"Won't people know you two did it?"

Arnie and Ben exchanged wicked glances at each other.

"Liberty Jones… we've got the staff on our side. And we've got an alibi. Once everyone's in here, Arnie's going to perform."

"Perform what?!"

"Irish step dancing."

"You can dance?!"

"Haven't done it in years but… McLeod's helped me out, thanks to Eugenie."

Eugenie. Didn't she have a crush on Arnav?

"What about you and Arnav?" I asked Eugenie.

She chuckled and pushed her headband into her hair, letting her bangs fall in front of her heart-shaped face.

"She hooked him up with Millie," Arnie filled in, "We planned it all last night."

"Great, couldn't you have included me?"

Ben shook his head.

"I told them you needed to rest before classes. You've got to beat this twat for valedictorian."

"Okay… and why did you need me here early?"

"I can't Irish step to nothing. You need to sing."

"You want me to sing in front of the entire school?!"

"Only the first round of breakfast."

I groaned.

"I don't know anything you could dance to?"

"Do a Christmas carol from choir!" Eugenie suggested.

I rolled my eyes.

"Fine. But if this goes wrong…"

Ben put his hand on my shoulder and my body tensed in natural response to him.

"It won't go wrong. Trust us. We're putting everything right at Rapetti. Once and for all."

The staff opened the doors and a throng of students stood in line, getting food and getting one of the students' favorite drinks: lemonade, that none of them knew Arnie spiked with hard liquor. Nick Knight came in with a crowd of Year 12s and flashed Ben a thumbs up. Arnie linked arms with me and dragged me to the front of the dining hall for our impromptu "alibi" — the performance of a shitty song and a likely even shittier Irish step dance.

"Here goes nothing," Arnie muttered.

He tapped his feet against the linoleum and I stifled a laugh. Our first mission: knock Millie down for size. And then Eugenie's plan for Danny. That would take a lot more work. No more being the victim. If someone was going to run Rapetti Academy, it might as well be me. And now that we found out who was blackmailing us, there was no reason for me and Ben to stay broken up. But we hadn't talked about that yet.

Arnie cleared his throat.

"ATTENTION!"

Because of the noise and the unusual morning commotion, the fifty or so folks who arrived at early breakfast turned toward us.

"As part of my Irish step class, I'm asked to perform spontaneously in front of a group... to er... represent what the Irish travelers would have done... er... back in Ireland."

"That never happened, mate!" an Irish student yelled.

A snicker rolled through the crowd, but Arnie didn't care.

"I brought my beautiful assistant to perform... It isn't a traditional Irish ballad, but a Christmas Carol. Ready Liberty?"

I nodded. My palms were sweaty already. How the hell did I let those idiots talk me into this? I caught the eye of a Year 12 in the back of the caf, who tilted her cup of lemonade to her lips and leaned over to whisper to her friend.

"And a 1... and a 2... and a 1...2...3...4..."

"We three kings of orient are..."

I sang the song, not missing a single note, which was lucky since it was early in the morning and I hadn't rehearsed at all. I couldn't tell if Arnie's dancing was any good, and I doubted that anyone else could tell, since the news about the lemonade tasting like alcohol had obviously been discovered. Arnie smirked as I neared the last verse of the song. At the back of the caf, Arnav slunk in and bumped fists with Ben before returning to the rugby table.

Then Marty Stuart and Zack Lewis ambled into the caf, and Ben gestured at them to join his table.

An alliance between the art freaks and the rugby boys? I never thought I'd see the day...

A Crazy Idea

Zack Lewis groaned as he leaned back.

"What are you up to wanker," he complained to Arnie.

Arnie leaned in and elbowed him.

"Try the juice, mate."

"Why?"

"Its spiked."

"Is that what you did?"

Arnie grinned.

"Nah, mate. Not me."

"Bollocks," Marty Stuart said.

Ben sat down and nodded to his twin brother. I think I was the only one who noticed the glance they exchanged. Eugenie sat between Arnav and Arnie, picking at a grapefruit.

"I think everyone's noticed."

"Good."

We sat back as everyone got drunker and drunker. Our diversion worked. I was in my morning class with Theo before I got word that Dean Warren had blazed into the caf furious. Half the school was standing on the tables, throwing off their school ties and grinding on each other. Rapetti students plastered videos all over social media. And there was a paper trail leading them straight to the culprit — Hope's sister, Millie.

But Millie was the least of my problems. She was mean too, but we still had to worry about Daniella. I still thought about what she said to me, and I didn't just want payback… I wanted to make sure nothing like that ever happened to me at Rapetti again. Maybe she was right. Eat or be eaten. Those were the rules around here. For too long, I'd try to play by the rules daddy gave me. Keep my head down and stay out of trouble. Look how well that worked…

Theo walked me to lunch after morning classes, and we sat at the tables we joined earlier in the day. Students sparsely populated the caf. Rumor had it a few suffered too much intoxication to handle attending class, and they'd either gone to the health center or back to their dorm rooms. Millie sat in the caf at her table with Amira to her left and her friend Charlotte to her right. She had her hair pulled back with a headband and her eyes watered. I couldn't help but smirk as I sat next to Eugenie.

Eugenie laughed as she cut off a piece of her haddock.

"Look at her crying."

Theo leaned over to Eugenie and elbowed her in the side.

"Is the haddock any good?"

"Yeah. It's fine."

"Cool. Cool. You eat a lot of fish?"

"Um... no. It's just what they're serving today."

"Right. Right. Your hair is... er... it's beautiful."

Eugenie wrinkled her nose and muttered, "Thanks."

Arnav and Ben came into the caf from class, walking past Millie's table without paying her any attention as they sat down.

"Eugenie," Arnav said, "You're experienced. We need you to settle a debate we're having."

"Um... okay... experienced with what?" Eugenie asked suspiciously.

"Dating. Men. Is it lame if a guy still plays video games?"

"No!" Eugenie said, "I love video games."

"Ha! Told you!"

"You're both wankers," Ben grumbled.

Theo leaned in to Eugenie again, "What games do you play?"

Eugenie ignored him. Was Theo hitting on her? And if he was, why was Eugenie giving him the cold shoulder? I guess she was back together with Arnie. Or somewhere in the middle of getting back together with Arnie and pursuing her new fling with Arnav. Either way, I didn't think she'd feel so opposed to Theo.

Millie stormed out of lunch early, and soon everyone left except the four of us who'd planned the entire scenario.

"It worked," Ben said, "She's in trouble."

Arnie leaned forward and fingered the large signet ring on his middle finger.

"Good. That still leaves that cheeky little fucker to handle."

"Daniella?"

Arnie nodded.

Ben shrugged.

"She has footage of you two having sex. She's untouchable."

"I'm with Arnie," I admitted, "I mean… you didn't hear what she said to me when I finally pried the truth out of her."

I told my story again, and everyone listened until the end. Eugenie sighed and shrugged.

"I feel a little bad for her."

I wished I could return that sentiment.

"I don't!" I confessed, "Honestly, she made some good points. And there were some points she didn't make. Rapetti's getting crazy. The Year 12s are getting out of hand. I mean… what happened to basic respect. In Year 12, we respected everyone."

Ben laughed.

"I've never respected anyone."

"I didn't go here," Arnie added.

Eugenie sighed again.

"We respected everyone because the older girls scared us shitless."

"Exactly. All this bullying is bullshit. I mean… we should all get along and everything, but if playing nice isn't going to work, maybe it's time we put the Year 12s in their place."

"I don't care about all of them. Just Danny…"

"That's only 'cause your ego's bruised," Ben muttered.

"Come on, Ben. I don't have to remind you of the lengths you've gone to maintain your status around here."

Ben turned red.

"I don't want you getting in trouble," he muttered.

"I don't care if I get in trouble. My hearing is right around the corner. I'm more stressed than ever… I want to shake things up, not freak out about getting my hands dirty."

"I mean, I'm not the one in the sex tape," Eugenie conceded, "But she stole Arnie from me. I can get revenge for that."

"Focus, people," Arnie said, "We need ideas. How the hell can we get back at her."

"And how can we get the other Year 12s in line?"

"You three are cruel."

"And you're incredibly boring when you're off the nicotine," Arnie said.

Ben scowled and shook his golden-brown hair out of his face.

"You'll regret that. Because I already have an idea. And I promise you… Dumps will hate it."

We Are Finally Getting Back Together

"We have to trick her into releasing the footage. That's the only way to get ahead of it."

"Sorry," Arnie said clearing his throat, "Do you think I want the entire fucking school to know I shagged Dumps?"

"Someone will have to take one for the team," Eugenie replied, giggling and shoving a spoonful of yogurt into her mouth.

"You're nuts," Arnie grumbled.

"She has a point," Ben said, "The best way to get rid of blackmail is to… you know, put it out there. I have Marley scrubbing the web to get rid of it anywhere it's put up. But she wants to control you here at school."

"So what? We show the sex tape to everyone… somehow… and what happens? I don't know. I think Danny's only part of the problem. All the Year 12s are out of line. What about something more sadistic?"

"Since when do you like sadistic?" Ben said.

"Says the guy I dated."

Ben's ears reddened. I hated referring to us dating in the past tense. But we weren't officially back together yet. It's not like I loved that either. But it was the truth.

"Let me handle it," Arnie said, "But Libs, you've got to do tonight's homework. And don't forget what we agreed."

Right. He needed me to cover for him. I hadn't forgotten, but I was still curious why. Arnie could be such a weirdo. Eugenie and Arnie left and Ben offered to walk me to my next class. We needed to talk. I knew that much. But it still made me nervous to be alone with him. What happened now? Did we get back together? Did we keep hooking up?

Ben held the door open for me and as I brushed past his school jacket, his strong masculine scent overpowered me. I could feel myself getting weak at the knees already. He was tall. Strong. And still so handsome. But had we been through too much to get back together?

Once we were out in the open air, Ben took my hand and stopped me on the path.

"We need to talk, Libs."

"Okay. Let's talk."

"With everything going on, I don't want you to be alone."

"Okay."

"Take me back. Please. I know I might not have proven it to you, but I love you. And I'll never leave you again... I promise. I was wrong about keeping you safe from a distance. I was just… wrong. But I care about you. I've never stopped —

It was my turn to stop him. I got on my tiptoes and kissed Benjamin Fox right on the lips. He grabbed my face and pulled it close, running his hands through my hair and sticking his tongue into my mouth. If a teacher caught us, we'd at least get a disapproving glare.

Ben pulled away from me, and he kept my face firmly in his hands.

"Say yes," he whispered, "Just say it. Please… I want you so badly, Liberty."

"Yes," I gasped.

And I stopped caring about getting caught. I only cared about kissing him. And having him. And being back together. And not having to worry or wonder or lie awake at night missing him. I wanted my Fox back. It wasn't enough to be friends. Or to have secret sex. I wanted us together… forever.

I pulled away from him this time, and Ben grabbed my waist, holding me against his torso.

"Tonight, I'll come to your room. Got it?"

"Yeah."

"Now… you head off to class. I'll see you later."

He gave me one last kiss and dropped me off outside my Physics class. Arnie wasn't there and like he asked, I covered for him. I didn't mind working alone. I preferred it. Plus, it was hard to zone out and dream about Ben with his twin brother yammering in my ear about Physics problems. After class, I had choir rehearsal, a fifteen minute meeting with Leonora Hargreaves, and then I walked over to Ben's rugby practice.

I could catch the last fifteen minutes of the game, plus it had been a long time since I'd hung out just Ben and Theo. As I approached the stands, I saw the last person I expected sitting there. Seriously? Wasn't she tired of bothering us? Wasn't she embarrassed that I called her out? Daniella rose off the bleachers, turning her attention from the shirts vs. skins game happening on the field.

"Hey Libby," she said, grinning.

"Hey Danny. What are you doing here?"

"Watching the game. Finding out who my next fuck is going to be."

"Don't you have anything better to do?"

"Maybe I'll fuck Ben."

"You can try," I answered, "If you want to embarrass yourself."

"Come on. Sit with me."

"I'd rather choke on my own vomit."

Danny snickered.

"Still mad? I think you need to get over it. Y'know, once the hearing's done, Yasmin will be on back on campus. It'll be nice to have my sister here again."

"I'm sure you'd enjoy that. You seem to have a thing for being the token black girl."

"It's better than being a white man's whore."

"Whatever, Danny. Buzz off. I'm here to watch my boyfriend."

"Boyfriend? Has he convinced you you're still important to him?"

"Danny, get the fuck out of here."

I sat down on the other end of the bleachers.

"You know, I've been texting Theo. I think he'd be down for a hookup. I don't even find that he's a fag."

"What the fuck, Danny. That's a slur."

"It's true, isn't it? I can't believe this place."

I ignored her. I was done playing games with Daniella Friedrich. I'd fallen for her poor little victim act, and she made me look like a fucking idiot. Was there anything wrong with looking out for fellow black girls? Absolutely not. But Danny took advantage of me. I shouldn't even call her Danny.

"I heard that ugly little art freak shagged Arnav. Maybe I'll take him next. But I've heard Indian guys have small pricks."

"Get the fuck out of here, Dumps."

Danny snickered.

"Seriously?"

"I get it now. Dumps. Because you're a piece of shit. Yasmin was at least right about that."

"Don't call me that," she snapped.

"Getting under your skin? You should have thought of that before you messed with me. Trust me, Dumps, I'm not the weak bitch you seem to think. If you were smart, you'd get off these bleachers before I walk over there and whack you in the fucking face."

"You wouldn't dare."

"Try me, Dumps. And by the way, Arnav and Theo aren't as easy as you think. Most people at this school aren't twisted little bitches like your sister and her friends. Like you. They'd prefer an 'art freak' to a stuck up skank."

Danny gasped.

"You did not just say that to me."

"Run along, Dumps. Don't make me ask you again."

She glared at me and I glared back. And I stared in a way that showed I meant business. I was done playing games with Daniella. Her sister. With everyone. My hearing was soon and by the time that rolled around, I had to be strong. Everyone at school would buzz about what happened all over again. I couldn't keep my head down and hide.

Danny stormed off and Ben finally caught sight of me in the bleachers. He waved and then poured a bottle of water over his head before running over to the edge of the field. Water soaked his gorgeous brown hair, sticking it to his neck and running down his chiseled abs.

"You good?" he asked.

"Yeah. Who's winning?"

"Skins, love. Obviously."

He flashed me a wink, and I smiled. Together. We were together again. And it felt fucking amazing.

"Cool. Want to get dinner after?"

"Sure. Heard from Arnie?"

I shook my head. I was supposed to cover for him. I think that meant with Ben too. I hoped Arnie would man up and tell me why soon.

"Whatever," Ben said, "He'll turn up when he wants. Can Theo come to dinner?"

I nodded.

"Haven't seen him in ages."

"Well he's got news. So… dinner should be interesting."

Ben trotted back out to the center of the field before I could ask what would make dinner so interesting. He tackled Nick Knight, who fell over, dropping the ball and allowing Theo to pick it up. Theo, bare-chested and tattooed, sprinted across the field, his hair a dazzling flash of blond as he raced to the other end. Another point for skins. I cheered, losing myself in the game's excitement.

At Night, Covered In Blood

After rugby, Theo and Ben put their arms around me while they were all gross and sweaty.

"Ew! You two are disgusting!" I squealed.

"What did Daniella say to you?" Theo asked, leaning over me and dripping sweat from his hair onto my uniform.

"Theo! You're dripping on me."

"Sorry," Theo muttered, shaking his head like a dog, causing me to shriek out loud as droplets of sweat splattered me.

"I'm going to kill you!"

Ben laughed and put his arm around me, nearly burying my face in his aggressively stinky armpit.

"I'm gagging!"

"Fine, will you wait outside the locker room? Clearly we need showers."

"And I need to change before dinner considering I smell like gross rugby boy right now!"

Ben and Theo laughed as they left me to sit on the bench outside the locker room. I hadn't been alone ten minutes when Arnav came out of the locker room, dressed down in a pair of khakis and a clean rugby polo.

"Oi, Libby. Mind if I sit here?"

"Sure..."

I wasn't really close with the other guys on Ben's rugby team. Hell, I was still figuring stuff out with Ben and I fit in better with Arnie's art freak male friends, even if they kept to themselves most of the time too. But Arnav was nice enough. And his sister Amira was beautiful, though she could have better taste in friends than Millie and her crew.

"I need to tell you something. I'd tell Benjamin but I know he'd panic."

"What is it?"

"Amira, my sister. You know her?"

"Yes..."

What did Arnav think? This school was so small that naturally I knew his sister. I knew almost everyone who went to Rapetti except for the true loners.

"She told me something and I don't think I ought to tell but... I have to look out for my mates."

"Go on..."

"Millie's got herself detentions for the alcohol incident. She suspects Ben and Arnie framed her and she wants to get payback. Amira didn't tell me how. She's trying to talk her out of it but... if you can be subtle, yeah, tell the twins to watch their backs."

"What do you think she'll do?"

"Dunno, really. I'm more interested in getting back with Eugenie."

"You two stopped... seeing each other?"

"She's right fit. But she likes Arnie. I got competition. No problem. I love competition."

Arnav thumped me on the back like I was one of the boys before he scurried off. I guess he wasn't the jealous type. I could only imagine what Ben would do if he thought some other guy was actively pursuing me. After a couple minutes, Ben and Theo came out of the locker room together. And they smelled clean. Thank goodness.

"I'm starving," I complained, "What's on the menu tonight?"

"Egg noodles," Theo said.

I groaned. British food could be trying. I longed for something delicious. Sweet potato pie, anyone? What about ribs? It's like British people thought good ass food was illegal or something!

Arnav and the rest of the rugby boys were already at the rugby boy table by the time we got there. Ben and Theo promised me "two-on-one" time and I wanted it. We sat down together and Ben leaned in.

"We have some serious matters to discuss," he intoned.

"We do?"

"First, your hearing is in a couple days. Second, halloween is right around the corner. We need to have a party."

"And third?" Theo asked.

"How'd you know?"

"We went over this without Libby."

"Right. Third, we need to handle the Dumps situation."

"I won't even correct you," I grumbled, "Did you see her at the field today?"

"Barely noticed, but yes," Theo replied.

"I can't believe she's so… two-faced."

Theo grunted.

"Neither can I. I dunno. I still feel bad for her."

"Don't," I snapped, "I wasted my time feeling bad for her and look at where that got me. Sorry, but I've officially turned to the dark side."

Ben raised an eyebrow.

"You? On the dark side?"

"Yup. I'm done. I can't take it anymore. You and Arnie are right. About everything."

Theo chuckled.

"Glad I'm not included on the dark side."

Ben scoffed, "You are! You just fake it better. Because you're blond."

"What's that got to do with it. Racist!"

"Racist against blonds?!" I teased.

Theo nodded.

"Just because it hasn't happened yet, doesn't mean it won't happen."

Ben rolled his eyes.

"Come off it. Now. Before we get into all of that, where the hell is my brother?"

Uh oh. This again.

"Ummm."

"You're covering for him, aren't you."

Ben put his hand on my thigh beneath the table and slid it up my skirt.

"Come on," Ben urged, "Tell me."

"The way you're eye fucking her is mad perverted mate," Theo grumbled, stabbing a flaccid egg noodle.

Ben slid his hand up further until I gasped.

"Fine! I don't know where he is. He wanted me to cover for him in Physics."

"Fuck's sake…"

"What? He's probably just… I don't know. Doing whatever weird shit Barnaby does when he's alone."

"It's probably nothing good," Ben grumbled.

"Don't worry about that. And I don't want to worry about my hearing either. After it's all done, they're probably going to come back here. They're only suspended."

Theo and Ben exchanged glances. Theo nodded and Ben said, "We have a plan for that."

"Do you two have a plan for everything?"

"Not for halloween. I think we should do a theme."

"Nice try changing the subject."

"Classic horror," Theo suggested.

"That's not half bad," I admitted.

"And as for Dumps... We'll leave it up to Arnie. Whenever he comes back."

"Doesn't he have class tomorrow?"

"Let's hope he returns in time. Wanker," Ben grumbled.

We left dinner and Leonora gave me my final update before the hearing. It felt like ages had passed, but it hadn't been that long. And soon, it would be over. And what would happen then? I still hadn't told Theo and Ben the details of how much was at stake. Of how much money Leonora would try to get out of the families. It didn't feel real. I couldn't imagine having money. Money of my own?! It didn't seem possible. And if I did have money... I couldn't imagine keeping it away from my mom.

In the evening, Eugenie snuck out to sleep in Isla's room and watch a new livestream of one of their favorite goth bands together. And Ben snuck in through the window in his pajamas.

We were alone again. And together. And right next to us, there was a bed. Ben kissed me softly on my lips and then forehead.

"I love you," he murmured, "I've waited all day for this."

One thing led to another with us. He peeled my silk nightie off and carried me into bed before spreading my legs and sliding between them. I'd been less than regular about birth control since we broke up, so we used protection this time until the pills kicked back in… I didn't need that type of drama in my last year of college. Before Oxford.

Ben and I made love all night. I came so many times that we had to change my sheets. And we curled up next to each other. That was almost better than the sex. The closeness. Ben raked his fingers through my hair and we faced each other as we cuddled. Ben's warm breath tickled my nose and lips. He smelled like mints and our legs twirled together. I could lie like this forever. But that wasn't going to be the case.

A knock at the window woke us in the middle of the night. I sat up straight, nearly jumping out of my skin when I saw Ben's face on the other side of the window. But it wasn't Ben. Benjamin lay next to me. And his brother Arnie stood on the other side of the window, terror in his eyes. Ben woke up as I leaped out of bed and flung my window open to find Barnaby Fox covered in blood.

"Arnie," I gasped, "What the hell happened?!"

Bloody Barnaby

"Why the hell are you covered in blood?"

"I-I walked. From my car… About a mile out. I… I hit something. I… fuck…"

"Did you hit a person?" I asked.

"I… I don't remember. I don't know what happened. I… They jumped out of nowhere."

"Hang on… Don't move…"

Ben leaped out of the window. I stood in my room, scared that someone would hear us and scared about what Barnaby had gotten himself into.

"What happened? Where were you?"

"I have to get the Range Rover… I… I can hardly remember."

Ben pushed his brother's hair back. Blood. So much blood.

"Why didn't you call the bloody coppers?"

"I… My phone's gone."

"Fuck's sake, Barnaby," Ben scowled.

"Libby, I've got to find his car. I'll get Theo. Can you get him cleaned up?"

"In case you forgot, this is a girl's dorm!" I hissed, "And it's after lights out!"

"Please… he's hurt. Get him cleaned up and take him to the health center. You won't get in trouble."

"Can you get through the window?" I whispered.

By now I was sure our commotion would wake someone. Barnaby nodded, but he groaned as he climbed through the window. He nearly collapsed as I pulled him through. At least Eugenie wasn't here. She would have freaked out. Ben ran into the dark. He probably already had Theo on the phone.

"I'll look into the hallway to make sure no one's there."

"Y-yes…"

He was stuttering and out of it. Shock. What the hell? I pushed the door open into the hallway. It was dead silent. As quiet as you'd expect for two or three in the morning. I could get Arnie out of here, especially since he was shaken up and unusually silent. I held Arnie by his arm, but his sweater was soaked. I pulled my hand away instinctively, and it was covered in blood.

"Arnie…"

"P-please… Let me get this off…"

I led him into the bathroom and pushed a chair under the door. At least it would deter any late night bathroom goers from walking in on us. My throat tightened.

"You're going to have to undress."

"I-I can't…"

"Arnie, why didn't you walk to a hospital or the health center?"

"H-help…"

"How am I supposed to get this off?"

"My pocket. I've got a knife."

I reached into Arnie's pocket as he leaned against the sink, his eyes wide and wild, ocean green as he stared out ahead. I didn't ask him any more questions about what happened. I found the knife in his pocket and rapidly withdrew my hand.

"So do I cut this off?"

"Yeah… I… my chest hurts…"

I stuck the knife through the fabric and ripped it through. When I pulled the fabric apart I gasped. Glass. Blood. Bruises. Whatever happened to Arnie was more than a car accident. Once I had the sweater off him, goosebumps spread across his skin. He was built like Ben but thinner, with less muscle and less of a tan since he spent his time indoors rather than tearing across a rugby field. And he had tattoos. All of them were bloody and dirty.

"Where were you?" I gasped.

"Get the glass out," he muttered, "Please. And… I might have been… shot."

"Shot?! Barnaby…"

"Don't you lecture me now. I need help. When Ben finds the car, he'll know what to do."

At least he was being less cryptic now and getting back into his old self. Maybe soon he'd tell me what the hell happened out there. And what he'd been doing.

"I can get the big shards out," I answered, "But you'll need a doctor."

"Fine. Ben will arrange that. He'll find the car."

"He doesn't even know what direction he came from."

Arnie chuckled and then winced. Laughing moved all the wrong parts of his body.

"We're twins," Arnie coughed, trying to hide how much pain he was in from me, "He'll figure it out. Plus, there aren't that many roads going in and out of this town. They keep us well isolated, yeah."

I pulled the first piece of glass out, and Arnie swore. I clamped my hand over his mouth and our eyes met.

"Quiet," I whispered, "This is a girls' dorm. We're breaking like ten thousand school rules."

I slowly removed my hands from Arnie's mouth, and his cheeks turned dark.

"Sorry," he groaned, "There's only fucking glass in my chest."

"I don't want us to get in trouble," I whispered.

"Got it. I need a distraction."

"Like what?" I said, "I have to focus."

"Talk to me. Tell me something about your life."

"You know all about my life."

"I know we're identical, but I think you're mistaking me for my brother. I know nothing about you except Ben's obsessed."

"He's my boyfriend. You make it sound like a bad thing."

"Maybe it is, maybe it isn't. The point is... he knows something about you I don't."

"There's a lot you don't know about me."

"How did you end up here? In England."

"You could figure that out," I muttered.

Arnie sucked in air sharply as I pulled more glass out of his chest. I wet a cheap one-ply paper towel and wiped away some blood as I worked.

"I could. But I haven't. Because unlike my brother... I'm not obsessed."

"I'm here on scholarship."

"That explains why you're my biggest competition."

"The last thing you need to worry about is your grades," I muttered, "I don't know what the hell you've gotten into."

"I've messed up. I've messed with the wrong people. And I'm not safe. None of us are safe."

"What do you mean 'none of us'?"

"Distract me. Please. This hurts like hell."

"Okay. Yeah. I came here because… my dad's dead."

"Really? I assumed he'd run off on you or something."

"Honestly, Arnie. When you're racist, it makes me want to pull out glass like this!"

I yanked and Arnie yelled. I clamped my hand over his mouth again and Arnie groaned for a bit. I guess that was my fault.

"Fuck," Arnie grunted, "You're a malicious little cunt, you know that."

"I'll let that slide because you hit your head."

"Did you hit yours? That hurt."

"I got the biggest piece. You should be proud of me," I answered with a smirk.

"I see why Ben likes you. You're both miserable sadists."

"Don't be so sensitive. Aren't you supposed to be unfeeling? A cold-blooded murderer?"

"That was once," Arnie grumbled, "And I learned my bloody lesson. Believe me."

"Excuse me if I don't trust you 100%."

"I know I'm fucked up. All of us are. Charlie can't keep a relationship. Ben's mental. Arthur's a twat. Eva's got an eating disorder and well… Ara's dead."

"I'm sorry."

"This isn't about me. You're good at that, aren't you? How did your dad die?"

"Cops shot him."

"Shit. Was he a criminal?"

I gently pulled out a piece of glass, trying not to let Arnie's question get to me. It wasn't his fault I hated talking about this.

"He wasn't. But that didn't matter. My sister died too."

"I didn't know you had a sister."

"Not anymore," I sighed.

Thankfully, we were nearly done. But I was getting uncomfortable in this bathroom with Arnie shirtless and covered in blood. He had bruises all over his torso and shoulders. But if someone shot him, there was only a graze. The bullet might be in the car. I wanted Ben to call soon. I wanted to get out of this bathroom. I hated seeing blood.

I'd worked well under pressure. But now there were bloody shards of glass, a torn sweatshirt, and Arnie's golden brown hair stuck to his neck as he stared down at me.

"Liberty?" He murmured, "You okay?"

No. I wasn't. Talking about my dad. All this blood. I felt sick to my stomach.

"Not really."

He put his finger beneath my chin and lifted my gaze to his.

"Look at me," he murmured, "I'm sorry for asking."

I pulled my face away from his. Arnie shouldn't do things like that. He shouldn't touch me like that. Not when I'm dating his twin brother.

"It's fine."

The strange energy between us dissipated when Ben rang my phone. I picked up and whispered, "Yes?"

"Liberty. This is bad. I need you to get Arnie out of there and bring him to the edge of campus. Immediately."

"Okay. Fine. I'm coming."

"We need to go. I'm guessing Ben found your Range Rover."

"What's left of it," Arnie murmured, "And fine. How are we supposed to get out of here without waking anyone up?"

"Back out the window," I said, "Sorry. Do you think you can make it?"

"My body hurts. But I can handle it. My head's getting clearer."

"So are you going to tell me what happened?!"

"Yes."

Things Are Happening Fast

Barnaby swore endlessly as I helped him out the window. I had one of Ben's rugby polos lying around my room from the summer and Arnie complained endlessly as I helped him put it on. But he could hardly raise his arms. Barnaby had hurt his torso. Badly. Maybe he even had broken ribs.

I jumped out of the window behind him and we started towards the school gates. I was still so desperate for Arnie to give me an explanation. We leaned against the campus gates, hiding behind the tall stone in case a teacher on a late night jaunt caught us. Arnie's cheeks were still red. He stuffed his hands in his pockets and groaned.

"I need fucking drugs."

"You need a doctor."

"I messed up. I've been talking to Marley about Daniella. The video. And the situation with Yasmin… And then I started talking to Yasmin."

"What?!"

"Her and the other girls are thirty minutes from campus. They'll be there until the hearing."

"Unbelievable."

It was like Arnie did everything in his power to piss me off whatever chance he got. Why the hell was he even like this?! I wanted to smack him across the face.

"I… I got entangled with her. I thought I could find something to use against Daniella."

"Why the fuck would you do that?" I hissed.

It was taking everything in me not to scream.

"You don't understand," he growled.

"Make me! Because I am ready to punch you in the fucking gut."

"I went to see Yasmin so I could get something on Danny. Since the party in the caravan, I've suspected Danny was up to something. She was strange around me. And… it wasn't right. I had to get close to her sister in case anything went wrong."

"This is your problem," I snapped, "You're always trying to be fucking strategic!"

"I don't need a lecture from you," Barnaby sneered, "I know I can be… brash. I needed you to cover for me because I was going to do it. Sleep with Yasmin. Get details about Danny. I went too far. Her dad's a fucking billionaire jand… there were guards. She ratted me out. They knew I was coming. They chased me. And… I don't remember. I must have wrecked the car or something."

"We need to call Theo's sister."

"Leonora? What does she have to do with this?"

"Maybe we can use this. If there's any damned evidence left."

Ben pulled up in his Range Rover. I climbed into the back with Arnie.

"How is he?" Ben asked.

"He's fine. But he needs a doctor and we need to talk to your sister, Theo. Now."

"We pulled the car off the main road. But… Barnaby. You hit someone."

"No… That can't be right."

"Seriously?" I gasped.

"We called an ambulance. They got them off the road but… we heard the nurses talking. The person he hit was probably working for Mr. Friedrich, but… he's Russian. And… we think he's connected to your mom."

"What?! I thought we told her not to be here."

"Keri. They mentioned her by name."

"I don't understand," I said.

"Father's got his connection in this town to open his clinic. We're taking Arnie there and then tonight we're going to stay at a hotel. Dad's sending guards in the jet. It's probably about the settlement. If I'd hazard a guess, Mr. Friedrich thought he could trap Arnie and get information to… send a message. Get Liberty to drop the case."

"Why would her mom get involved in that?" Theo asked.

I scoffed, "You don't know my mom."

Arnie groaned, "Can you all shut up!?"

"You're the arsehole who went to see Yasmin!" Ben snapped, "What the hell were you thinking."

"Information about Daniella. I wasn't worried about Libby's stupid case."

"Congratulations, wanker. We're officially all in trouble."

"How are we going to explain that we disappeared? Again."

"I just texted my sister," Theo chimed in, "She's going to move the hearing to tomorrow morning. I explained everything to her."

Arnie groaned.

"My stomach hurts."

"Serves you bloody right," Ben growled.

"Wanker! I lost my car. And someone fucking shot at me."

Theo glanced over his shoulder, desperate to provoke Ben to sympathy, "He looks awful."

"Lucky for us, we're here. At the clinic. But we have to hurry, so hopefully this bastard doesn't need serious medical treatment."

Arnie limped out of the Range Rover. Ben and Theo held him up and led him inside. I wanted to wait in the car, but Ben looked like he'd throw a fit if I thought I'd stay out here alone. So I followed them inside. It took around thirty minutes for the doctor to finish stitching Arnie up and giving him enough painkillers to last the night.

Arthur Fox wasn't taking any chances, apparently. Because we didn't have to get to a hotel for private security to come pick us up.

Ben had to leave his Range Rover behind and then we all climbed into armored cars. We drove for an hour until we got close to the shore. And by the time we arrived, we got word from Leonora. She spoke to the other lawyers, and they agreed: my hearing would be tomorrow.

The Result of Libby's Hearing

My hearing was the first time I'd seen Yasmin, Hope or Claire since the incident. None of us would speak. This was a private hearing, not an official courtroom. The judge would listen to the lawyers and present his decision. The only real point of the hearing was so that the school's decision could enter the public record too.

That would be the difficult part. Handling the school's decision. That and dealing with the new private security. Ben was there for her, but he couldn't walk into the hearing room. Theo came too, but he was mostly there to talk to Leonora. Eugenie and Arnie waited at the hotel. When Eugenie found out how badly Barnaby had been hurt, she'd rushed away from school, half-cocked, spending over a hundred pounds on a taxi to meet him.

Daniella showed up to the hearing. She sat behind Yasmin and between their parents. Yasmin's father, Mr. Friedrich, had a cold face with sharp angles that betrayed nothing. It was hard to believe he was the one who'd called a hit on them. Yasmin's mother sat on the other side of Daniella, occasionally whispering to her in Spanish. She looked like Yasmin, a round face with chiseled doll features and a stiff, snooty stare.

Their father never looked at Daniella. He focused his attention on his beloved daughter, Yasmin. Millie came to represent Hope. Their parents didn't bother to show up. Claire's parents came but didn't bother with a warm reception. Her mother wagged her finger at her, and Claire's mild-mannered father had to pull her away. They'd paid for legal defense, but they weren't pleased with the position their daughter ended up in.

Moments like that one, sitting in a makeshift courtroom for a school hearing to decide my fate made me wish I had parents who could be there for me. Against her better judgment, my mother walked through the door. And I immediately regretted even the passing wish that I could have parents be there for me.

I didn't know how she got past Ben or the security team outside. I guess because she was my mother, they couldn't keep her away from the hearing. She carried a bundle in her arm and my throat tightened. The sibling I never knew. The sibling I didn't want. My mother waved at me and smiled. She did that sometimes. She acted like everything was normal when it wasn't, like that could make me forget all the ways she'd fucked my life up.

Sometimes it worked. I just wanted a mother. I'd always wanted a mother. And I'd never felt that need so strongly when Daddy was alive.

He was a good parent. He was both my mother and my father. And he'd meant the world to me. When he left, everything changed. I didn't know where I was going. Or what I was doing. Leonora slid a glass of water over to me and whispered, "Are you nervous?"

I nodded. She smiled and pinched my cheeks as if she were several years older than me than she was. I didn't even mind the gesture, even if perhaps I should have. She rose and presented her case to the presiding officer of the court. The judge listened carefully, and I tried to listen, but I couldn't. It was even harder to focus when the lawyers for the three other girls spoke. They couldn't argue against what happened — the facts weren't up for debate. All they needed to debate was the settlement.

To drag the hearing out further, the school read their verdict first. Yasmin would face a one year suspension. Claire and Hope would return to school with counseling and 100 hours of community service each. Then the judge read his verdict.

"At this time, due to the troubles and the desire both for privacy and an absence of consequence from the private institution, Rapetti Academy has awarded Liberty Jones with a sum of £75,000 for her troubles which come at the expense of a non-disclosure agreement and a press gag. From the three families, the net total as determined by the court is a sum of £15 million to be paid in a lump sum by the end of the year into a private trust, created and managed by Honorable Leonora Hargreaves for Miss Liberty Jones..."

My ears buzzed and rang after that. £15 million pounds, plus a sum of £75,000 from the school. Millions. Millions of pounds to keep this quiet. Millions of pounds to keep their honor intact. Money that was everything to me had been nothing to them for the price of my silence. Silence I would have kept anyway, because what would be the point of bragging about being a victim? I'd never been keen on the role of victim.

The judge banged his gavel, and everyone rose except me. Realizing that I wasn't standing, Leonora smoothed her skirt and touched my thigh.

"Liberty. It's over. We got the money. Plenty of money. Aren't you pleased?"

I was numb. I mean, I was happy too. But I couldn't imagine it. I'd grown up poor. I'd never had money of my own. I didn't know what I'd do with £15 million pounds. Not even the police department had given that much money after the settlement over my dad's death. Not like I would have seen any of that money with my mother hovering around, reading to hoover up any dollar that came from my dad's death.

As I sat frozen, I could smell her perfume as she came up behind Leonora and me. I turned to look at her and her face softened in a smile. Understanding the pain between us, Leonora rose, pressing her hand to my back.

"Hello Keri," Leonora said stiffly.

"I want my daughter to meet her sister," she said.

"I don't think now is the right time."

Leonora could muster a stiff English upper lip whenever she wanted. And perfectly alternate this persona with her gentle school marm appearance.

"We'd better go, Libby," Leonora said firmly, "Your boyfriend and my brother will be waiting outside."

"Yeah…"

"Don't be scared. I'll help you with everything that comes next. This is a good thing."

Her words soothed me, but not entirely. Overnight, I'd gone from a poor scholarship student to a multi-millionaire. Holy shit. Holy fucking shit.

The Aftermath of the Hearing

I didn't know when I'd get used to this or if I ever would. Leonora's trust meant I'd get a monthly income for spending money and then I'd talk to my "financial managers" for any large expenditures. I had to call Oxford and tell them I didn't need my scholarship anymore. I had to pay my last semester's tuition at Rapetti Academy out of pocket. That saying "more money, more problems" was right. But having problems when you had money was different, because at least those problems had solutions that didn't involve eating tinned sausages or skipping dinner.

It was hard getting used to the girls back at school. Hope tried to talk to me. To say she was sorry. I thought she meant it, but I still could never trust her again. I said hello in the hallways, but that was about it. We'd never be friends the way we were before. Her sister Millie still hated my guts. She'd been loyal to Yasmin, and even if the financial terms of the arrangement were private, everyone knew what happened to the girls.

Claire avoided everyone, especially the popular girls. Her parents had gone bonkers, I'd heard, and their punishment had been far worse than what our hearing decided. Ouch. I might have felt bad if she hadn't been responsible for tormenting me. Mr. Friedrich's exposed mafia ties had been squelched, too. So we didn't have to worry about random attacks.

The one person I couldn't seem to shake was my mom. She didn't care about Leonora's frequent threats to sue. And I told Leonora I didn't want to take things further. I didn't want to take my mother to court. I didn't want to deal with her at all. Each time an unknown number called my phone, worry took over. Ben noticed how distracted it made me, and he offered to take care of things.

I didn't know if Ben's idea of "taking care of things" would do more harm than good. I think the only reason he didn't "take care of things" his way was because I'd begged. Halloween was a couple days away and aside from my mom, our only other enormous problem was Daniella.

Our plans to mess with her were on hold. With the hearing and the aftermath, not to mention classes and regular commitments, Danny became irrelevant. But she still had dirt on us, which was a huge freaking problem. Ben didn't seem worried when I brought it up. He was only worried about two things: rugby games and Halloween.

Now that we were back together, I reminded him of the "deal" I'd made with his dad about his grades. Ben rolled his eyes.

"I'll have Barnaby take my exams for me."

"How would that help? He's not even in half your classes."

Ben shrugged.

"Stop thinking about that. We need to think of something important."

"Like Halloween?"

"Theo's renting a manor for the party. He's dressing as Beetlejuice. We should match. Posh and Beckham?"

"No!" I said, "How the hell am I supposed to be Posh? I'm black."

Ben shrugged.

"Fair point."

Ben stroked his stubble. He'd started growing his facial hair out before their next game. I leaned over and kissed him. I loved the way his beard tickled my face. I love just… being with him.

"We could go as Beyonce and Jay-Z."

"I'm not doing blackface."

"Who said anything about blackface!?"

Ben grinned.

"Sorry. Just letting you know."

I strained my voice from all my choir practice. Ben pressed his nose against my cheek.

"What if we went as an angel and a devil?"

"A devil?" I said, shifting uncomfortably, "Isn't that a bit… I dunno… evil."

"Evil? Since when are you religious?"

"I don't want to be a devil. That's all I'm saying."

Ben snickered.

"Did you really think I'd be the angel? Plus... you'll look phenomenal in white."

He kissed my neck, and I leaned over to kiss him back. I ran my fingers over his beard and whispered, "Fine. I'll be your angel. But you... need to study. Rugby doesn't count as studying."

Ben groaned.

"My grades are fine," he complained, "They're slightly better than last year."

"Slightly?"

"I'm working on it."

"Work harder. Arnie can help if you need it. But he shouldn't take your tests for you."

Ben scowled.

"Do you really think Arnie's that much smarter than me?"

I shrugged.

"He gets better grades. He's right on my tail for valedictorian. But he bombed his last physics quiz."

Ben scowled. We'd gone from playful to a tense in a matter of seconds. I didn't get it. I wasn't trying to be rude. Barnaby had better grades. It wasn't a judgement. It was true. He shrugged me off his shoulders.

"Yeah. He's so bloody brilliant."

"I meant nothing by it."

"Sure you didn't. Just like you mean nothing when you spend every bloody day in the library with him."

"You aren't jealous, are you?"

"Why would I be jealous?" Ben sneered.

"You sound jealous. And he's my lab partner. I have to hang out with him. I thought you'd given up this weird problem you have."

"I don't have a weird problem. It's just... you know what. Never mind. I need not be so... childish."

I reached for Ben's hand. He squeezed back. He was frustrated, but not properly vexed. Which was good. I kissed his shoulder through his shirt.

"Tell me."

"It's a problem with having a twin brother. Especially one like Barnaby. Before... everything. He was always the one people liked. He was popular. I was in his shadow. It's hard to let go of."

I'd heard the way everyone talked to Ben in his family. His dad, his mom, his siblings. They all punched down. And there were still some tender spots. I pressed his hand to my lips.

"I choose you. And finally... you've chosen me."

Ben twisted his face in mock offense.

"I've always chosen you."

"You dumped me."

His green eyes met mine.

"I always do what I think I must so I can protect you."

I grinned.

"My little devil."

"And you're my angel."

We had Halloween costumes set, which was half the battle. Ben's phone buzzed. He picked it up and groaned.

"It's Barnaby. He wants a Halloween costume idea."

"Freddie Krueger," I suggested, "Or Jason from Friday 13th."

Ben smirked and kissed my hand.

"Fuck, those are good."

He tapped a quick message off to his brother and leaned back. Arnie replied and Ben nodded.

"What did he say?"

"He's going as Freddie. And he's inviting Charlie."

"Does Theo know?"

Ben messaged Arnie and waited for a message to return.

"No. Theo doesn't know."

"Are you going to tell him?"

Ben shrugged.

"I don't know what the hell goes on between those two."

"I guess we'll find out at the party."

Ben stroked his chin.

"Yes. And then there's the Dumps issue."

"The Dumps issue? I thought we wouldn't do anything."

Ben grinned.

"Theo invited her. And we're sure Barnaby will be her date."

Perfectly Orchestrated Revenge

I was nervous about showing up to Halloween dressed like this. My costume was cute, Eugenie helped set it up. White wings, a halo hanging above my picked out natural hair, a tight white dress that hugged my curves plus silver makeup that made every inch of my skin glow.

Eugenie dressed as the Red Queen from Alice in Wonderland. Her costume was short, cute and a bit goth. Her cheeks glowed red from blush and we'd spent nearly an hour getting her lipstick to a perfect heart shape. She knew Arnie planned to go to the party with Daniella, and that fact didn't bother her anymore. He was dressing up as Freddie Kruger. And if that bothered her, Eugenie didn't show it. I wasn't nervous about the party. I was long past getting nervous about Rapetti off campus parties. It was weird... being one of them — a student who didn't have to worry about losing her scholarship. I didn't think I'd get used to it so quickly. I didn't want to lose myself.

"Isla and Marty are going together. Did you hear?"

"No. Are they together?"

"I dunno. I think Marty likes her. They're going as Jamie and Claire from Outlander. He's got a full highlander getup and everything."

"Sounds cute."

"They're so into it. I think they're going to hook up."

"Is Louisa coming?"

"She's already over there with Zack, helping Theo to set up."

We met Ben at his secret parking spot. He looked… phenomenal. He wore a black blazer over his bare chest. Dark liner beneath his lids and devil horns. He grinned and wrapped his arm around my waist, squeezing me close to him as he whispered, "Good evening, my little angel," into my ear. Eugenie wrinkled her face in mock disgust.

"You two are disgustingly cute."

"Don't be jealous, dear."

"I'm not."

We were all giddy. Not just because of our costumes and the promise of a wild Halloween, but because of Barnaby's plans. Marley was nearby too, but he wouldn't come to the party until he'd done everything Ben asked. Charlie brought him down to England. This was it, the last job Ben had for him. Marley had earned a place with a Scottish orchestra. He was fantastic at the cello, and working for Ben allowed him time to practice and go to auditions. We weren't as close as we'd been before, but… I wanted to see him. I wanted to know he was doing okay.

He hadn't heard details about the settlement, and I didn't know how to tell him.

"Hey Marley I'm filthy fucking rich now because a crazy white girl nearly shoved a giant dildo up my ass."

I didn't think there was a simple way to slip that into conversation. I'd hoped Ben would tell him, but Ben didn't gossip with Marley. He wanted him around to monitor him. To make sure Marley didn't get the wrong idea about me. He was over me by now. I was certain of it. He'd met a girl in the orchestra. Mixed. Jamaican and Scottish. They were "friends with benefits" which suited Marley fine, according to Ben.

I hadn't heard from my mother in a week. I blocked all the numbers she normally called from and I hoped that she gave up on trying to get a hold of me. Knowing her, that wouldn't last. At least I'd have Halloween. My last Halloween at Rapetti Academy.

I'd have to make it count. When we arrived at the party, Ben declined the drinks Theo offered him at the door. Everyone poured inside and Theo tugged at my forearm.

"Don't go in yet."

He nodded at Ben, who shrugged and wandered inside, leaving me on the steps of the rental to talk to Theo.

"Why didn't you tell me Charlie would be here?"

"Um... I... I didn't think you'd want to know."

"You don't get it. I'm not getting back together with Charlie."

"I didn't think you would," I lied. I assumed they'd get back together. Theo ran his fingers through his hair, reaching reflexively for the spliff behind his ear.

"You don't get it. I like Eugenie now."

"What? She's practically dating Barnaby."

"So?"

"In case you forgot, Barnaby's crazy. I wouldn't touch a girl he liked with a ten-foot pole."

"She deserves better than him."

"What about Charlie?"

"He's a wanker. No offense, but… that's all the Fox brothers. They're exhausting. I just want… someone nice. Someone to love me."

"Charlie loves you," I said.

Theo's cheeks darkened as he inhaled. Once he blew out pungent smoke, he shook his head.

"He doesn't. He likes the idea of me. And that isn't enough."

"Give him a chance. Even if you like Eugenie… You and Charlie have history. If there are still feelings there… don't you owe it to yourself to explore them?"

"Fuck."

"What?"

"I hate that you're right all the time."

"You two work together. Maybe it's a little toxic. But just the right amount."

Theo smirked.

"Go on. See what he's dressed as. Maybe you'll change your mind."

I came close. Charlie stood in the middle of the party dancing his ass off — dressed like Tarzan. Which meant an offensive dreadlocks wig and a loincloth. And unfortunately, he didn't care if every single person there caught sight of his jiggly bits.

"Charlie!" I shrieked, as he bent over in a six o'clock position right in front of me as I walked toward Ben.

"Liberty!" he shrieked, standing up properly and lifting me up, spinning me around. I screamed until he set me down, kissing my cheeks.

"You look fit."

"You look… naked!"

Charlie winked, "Nothing the lads and the lasses don't enjoy."

I rolled my eyes, and he tilted a bottle of wine back into his mouth.

"Want some?"

I shook my head and continued wandering towards Ben. He put his arm around me and kissed my cheek.

"Libs, it's nearly time."

"This is crazy," I whispered, "We could get in trouble for this. Maybe I'm not cut out for this."

"Shhh," Ben whispered, "This will work. Promise. Look at them."

He pointed towards a corner of the room. Arnie had his tongue nearly halfway down Daniella's throat. She had her hand on his butt, squeezing it and running her hands up his back. I thought they'd start having sex right there. I wrinkled my nose.

"Ew. Makes me sick."

"Patience, my love," Ben whispered, "Nearly everyone's here."

It took another 40 minutes for everyone to arrive. But we had to wait for Marley. When he entered the parlor where everyone was dancing and acting foolish, I nearly didn't recognize him. He'd lost weight. And he'd cut his hair. I ran over to him and hugged him. He'd dressed up as Black Panther from the movies and his costume looked professionally made. He held me tightly and pulled away, eyeing me up and down.

"Did that white boy make you wear that?"

I rolled my eyes.

"No. It's a couples costume."

"You look great."

"So do you."

"It's been a while," Marley said.

"Yeah."

"I'm sorry for everything, Libby. For not being there for you. For the stuff with your mom."

"Don't keep apologizing."

"We'll never be friends like we were before," Marley said, "I get it. But I have regrets."

"I don't."

Ben climbed the stairs in the middle of the room. Wide, ballroom stairs like you find in rich people's houses. He nodded at Marley who turned to me.

"I did it. I got into that girl's room and destroyed every copy. The only one out there is the one your boyfriend's got."

"Good. Thanks."

"Twins. You ever think you chose the wrong one?"

I snorted.

"No way! Arnie is… different."

Marley grinned.

"He's fucking crazy. I barely know the dude but… he's bat shit."

"Tonight we'll prove that," I muttered.

Ben had a microphone. And it was a party, so there was a speaker system. Ben gave the DJ the signal, and the music quieted. He tapped the microphone and everyone's eyes turned to him at the top of the stairs. A large white projector sheet fell behind him. I searched for Arnie in the crowd. He gripped Danny's hand and led her up the stairs so they stood a few steps below Ben. She giggled. She seemed tipsy.

Too late for me to back out now. I'd helped them coordinate this. I'd planned this. Marley took my hand and led me through the crowd of Rapetti kids until we found Theo. He fist bumped Theo and nodded quickly as Charlie before he disappeared. He wasn't finished with his work.

Ben cleared his throat.

"Friends and foes in this crowd, welcome. Everyone at Rapetti who matters stands here tonight…"

Everyone cheered. Millie whispered something snarky to Amira. I knew it was snarky because of how Amira giggled and smacked her forearm. Hope leaned against the wall, ignoring Edward Chapman blatantly hitting on her and trying to touch her body in her skintight Catwoman suit.

Ben continued, "I have a video to play for you tonight, but before I play this video, I want to tell you a story. A story of a two-faced girl who lied to everyone here and played the victim when she was actually the villain."

Arnie pressed the clicker. I'd made the slideshow. And I was proud of it. Screenshots of Danny's texts flashed on the screen. Everyone gasped. Arnie gripped her forearm with his other hand. She couldn't run. Ben spilled everything. The entire truth. And then when he got to the sex tape. He played it.

I couldn't believe Arnie agreed to this.

"The best way to get ahead of blackmail is to release it yourself," he'd said. Eugenie disagreed at first. She liked him. She didn't want people to know what he'd done. Arnie didn't care.

"It's for a good cause," he'd said.

Snickers erupted in the crowd and then snide comments. It's easy to change the tone of a crowd. Marley yelled from the other side of the room, "Slag!"

And that was it. Laughter to insults. And then Ben finished his speech, "I guess that's why they call her Dumps. And tonight, you're going to make that nickname even more true. We have tomatoes, eggs, whipped cream, rotten fruit and a week's worth of waste from the cafeteria. And we have tonight's guest of honor. Daniella Friedrich."

Theo reached into his pocket. He was ready to throw the first fruit, strike the first blow. The pungent rotten tomato soared through the air. He was an athlete and had perfect aim. It hit Daniella's dress, and she screamed while the entire room laughed. Arnie held her there. Still. Not like running would have done her good. Running would have made it worse. Ben walked down the five steps to meet her and he poured his drink over her head as she shrieked.

More laughter.

Let the games begin.

Crazy Sex-You're-Not-Supposed-To-Be-Having

Cavorting laughter filled the manor. Raucous laughter. And by the time Daniella ran off, crying, we were all satisfied entirely with our revenge. She could consider this a valuable lesson learned.

I wanted to feel bad, but I didn't. And Barnaby was right. The best way to stop a rumor in its tracks, to deal with blackmail, was to get ahead of it. The DJ started playing Michael Jackson's Thriller, the perfect Halloween song. Ben grabbed my hand, and we danced out to the center of the dancefloor. Then Charlie came up behind me and gyrated on me until Theo pulled him off us. They appeared to be arguing.

Ben's hands held my hips as we moved together. I liked to think I was rubbing off on Ben because he was becoming a better dancer. One awkward white boy move at a time…

Charlie pushed Theo. Then Theo pushed back. Then Charlie grabbed Theo's collar, and they kissed. Hard. Holding onto Theo's lapels, they moved to the edge of the room and Theo turned Charlie around, pressing him against the wall, kissing him. Ben wrinkled his nose and spun me around so he didn't have to look at his best friend and his brother making out hard against the stone walls.

Eugenie and Arnie danced for a bit, but then they split off to dance with other people. Eugenie had her arms around Arnav, who grinned from ear to ear. He'd dressed up as a soccer player, which meant wearing his rugby uniform with a soccer jersey instead. A very lazy costume. Out of the corner of my eye, I noticed Barnaby talking to Hope in the room's corner. I could hear a couple words floating above the music. They weren't talking. They argued.

And then… Arnie kissed her. Kissing was in the air. Ben grabbed my cheeks and kissed me too. Everyone dancing around us disappeared, and I felt the intoxicating need for Ben building inside me.

I grabbed his hand and tiptoed around the cleaning crew as I pulled him upstairs. There had to be an empty room up here somewhere and I needed Ben. Badly. He looked nearly like his brother with dark liner smudged between his lids, but thankfully he was Ben. My gorgeous rugby player boyfriend. I found an empty room and shut the door behind us. Ben grinned at me.

"You are… so different from when we first met."

"Shut up… Before Charlie notices and thinks its hilarious to walk in on us."

Ben grabbed my hips and pressed me between his body and the door. My hands rushed to his chest and I could feel his heart pulsing between my fingertips as desire surged between us. I bit down on my lower lip as Ben grinned at me.

"I love you, Libs," he whispered.

"I love you too."

"But tonight… you're not being very angelic…"

"No," I whispered, "I'm not…"

"I haven't ruined you, have I?"

I laughed.

"Oh, you definitely have."

Ben chuckled and stroked his horns.

"Was it my devil's tongue?"

He kissed me again, and he smelled so good. What is it about boys? The sweatier and more disgusting they get, the better they smell. I wanted to bury myself in that smell. To take his clothes off and have him enter me with that scent surrounding me. I stroked his chin, running my fingers around the chiseled jawline.

Even in the dark, I could tell how perfectly green Ben's eyes were, and I wanted to watch them shudder and flutter closed as he entered me.

"You've made me a better person," he whispered, "I hope I haven't made you worse."

"Only in the best ways."

"Before I fuck you against this door," he whispered, teasing my earlobe with an eager tongue, "I need to ask you something. Something important."

He stopped kissing me and gazed at me with unexpected intensity. My heart raced. I wanted him. More than anything. But the uncertainty of some important question hanging between us both frightened me and made me want him more.

"Christmas. I want you to spend Christmas with me."

I giggled.

"Yes... Yes, yes!"

He tugged on my lower lip, sucking on it a bit before letting it go. I wanted him so badly then, that I would have said yes to anything. Run around the room barking like a chihuahua? You got it, Ben... He didn't know he had that hold on me. Or if he did, he held his control graciously.

"So," he murmured, "I see you're wearing it tonight."

I didn't think he'd notice. I put the promise ring back on. I'd never let it get too far away from me. I'd always hoped that somehow, I'd get Benjamin back. And I had him. And nothing would take him away. Not now, at least. He ran his fingers over the jewelry and I nodded, pulling on the lapels of his blazer and kissing him again.

"Thank you," he whispered, "For taking me back when I've been an utter prick."

"I love you," I said, "And I meant it when I said forever."

"So did I," he said, "And I will never leave you again. Now... how the hell do I get you out of this thing."

"There's a corset. You'll have to unlace me."

His fingers strummed the strings of my dress and he ran his hands over my angel's wings.

"I have an easier way in," he murmured, hiking my skirt up and running his fingers along the outside of my underwear.

I bit down so hard on my lower lip I thought I'd start bleeding. I wanted him. Here. Now. Always.

He lifted me off the ground and unzipped his pants, pressing the tip of his dick against my entrance and urging his hips forward. I moaned as he entered me, and he slammed my body hard against the door. Each time Ben entered me, I forgot how big he was. He was huge. Definitely above average. Way above average. He filled every inch of me and the first thrust always came with a bit of pain. Pain I had to deal with. Pain that made the pleasure so much better. He pinned my hands over my head, taking away my control.

"Look at me," he grunted, and I obeyed him, gazing into his green eyes as he ardently thrust between my legs. I was so wet. My pussy dripped mechanically, and each thrust caused an explosion of juices between my legs until I came. Quickly. It's hard not to cum fast when a big fat cock pumps between your legs, stretching you out and pleasuring you deep.

Ben's lips and tongue on my neck only made me hotter. And hornier.

"Fuck me. Fuck me hard…"

He grunted and pushed his hips inside me deeper. I came again. And again. I lost track of how many times I came. Ben pulled out of me and pressed my chest against the door and we groaned simultaneously as he entered me from behind, pounding away at my pussy with his gigantic cock as my ass bounced back against his dick.

"Yes… yes… Give me your big white cock," I gasped.

He fucked me harder. Like hearing the words big white cock forced him to lose control. He grabbed onto a handful of my hair and craned my neck back. I gave every ounce of control to him as he fucked me against the door. His hips moved slower after I'd cum so much I thought I'd faint. He pulled out of me and whispered, "There has to be a bed in here somewhere."

He lifted me off the ground effortlessly as I squealed and threw me back onto a bed that looked way too fancy for tipsy nineteen-year-olds to have filthy Halloween upstairs at a party sex-they're-not-supposed-to-be-having-sex on. Ben didn't care. My knees tilted up, and he guided his dick between my legs. I screamed as he hit me deep and juices splattered out of my pussy all over his abs and thighs as he slid up to the hilt in my dripping sex.

He slowed his stroke down, gazing into my eyes as he murmured, "I'm going to cum inside you…"

I nodded, urging him on by digging my fingernails into his ass, "Cum inside me… use your big white cock…"

"I'm going to cum inside your tight black pussy, babes…"

I bit down on his lower lip with my tongue, drawing him into me, drawing his heat and sweat and dick into me deeper. I gasped as I came one last time and Ben's cock burst inside me. A gush of hot liquid squirted between my legs and his dick pulsed inside me as I cried out and Ben groaned, collapsing on top of me as spurt after spurt of his cum coated my pussy. He let me take his lips between my teeth and when his eyes fluttered open, he grinned.

"You… are fucking hot. And I'm going to fuck you again tonight."

"You just came!"

Ben grinned.

"We'd better go dance until I'm ready again. Because trust me… I'll want you again before the night's up."

"We'd better go dance until I'm ready again. Because trust me… I'll want you again before the night's up."

4 Words No One Wants To Hear

The night ended as it normally did. Rapetti kids drunkenly slumped over couches. Charlie and Theo wrapped around each other in a bed upstairs. Eugenie and Arnie sleeping in another bed. I guess whatever flirtation he had with Hope didn't pan out. Good for them. I noted that Arnav slept in their bed, but he might have wandered in there in the middle of the night. I didn't speculate much. It was probably something crazy knowing Barnaby.

The clean-up crew tiptoed around the passed out kids as I tiptoed into the kitchen. The after party crew had orange juice and bagels out for us. I greeted the kind-faced Romanian lady who handed me an extra strawberry for breakfast. I scarfed down the bagel and nibbled at the strawberry before I wandered outside of the manor in my costume — without the wings and halo. I'd forgotten how cold mornings in the English countryside could get. I sank my toes into dewy grass as goosebumps traveled from my toes up the sides of my legs. Ben and I were back together again, and it felt good…

I offered to help the clean-up crew, but they respectfully declined my help, so I snuck back upstairs and into bed with Ben. He groaned.

"Cold," he moaned.

I snuggled close to him.

"Cold toes," he mumbled.

I giggled and ran my toes over his bare calf. Ben wrapped his arm around me and sleepily pulled me towards him, his raspy English accent drawing me deeper into him.

"Come here, you…"

He attacked me with a famished kiss and wrapped his warm, bare leg around me. His hairy leg tickled my thigh and I giggled and whimpered at him to stop. Which he didn't. Ben pounced on me, spreading my legs apart and resting his body against mine. His eyes were barely open.

"Where'd'you go?" He mumbled, "Why are you so bloody cold…"

He kissed my shoulders, my cheek and my neck, warming up with rough morning lips and peeling my thin dress strap over my shoulders to kiss them properly.

"I went outside. To survey the damage."

"Hm," he murmured, "Did we fuck it all to hell?"

"Yes. We did. And they won't let me help clean up."

Ben chuckled.

"Do you ever tire of being such a good girl?"

"No," I whispered, raking my fingers through his hair, "But I'm not a good girl."

Ben chuckled.

"Are you talking about what we did last night?"

He ran his tongue along my neck.

"No," I insisted, drawing a sharp gasp as he tasted my neck. And then my shoulders.

"I'm talking about Daniella."

He sounded out every letter of her cruel nickname.

"Dumps."

"Yes. I'm feeling… guilty. Maybe we went too far."

"She didn't worry about threatening you. Or blackmailing all of us."

"I know. But… the look on her face. Maybe she's not entirely evil."

Ben grinned.

"Why are you smiling?"

"You are such a good girl."

"I am not!"

"Yes, you are… And don't worry about Daniella. We ought to get back to campus."

Ben climbed out of bed and stretched, every perfect muscle on his body glinting in the morning sun. I wanted to pull him back into bed. Immediately. He stared out the window, leaning against the sill, the muscles in his pale arm flexing as he stared over the manor grounds.

"Christmas," he murmured, a smile crossing his face, "You'll be home at Christmas."

Before I could plead with him to get back to bed, our door burst open without a knock. That could only be one person. Arnie.

"Arseholes."

"Good morning," Ben muttered sarcastically.

Arnie was remarkably unscathed for someone who had been through an accident. There were a couple bruises on his bare chest, thinner and less developed than Ben's. And very tattooed. That was a big difference. Eugenie appeared around the corner, wearing his Freddie Kruger costume sweater.

"I'm hungry," she whimpered, "Let's get breakfast."

Arnav appeared behind them and slid his hands around Eugenie's waist. Arnie winked at us and wandered off with his duo.

"What the heck is going on with those three?" I muttered.

I had a second breakfast, Ben had his first, and we drove back to campus. I took a nice long shower. Ben texted me he was in the library doing homework. I did some homework on my own and then met Barnaby in the library with his brother where we worked on our physics project while Ben occasionally scowled at us for arguing too loudly.

After that, Ben wanted to take me out to dinner alone. Off-campus. On a proper date.

"We need to talk tonight," he said, "It's about something important."

Great. We need to talk. The words that send fear into every woman's heart. But date night. That meant it couldn't be that bad. Whatever Ben had planned for me wouldn't be scary or awful. And it wouldn't be awful, because he told me he loved me. And he was excited to spend Christmas with me.

I walked out of my dorm in a cute pair of jeans and a sweater. It was getting chilly at night. I'd pulled my hair back in two-stranded twists and waited outside near the main road. When I saw headlights, I put my phone away. It took me a minute or two to register that this wasn't Ben's car and I was probably in enormous trouble.

"What are you doing here?"

"Get in the car."

"No! I'm not getting in the car."

Zinfandel

I did *not* want to get in the car with my mother. But then... she pulled out a gun. I wasn't exactly scared. Well, I was as scared as anyone would be if their mother pulled a gun on them. But there was no way in hell Keri would actually hurt me. Would she?

"Are you seriously pulling a gun on your own daughter?!"

How the hell did she even get a gun? Weren't these super illegal in England? Not like Keri gave a damn about what was legal and where.

"I said, get in the car young lady. I've got your sister in the back seat."

"My sister?!"

If there was one thing I could count on Keri for, it was to become the perfect example of what *not* to do as a mother. I didn't plan on being a mother anyway. I planned on going to Oxford. And ending up with Ben. My voice was still strained from choir practice.

"You're pulling a gun on me with a baby in the back seat?"

"Liberty Jones, stop fucking playing with me and get in this goddamned car."

I'd stalled long enough. Ben rammed his Range Rover into the back of Keri's car. Not enough to hurt anyone, or even dent the car, but enough that she checked her rear view mirror and stomped on the gas, pealing out of the campus gates. In a community based on "trust" and perfectly tucked away in the middle of the wilderness, they didn't expect to need high-level security.

Ben parked and leaped out of the car, running his hands over my shoulders, grounding me. Reminding me that for all the bullshit Keri put me through, I was still here.

"Who the hell was that?"

"You ran into someone's car and you didn't know them?"

Ben shrugged.

"You seemed scared. And angry. I figured I'd give them a fright."

"It was my mom. Wielding a gun. With my damn sister in the back seat."

"Oh. Libby…"

He wrapped his arms around me. I didn't feel sad. By now, Keri's antics were old hat. I couldn't let her get to me like that. He kissed my forehead.

"Do you still want to go out?"

"What kind of question is that?"

Ben's cheeks darkened.

"Well. It's just that... We need to talk and I don't want to upset you."

"Upset me?"

"Don't worry about it. Let's go eat. Are you hungry?"

"Starving."

Ben kissed my cheek.

"I knew it."

I got into his car, glad that at least he'd come in time. I was nervous as we drove a couple towns over. I kept worrying that Keri would come back. That I should do something to stop her. I had money now. Maybe I could use some of it. Then it occurred to me... Ben shouldn't have to pay for everything anymore.

"Do you want to split dinner with me?"

Ben scowled.

"What?"

He might have been scowling because he had to parallel park, which he hated. He'd crashed three previous cars that way — a feat, since he'd only had his license at 18 and driven illegally two years beforehand.

"I can afford to pay for half a dinner now. Even somewhere like this."

The restaurant was fancy. And French. A place where the waiters treat you like garbage, but you'd kill your own roommate for the food. Sorry, Eugenie.

Ben shook his head, golden-brown hair cascading down his back.

"Don't be ridiculous, Liberty."

"I can afford to. I should pay half and half for everything now. I'm..."

"Don't say rich," Ben finished for me.

"It did feel weird."

He smiled.

"I don't care if you can afford to. Because I can afford to and you're my girl. Plus, I'm pretty sure I owe you like a year of dinner because of what I've put you through."

"And what you're about to put me through," I added, the painful "we need to talk" still hanging between us.

Ben grunted and we took our seats. As usual, Ben made a reservation and pre-ordered wine, which he didn't touch, but I enjoyed a few sips of Zinfandel as his brow furrowed at the menu.

"Duck," he said, "Want to split the duck?"

I agreed and Ben leaned back.

"This isn't easy for me to talk about."

"Now you're freaking me out."

"I'm scared to ask you. So freak out."

He leaned forward and smirked. Why was I more scared of Ben's green-eyed devil smirk than my mother waving a gun at me — and potentially returning to campus to find me later too.

"Can you ski?" Ben asked.

"Stop changing the subject."

"I'm not! That *is* the subject."

"What?!"

"Can you ski," Ben repeated, as if I'd been serious about needing him to repeat it.

"Um... no?"

He exhaled loudly.

"Well that's a bloody relief."

"What?! Why did you make such a big deal out of asking me if I know how to ski."

His cheeks darkened.

"I didn't want to be... I didn't want to be..." he leaned in, so close I could peck him on the lips if I wanted to. Or slap him across the face.

"I didn't want to be racist."

Now I want to slap him.

"What's racist about asking if I knew how to ski?"

"I didn't ask because you're black!"

His tone made it seem that my blackness was at least 40% of the reason, but he'd talked this up.

"Why are you asking at all?"

"Because. Mum and dad want to go away from Blackmoor for Christmas. We have a lodge in Gstaad."

"What word did you just say? And Jesus, how many houses do you people need?"

Ben's cheeks were properly red now and he eyed my wine like he didn't care if he had to drive home, he wanted a bloody drink.

"Gstaad. Switzerland. It's a quaint village and if you don't want to go skiing because it's too... white... you don't have to go."

I giggled. I couldn't help it. But it was Ben, taking racial sensitivity *so* seriously. And I couldn't figure out why for the life of me.

"Why are you acting like this again?"

"I had a talk with your friend."

"Um...okay?"

"Marley told me I had to start taking racial sensitivity seriously or..."

"Or what?!"

I didn't exactly like the idea of the two of them discussing me like that, although it was probably inevitable.

"Or I'd fuck this up. Again. He wanted to kill me when I dumped you. I mean, he understood but... he still wanted to kill me. Luckily he's smart enough not to bite the hand that feeds him."

Ben winked and I rolled my eyes.

"I appreciate your *sensitivity* but um..." I snickered.

"What's so funny."

"You've never really talked about the race thing with me like this."

"Yes I have!"

"When?!"

"In bed."

It was my turn to want the ground to swallow me up. Ben didn't really think dirty talk about his "big white cock" was the same thing as discussing racial differences, did he? If he did, he'd genuinely lost his mind. Wait, scratch that. Ben was already crazy. That's what I liked about him.

"That doesn't count," I muttered.

Ben grinned.

"Ha! I think it does."

"It definitely does *not* count."

"Then tell me... what do you want me to do... better. How can I be like... good at this race stuff. Because if we have a kid one day... like... I want to be a good dad."

My stomach wadded up like wet cotton. A kid? We were only nineteen. And about to start university in the fall. I'd rather talk about ski vacations than having a kid. Period. Ben noticed my discomfort and thankfully, I didn't have to tell him what I feared: that I'd never want a kid.

That I was too screwed up from daddy dying, from losing Niecy, from my mom being absolutely nuts.

"Hey," he said, reaching across the table and touching my hand, dragging me back into reality, "Are you thinking of your mum?"

How did he get to know me so well? How did Ben unravel me like this?

"Yes," I replied, honestly.

"We'll have to do something about her."

He pulled out his phone.

"What are you going to do, call her?" I asked sarcastically.

"Yes," Ben responded.

And I had about fifty-seven more questions for him while he dialed.

Catching Up With Theo & Arnie

Ben was crazy. Super fucking crazy. And since when did he have my mother's cellphone number? Ben could be unpredictable like that. She didn't pick up, so he left a message.

"Keri. It's me. Nice to run into you today. Call me."

He hung up and tousled his hair.

"Are you serious?" I whispered, as if she could hear me through the phone even if he'd already hung up.

"Marley got me her number after she first showed up. I figured it could come in handy. What does she want," he wondered bitterly.

"I don't know what she wants. I never know what she wants. Usually money. Sometimes attention."

"Money," Ben muttered, rolling the word over his tongue playfully. We finished dinner, making idle conversation, but my mind wandered back to my mom. I didn't know if she was ignoring Ben's phone calls on purpose, but I knew we probably hadn't seen the last of her. After our date night, we both went to bed early. It felt good to stay up texting him again. In the morning, I found myself nervously glancing around campus for my mom's car — at least the car she showed up in.

My project with Arnie was going well, and I was still ahead of him in all our classes to his chagrin. He was starting to get bitter about it — pulling my hair during quizzes or poking me his pen repeatedly during class. Annoying, but totally Arnie. Eventually, I decided to ask him about Halloween. He grinned in a way that looked just like Ben for a second.

I could forget they were *related* until moments like this, when how "identical" they were became obvious.

"That was an entire week ago," he answered, leaning in and raising a thick eyebrow, "Have you been thinking about it. Wishing you could join?"

He bit down on his lower lip. Arnie had a very punchable face. Very.

"I hate you."

"Why do you care, if you're not... interested."

I ignored his suggestive, wiggling eyebrows. Ew.

"I could ask Eugenie but I don't want her to think I'm judging. I know *you* don't care."

"Ouch."

"What about that was offensive?!"

"I dunno," Arnie mumbled, "But I'm taking one of your candies."

He stole a gummy bear and plopped it in his mouth. It was taking us forever to get homework done, partly my fault because I kept distracting him and this was yet another distraction.

"Fine. Have some more. And tell me... what the hell happened?"

"Bliss, Liberty," he said dramatically, "Pure bliss. *Sharing* her."

"Did you really?"

Arnie winked.

"You'll never know."

"You're a freak."

"Proud of it, love."

We finished our homework and I met Ben at the library's entrance. He wore his rugby uniform and he was gross and sweaty.

"Jesus," Arnie sneered at him, "Didn't you think to shower before meeting your girlfriend?"

"Shut up," Ben grumbled, "I took a nasty fall earlier. And... I walked off the field. Coach is a fucking madman and if he doesn't get his act together, we'll lose the bloody tournament."

I felt guilty that I'd forgotten about Ben's rugby tournament. I'd been so busy with my grades, choir practice, the bliss of us getting back together, hanging out with friends and worrying about my mother that I forgot this was his final rugby season.

"Tournaments. Rugby. Don't you Neanderthals ever get tired of running into each other?"

Arnie elbowed Ben in the side and he let out a blood curdling scream. I lifted his shirt and gasped.

"What the hell happened to you!?"

"I told you," he scowled, "Nasty fall."

"You look like you have internal bleeding!"

"I don't. I'll be fine. I just... I wanted to see you. I forgot you were spending time with this imbecile."

Ben squeezed my hand and I kissed his lips. They tasted salty. He grabbed my waist and kissed me so hard, we both nearly forgot Arnie was standing here until his cleared his throat.

"Are we going to get dinner or will I have to watch you two idiots fuck each other outside the library."

Ben pulled away from me and shrugged.

"You two get dinner. I've gotta run. I only wanted to see you."

He ran off and Arnie rolled his eyes stuffing his hands in his pockets.

"It's absolutely gross how smitten he is with you."

"Gross?!"

"Yes, gross."

"Haven't you ever been in love before?" I teased.

"I love fucking Eugenie."

"That's not exactly *love.*"

"She has a perfect arse though. That has to be something."

"No... It isn't. I think you act like this, but I think you know... I think you loved Hope."

Arnie grinned.

"Hope."

"I saw you talking to her at Halloween."

"Christ, woman. Do you have a GPS tracker in my bloody pocket?"

"No!" I answered defensively, "I only saw you two and wondered."

"You love gossip nearly as much as my idiot brother."

"Hey! He's not your idiot brother. He's a total marshmallow."

"I'm going to vomit..."

"Arnie, don't!"

"Fine. I asked Hope to get back together and she said no."

"What?!"

Arnie shrugged, "The hearing is in the past."

"Don't you think that's a little... disloyal? I mean she was with a bunch of girls who tried to shove a dildo up my —

I trailed off and Arnie didn't have trouble filling in the blanks himself.

"Yeah," he said, "I know. But I really don't want to go on the family ski trip. I need someone who's going to go somewhere warm. Like St. Tropez or Bali."

"This is just about getting out of your family ski trip?"

"My parents hate me."

"They don't like Ben much either," I muttered.

Arnie snickered.

"Their golden boy? You must be joking."

"I'm not. I've heard them saying awful things to him. He'd never complain about it. Certainly not to you."

"Hm."

"What?"

"I guess I'll have to go on the ski trip now. Out of the goodness of my heart. To protect my dear brother."

He staggered into me dramatically and I pushed him off.

"You are *so* annoying."

"Not any worse than you. By the way, do you think you can read my English essay over? My grammar's atrocious."

I agreed to read over Arnie's essay. I took his printed essay to choir practice. It was just me, rehearsing my solos for the winter show — only four weeks away at this point. Theo met me after choir at Ben's behest to walk me back to the dorms. We'd barely seen each other since Halloween.

We chatted about everything except him getting back together with Charlie until we got to the dorm room.

"I'm coming on the Fox ski trip, thought you might want to know," Theo said.

"Are you serious?"

"Charlie invited me."

"So you two are..."

"Reluctantly giving things another go. He's patched things up with his father. We think."

"They were awful to him."

"I know. But... it's Charlie. He has a way of weaseling himself in."

He dropped me off at the dorm and then he said, "By the way, I saw your mum on campus yesterday."

"What?!"

An Unexpected Phone Call

"She was lurking on the edge of campus. I don't know why."

My heart pounded in my chest again. What the hell was she doing? What did she even want?

"I figured you knew," Theo said.

"I didn't. She shouldn't be here. I think your sister has threatened to sue her multiple times."

"What could be important enough for her to risk that?"

"I wish I knew. Ben tried talking to her."

"Be safe. Have a good night."

I couldn't sleep thinking about my mom out there. Why wouldn't she just go away? I didn't get it. She might have fooled herself into thinking she cared about it once or twice, but at this point... I didn't want her around. It hurt too much. I'd given her chance after chance, and the truth was... I didn't need her.

In the morning, my phone rang.

"Hello?" I whispered, scurrying out of the room so I wouldn't wake Eugenie up. She had a late class, and I'd gotten dressed early.

"It's your Aunt Rita."

I knew that. I recognized the number. But I wasn't used to Aunt Rita calling to check in on me. I'd honestly forgotten about her. It's not like she was anything close to a parent, and her only concern seemed to be making sure I wasn't pregnant and making sure I didn't need money.

"Yeah. Isn't it like… 3 a.m. over there?"

"Yes. I stayed up to catch you before classes. How are you?"

I was instantly suspicious. People in my family didn't call to "catch up". Especially not Rita.

"I'm fine. Are you fine?"

She noticed the edge to my voice because she cleared her throat.

"Yes. Yes, I'm fine."

"Okay…"

I'd exited the dorm, and I was losing my patience with Rita quickly. If she had a reason for calling me, I wished she would get to the point before wasting any more of my time.

"I wanted to talk to you about your mother."

"What about her?"

"She says you aren't talking to her."

"I'm not."

"I have a few words for you. Mark 11:25."

Okay, just because I was in choir didn't mean I was churchy enough to understand what this cryptic Bible verse mention meant.

"Great. Thanks."

The pitch of my voice grew higher as I tried not to reveal the depths of my frustration.

"It's important to forgive those who have wronged us," Rita said, "That's one of Jesus' many lessons."

"Yup. He has many lessons."

I rolled my eyes. I noticed Ben and Arnie walking to breakfast together ahead of me — from behind it was harder to tell them apart. I'd much prefer hassling the twins than dealing with my annoying aunt on the phone. Did she really call me to quote Bible verses?

"Do you talk to your cousin?"

"Who?"

"My... um... my step-daughter."

"Um... no..."

I hardly thought Rita's step-daughter counted as my "cousin". I'd met the girl once. She was a sullen biracial girl. I guess my uncle had a type. I think Aunt Rita had four step kids.

"Well, she wants to go to University in England."

"Great!"

"Yes. But university is very expensive. And your uncle and I have so much to handle here. I got laid off last week."

"I'm sorry to hear that."

Where the hell was this conversation going? The impulse to let out a shriek and throw my phone into the grass grew stronger. Arnie and Ben noticed me and waited for me to catch up, which only increased my desire to fling my phone into the abyss.

"When are you coming back to America?"

No one in my family knew about the deal I'd made to get away with… well, murder. It was technically self-defense, I guess. But a deal was a deal, and I had no reason to go back. I didn't want to think of it either.

"Not for a while."

With my student visa, I didn't have to go back at all until I finished university, right when my "five-year ban" from my country ended.

"Your mother told us about your hearing. She mentioned that you are now a millionaire."

Oh. I should have seen this coming. Keri running her damned mouth and the people who treated me like dirt coming out of the woodwork to bug me. I'd caught up to Ben and Arnie. Before I could respond, Arnie yanked the phone out of my hand and said, "Hello? Liberty's busy. Try again later."

And he hung up. Ben laughed.

"What the hell, Arnie?! Have you lost your mind?"

"You looked uncomfortable."

"I was, but still! That was my aunt!"

"What did she want?" Arnie asked.

Ben had heard enough about my Aunt Rita to guess before I had.

"Money," Ben said, "Obviously."

He knew me too well. Arnie wrinkled his nose.

"Hasn't she got a job or a trust fund or something?"

"Normal people don't have trust funds," I snapped.

Arnie shrugged.

"They ought to."

"Barnaby," Ben said, "As an ally to the working class, I challenge that assertion."

I wanted to sink into the ground. Was this Ben's idea of getting woke? Where the hell had he heard about this working class mess.

"Can you two stop talking? I'm starving."

"And," Arnie reminded me, "You need to give me feedback on the essay."

We walked into the cafeteria together as I laid out my pointers for Arnie. I gasped when we entered the cafeteria. Hope, Millie, Amira and three of the rugby boys gathered around Daniella and they were throwing a mixture of scrambled eggs and milk at her in her uniform.

Ski Trip Plots

Ben tried to hold me back, but I yanked my arm away from him and marched over to the crowd surrounding Daniella. I guess I wasn't 100% done with being the good guy.

"Leave her alone!" I yelled.

Everyone jumped back. Arnie and Ben were on either side of me, which probably helped. Daniella whimpered and wiped milk off her uniform. Ew.

"Go back to your room and change," I snapped at her.

We'd already punished her enough. She didn't have to become the entire school's punching bag to learn one stupid lesson.

"Thanks," she answered sullenly before storming off. The surrounding crowd subsided. I could tell Ben and Arnie disagreed with me without bothering to look at them. We got breakfast and sat down.

"So," Arnie said, "Have you become a Christian?"

"What are you talking about?"

"Dumps," Ben said, "Since when do you care what happens to her?"

"I don't. I just… I don't think it's right."

Ben and Arnie exchanged glances again and shrugged.

"Do you have ski pants?" Ben asked.

"Jeans?"

"No, Libs. You can't ski in jeans."

"What do you ski in then? Leggings?"

"Good luck," Arnie muttered to him in a sing-song voice.

Ben showed me what he meant by ski pants on his phone. Right. I could easily allow myself to forget that I'd promised Ben to take part in the whitest activity I've ever heard of. I wondered what Marley would think. I mean, maybe race has nothing to do with it, but it's somehow very white to attach yourself to thin boards and fling your body down an icy hill at top speed.

I grimaced.

"If you hate skiing, we can hang out in the lodge. It's cozy."

Arnie rolled his eyes.

"You two disgust me."

Ben grinned mischievously.

"You could try not being a miserable prick. Maybe then you'd have a girlfriend."

"I don't need a girlfriend," he said, "I'm 100% fine, riding solo."

It was my turn to exchange glances with Ben. We didn't bother arguing with his brother. I couldn't stop thinking about Rita's call. Did my mother tell her I had money? Why did she bother coming to me? Rita… the same woman who wouldn't give me $500 when she had it thought I'd pay for some step-cousin's entire college tuition?

Maybe I should change my phone number…

After classes, I had choir practice.

Each day after that was uneventful, loads of hanging with Louisa, Isla and Eugenie, working on Physics, hot hookups with Ben, and the occasional hang out with Theo.

Ben's team won the rugby tournament, and he was super depressed about the last day of the season. Theo and I tried to cheer him up, but nothing worked. At least he spent a lot of time studying, which meant his grades would improve. Rugby would start up in the spring again for a brief season, but autumn rugby was way better and Ben knew this marked the end of an era. The end of our time together at Rapetti rushed toward us. If I thought about it too long, I'd get super sad. So I tried not to think about it.

By then, the Lessons & Carols winter concert was only three days away. I couldn't wait. Practicing so much tired me constantly, and I had to stay up late to study all the time. I cheered myself up by remembering that soon, I'd spend my time snuggled up next to Ben in a comfy ski lodge in Switzerland. I still couldn't pronounce Gstaad properly, and Ben stopped trying to teach me. I'd find a way around saying the name out loud.

Before I went to bed, Eugenie helped me order ski outfits and then she took my hands in hers and stared into my eyes before saying, seriously, "Please, pretty please Liberty, you need to get some cute lodge looks. Like… lingerie."

"Lingerie?!" I giggled.

"It'll be warm in there and cold out there. Trust me… you can seduce Ben with like… a see-through dress."

"Eugenie!"

"Try it! I found this website…"

We huddled in Eugenie's bed shopping for lingerie and she talked me into some scandalous outfits. What the hell would Ben think when he saw me in those? I was sure he still saw me as a total nerd. I mean, he was attracted to me, but I wasn't exactly the girlfriend who showed up dressed all sexy. It was too late for me to cancel the order and Eugenie talked me into it, so I'd have to be… sexy.

I went to bed way too late and in the morning I woke up to Arnie climbing in through my window. Without knocking. Eugenie had left for the morning and I threw my pillow at him as he stumbled in.

"Liberty!" he complained.

"Get. Out."

"Our Physics final is today."

"I know. I studied."

"So did I, but you need a power breakfast. Come. Now."

"Why the hell are you in here? If Ben knew he'd kick your ass."

"He's outside."

I groaned.

"I hate both of you," I mumbled, dragging my pillow over my head.

Arnie didn't care. He dragged me by the legs and ripped me out of bed.

"Arnie!" I screamed.

I tried to slap him across the face, but he grabbed my hand and stopped me.

"Get dressed."

"Get. Out!" I yelled, "I'll meet you two idiots outside."

"Three idiots. Theo's there too."

I groaned.

"I hate all of you," I mumbled.

I triple checked the lock on my window after pushing Arnie out and dressed in sweats. We could wear whatever we wanted for finals week — thankfully. Studying for Physics had been brutal, and I'd barely slept. My hair looked like a house for several small rodents, but I wrangled it into a puffy, unruly bun and threw my hood over my head.

"You look like shit," Arnie said.

Ben punched him hard.

"What! I'm being honest."

"Shut it, you idiot," Theo grumbled, "It's a power breakfast, not smack talk."

"Whatever," Arnie shrugged, "I'm going to get the highest grade in the class. So it doesn't matter what she does."

He was talking up a big game. Arnie got two Cs on some quizzes. He'd have to get 100% plus all the extra credit questions to bring his grades up and everyone knew Physics extra credit was impossible to get perfectly. He wasn't wrong about everything. I looked like shit. And I completely shot my voice from singing. I couldn't wait for finals to end and best of all, for the concert to end too.

The day after the concert, we'd leave on winter break, and I would finally be free of school stress. I could spend proper time with Ben and show off my sexy new clothes...

Life Lessons & Christmas Carols

"I look ridiculous in these choir robes," I lamented, "Couldn't we sing in something... I dunno... sexy!?"

Ben laughed.

"You look cute. Like a little... priest."

"Ew!"

"You'll do fine. Ready for your solo?"

"Unfortunately," I sighed, "Yes. I can't believe we're already here. The last day of proper school for the semester."

"Don't get all sentimental, Liberty. We're getting right on a jet to Switzerland tomorrow night, and there's plenty to celebrate."

"I don't even know what I'm getting you for Christmas yet. Leonora's making the accountant give me a lecture about holiday spending. I've barely spent $500."

Ben snickered.

"It's all standard. Don't worry. You get used to it."

"It's weird…"

Ben grabbed my shoulders and kissed me.

"Run along, my little mushroom. Arnie's saving me a seat in the pew."

"I can't imagine you two entering a church and not having the whole thing burst into flames."

"It's a chapel. Quite different. Plus… Arnie snuck in a flask."

"Ben!"

"You know better than anyone that the Foxes are better singers when we're drunk."

I couldn't argue with him about that. I gave Ben a hug, and he rushed off to grab his seat. I grabbed my music and walked to the chapel. The Christmas spirit buzzed everywhere. By this point back home, there would probably be snow on the ground. But it was only chilly here, and not unreasonably so. I clenched my fists as I approached the pulpit for my solo.

The chapel organ rang out, and I began singing. I thought performing would scare me more. I was nervous, but once I started, my singing came naturally to me. It was easy to find the next words, the next notes, the power in my voice. The meaning behind the lyrics. And it meant something to me to be the one who filled the school with Christmas spirit.

No eyes left me throughout the solo and when I rejoined the choir, a few people clapped which defied all church etiquette but flattered me plenty.

Caroling and Christmas lessons made me feel all warm like a cinnamon bun and after, Ben waited in his pew as the choir marched down the aisles and turned the corner to head to the back of the chapel where we returned our robes and hugged each other.

"That was beautiful, Libby."

"Yes. It was so lovely."

"Your voice is amazing!"

Ben stood in the doorway. He'd snuck into the back and no one had the heart to chase him off. He hugged me and kissed my forehead.

"Your voice," he whispered, "It's angelic."

Everyone giggled and cooed at Ben and I for our romantic display. I felt shy, but Ben didn't seem to mind. He slipped his hands into mine and nodded toward the exit.

"Celebratory dinner?"

I'd finished my finals. Ben still had one more.

"Are you sure? Shouldn't you study?"

"If I think I'll fail, I'll have Arnie take it for me."

"Ben!"

"Joking. Joking. I only had a few sips of booze so if we get dinner, that'll give me time to sober up and we can study together. How does that sound?"

"Fine. Is anyone else coming?"

"Theo, Charlie, and Arnie."

I groaned.

"Charlie was here?!"

"He wouldn't miss your concert."

"Only because he wants to mock me."

Ben snickered.

"Yeah. He fell asleep. Don't worry about that."

"He fell asleep in chapel!?"

"Typical."

He was right. This was typical Charlie. I was so distracted by Ben and excitement from the concert that I didn't notice her until we'd walked down the chapel stairs. She leaned against a lamppost with a baby carrier. I froze, and then Ben noticed her and stuffed his hands in his pockets.

"Maybe she hasn't seen us," I whispered.

Obviously, I was wrong. Keri approached.

"Liberty. Benjamin. That was a lovely concert, darling. You must get your singing voice from me."

"I got it from months of practice," I snapped.

I didn't have patience for her anymore.

"Here," she handed me the baby carrier, and because I couldn't exactly let the infant fall to the ground, I took it from her.

"What do you want?" Ben said, sternly.

"I'm going back to America. And you won't be hearing from me anymore. I've been trying to talk to you so I could say goodbye."

"You pulled a gun on me!" I hissed.

There were still Rapetti students milling past us, including choir members. I didn't want anyone overhearing this humiliating conversation with my mother. Or hearing the fact that she pulled a gun on me — embarrassing for several other reasons.

"I needed to talk to you. This child… you need to take care of her for a while."

"What?!" I yelled.

A faint gurgling came from the bundle of blankets I carried.

"No! You take her back."

"I'm sorry, Liberty. Goodbye now, okay?"

"What the hell is wrong with you?" I snapped.

My mother leaned forward and flashed metal from her trench coat pockets. She was armed. Again.

"What are you going to do? Shoot me while I'm carrying your child? Like I couldn't think any less of you."

"No," she said calmly, "I'll shoot him. And I won't miss. So you let me go."

"Take her back!" I snapped, pushing the baby into her chest. Keri stepped back and the baby nearly fell to the ground. She made no moves to catch the carrier, so I did. Barely. And the baby gurgled and started to cry.

Keri pulled the gun out, concealing it with her palms.

"Let me go," she whispered, "I need to go before I get myself in any more trouble."

"What about me?!" I screamed, "You embarrassing useless bitch!"

Now a few people turned to look at us. It was too dark for most of them to see Keri carrying a gun.

Ben snarled, "Go. Go, Keri. Because if you shoot me, I must do something about that. And I don't want the responsibility for taking someone else from Liberty."

He threw his arm over my shoulder. I was in shock. My fingers were growing cold against the handle of the baby carrier. My mother disappeared into the night, meandering calmly like she hadn't pulled a gun on her daughter. Again. Ben's arm wrapped over my shoulders. No. No, no, no. This couldn't be happening.

My mother didn't just dump a newborn baby on me.

"Ben," I inhaled sharply, "What the fuck just happened?"

Before he could answer, the baby started to cry. I hadn't even looked at her. Blankets covered the infant's face, and I thought I would pass out, except I was holding a freaking baby and unlike my mother, I couldn't let this child fall to the ground. Her child. My sister. This wasn't happening. This couldn't happen. My mother couldn't sink this low.

Ben took the carrier from my hands and peeled the blankets back.

"So," he murmured, "This is what she wanted."

"She can't do this to me," I whispered, "Hasn't she done enough?"

"Come, Libs," Ben said firmly, "We need to get you out of the snow."

I hadn't even noticed that it started to snow.

Turn the page to continue reading Book #5.
Click here to get a text when my next book comes out:
bit.ly/benandlibby5

BOOK #5

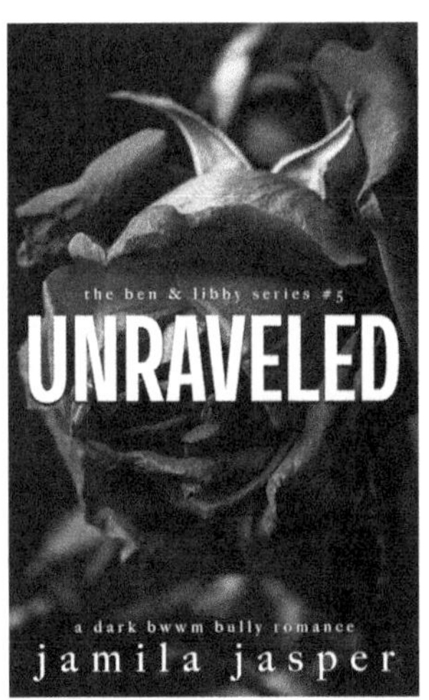

bit.ly/benandlibby5

UNRAVELED

jamila jasper

Description

An unwelcome Christmas miracle lands on Libby's lap.
Her estranged mother left her with a Christmas gift that cries... and needs new nappies every few hours.
Libby prepares to attend Oxford with Ben with a bouncing baby that was never part of her plan.
With her mother on the run and full custody of her new sibling, Libby's relationship may fall apart.
Benjamin Fox isn't about to let that happen.
He's worked hard to win this woman's heart...
He's not about to let her go...
Or to let her fail.

Jet To Switzerland

Charlie, Theo, and Barnaby were asleep on the jet. They accepted the fresh addition without protest, like they half expected one day Ben and I would show up with a mysterious biracial baby with no explanation. Ben held the bundle. I was in shock. There were no documents. No birth certificates. I didn't know the kid's freaking name.

A girl. A baby girl. Another baby girl for her mom to fuck up. Scratch that. Now her mom left the baby girl for me to fuck up. We didn't know what to do about my mom. What the hell could I do about her? She'd finally lost it.

Ben leaned over and touched the baby's nose, ignoring the gravity of the situation. "She must have a name. Maybe she can tell us?"

I wasn't sure if Ben was joking or if he really knew nothing about babies. I knew nothing about babies, either. But I knew this one was too young to talk.

"

"Are you joking?"

"Yes. Come along."

Ben carried the bundle onto the jet. I settled into my seat next to him. Theo and Charlie fell asleep intertwined before we took off. Barnaby flipped through a well-worn copy of Crime And Punishment. We didn't have any paperwork for the baby. Could we really enter Switzerland with a mystery baby and get away with it? What the hell would I do when this kid finally woke up. How the hell could my mom do this to me and why the hell was Ben so damn cool about it.

It's like he was ready to be a parent and he just... stepped in. Doing everything. This wasn't his problem. This was my problem. Kerri's problem.

"Your parents are going to think the baby's mine," I whispered with deep concern. Ben was cool, as usual.

"She's still asleep," Ben whispered, running his hand over my fleece-lined leggings, "Your mum didn't bother to leave us any clothes for her."

"She doesn't bother doing anything that could be remotely helpful," I hissed, surprised at the fury in my voice. I had a right to be mad. After everything, I at least reserved that right.

The bundle made an odd gurgling sound.

"What's her name?"

"I don't know! She didn't tell me..." I whispered.

My voice trembled. I wanted to act normal. But this wasn't fucking normal. I trailed off and when I found my voice again, I said definitively, "We need to find her and give this baby back to her."

Ben grinned.

"We'll at least spend Christmas with the girl."

"You say that like it's a good thing," I hissed.

Ben sighed.

"Relax. Your mum's gone mad — again — and now we have this baby. But... freaking out won't help anything."

Now he was Mister Calm. I couldn't do that. I couldn't be like that. Because this was fucking crazy. The flight was quick, only an hour and a half from Fenland Airstrip to Gstaad. Plenty of time to lose my mind, I thought. Ben couldn't have been more relaxed.

He leaned over, cooing and making all these sweet fluffy sounds which sounded dangerous coming from his bear-like body.

"We ought to name her," he said with his gruff, posh accent.

"Are you crazy?! She probably already has a name."

"We don't have a birth certificate. We don't have any proof."

"Here's our proof: my mom apparently has one goddamn purpose, and it's ruining my life."

"There are worse things that can happen than a baby."

Was this some kind of rich boy logic, where having a baby at nineteen wasn't the end of everything?

Instead of worrying about Oxford or studying for my A-levels, I'd have to change diapers.

Rapetti wouldn't allow you to attend with a baby. This was a private school — and an exclusive one. Rumors would spread.

They'd think I was some stupid stereotype. I had enough trouble with Rapetti bullies. This wouldn't make it better.

"I like the name Frederica," Ben said without a hint of irony.

I wrinkled my nose.

"She's not a British grandma. She's black."

Ben raised an eyebrow.

"What?" I snapped.

"I'm no expert... yet... but isn't it racist to say some names are black and some names aren't? I mean... we can't exactly name her Jasmine."

"Jasmine is your idea of a stereotypically black name?"

I tried not to laugh.

"I don't believe in stereotypes," Ben answered, leaning back and sounding far too cavalier.

The baby woke up. And Ben leaned forward.

"She doesn't smell, so we don't have to change her nappy. Maybe food. Can she milk those things?"

I stared at him blankly. Was he talking about...my boobs? Hadn't this boy ever taken a biology class? He was nineteen freaking years old.

"Are you joking?"

"Squeeze them," he insisted. "Like the nipples. Oh, God. That sounds sexual. Don't let the boys see."

"Ben. You can't just milk your boobs randomly."

"Oh. What if she latches on with her teeth or something?"

"She doesn't have teeth!"

Ben leaned forward and slipped the baby's mouth open. She stared at him with large cinnamon eyes. My throat tightened. I couldn't stand this. We didn't have any food.

"We have to feed her soon. She may start crying," he said solemnly.

"Warm milk," I said. "You must have milk on this jet... if for no other reason than to make White Russians."

I could count on the Fox family to keep a well-stocked bar.

"Isn't cow's milk going to give her diarrhea?"

I wrinkled my nose. Oh, God. We didn't even have a diaper. I'd have to fashion one out of a white t-shirt until we landed. Arnie groaned.

"Can you two shut it?!"

"What do we feed a baby?" Ben hissed.

"Milk, you idiot. But you need to warm it up and sterilize the bottles."

"What? How do you know that?"

"I nursed yaks in Mongolia for a month when I was fifteen."

"Wanker, she isn't a yak."

"Same difference." Arnie yawned sleepily.

My head hurt. Badly.

"Warm milk," I said, "We can handle that."

I mixed milk with warm water, which was the best I could do this far in the air. Why hadn't we been smart enough to get baby formula?! Oh yeah. We weren't fucking parents. This was my mom's idea of a birthday gift.

I fed the little girl with a tiny spoon, dripping it into her mouth as she gurgled and tilted her head in a confusion. It was messy. Very messy. And Ben was probably right about the pending diarrhea. As I fed her, he leaned over, backseat driving my airplane spoon and then blurted out, "Emma."

"What?"

"We could name her something traditional."

I pursed my lips. I'd rather not name my sister after a Jane Austen character. Ben was so... British the way he thought about names.

"I don't know," I whispered. "I wish my mom told us. Who does that? Who abandons a baby?"

Ben put his hands on my thighs again. He tried his best not to speak ill of my mother. He couldn't help himself sometimes. Kerri made it easy to speak ill of her. But he tried to understand that she was still my mom. And until recently, I'd hoped that we could be a family... an actual family... for the first time.

"What about... Missy?" I suggested.

"Short for Margaret?"

"Short for Missouri. But we'd never call her Missouri. Just Missy."

"That is so American."

Ben's voice dripped with disgust. I knew it wasn't on purpose. He was just tired.

"We're never going to decide," I groaned.

I'd finished feeding my sister, and she kept... staring. It made me feel guilty somehow. Like there was any part of me responsible for this mess.

"I'll think like an American then," I said proudly. "But not Missouri. A brand new name."

Ben sounded so insistent, like we were talking about naming our child and not the sister my mother dumped on us unceremoniously. I ought to stare out the window at the Alps, enjoying my youth, not naming my baby sister.

"Sophie," Ben whispered, "It means wise."

"It's pretty."

Ben failed in thinking like an American, but he'd thought of a name that didn't make me gag.

"We should change the spelling," I suggested.

Ben massaged his brow.

"No... we can't change the spelling."

"Fine. Sophie. It's cute."

"She is cute," Ben whispered, "And for now... she's ours."

There was something final about the way he'd said it that I didn't want to admit. I nestled close to him and I suddenly got the sense that Ben was acting like a father. I missed my own father. But maybe Sophie could have Ben, at least for now and at least while she was ours.

My heart flipped. Ours. There was no way we could handle this. We'd barely gotten back together. The last thing we needed was a baby.

The plane shuddered. Switzerland. I leaned over Ben and peered out the window at the Alps. Another winter holiday…

Now They Know About The Baby

One car took Arnie, Theo, and Charlie to the chalet. Ben and I had to buy baby supplies. We didn't have a clue what we were doing and by the time we got back to the car, Sophie was crying. A lot.

"I think she pooped," I said.

Ben nodded. "We're five minutes out from the chalet. We'll change her nappy there."

"Do you know how!?" I asked, panicked.

Ben grinned.

"I have cousins. Naturally."

"I'm sure I've done it," I muttered, but I honestly couldn't remember when. Maybe when Niecy was a baby. I tried not to think about when Niecy was a baby because that inevitably led to thinking about the fact that she never grew up.

We pulled up to the "chalet". I didn't know what I expected, but I didn't expect a massive wooden ski lodge with turrets and several floors. Enormous didn't begin to describe the place. Benjamin wrapped his jacket around his tall frame tighter. He scowled as the wind whipped his hair out of his face.

He shoved his hands into his pockets and offered to help with the baby carrier. I shook my head and pulled the little blanket over Sophie to protect her from the cold.

Sophie's diaper had crossed over from "maybe she did a poop" to "that shit stinks" and we hadn't greeted Ben's parents yet with the surprise. If they were even here.

Ben's family had always been notoriously cold-hearted. And if I was lucky, they'd live up to their reputation. I didn't look forward to the inevitable Emma Fox meltdown at the sight of a baby in her precious son's arms.

Arnie, Theo and Charlie weren't at the chalet, although there was evidence that they had been early, so maybe they'd given us a break and dragged Eva-Marie, Arthur Jr. and the parents out for a late dinner.

The staff at Blackmoor took care of King George when the family traveled to Switzerland, so I didn't have the dog's familiar howling or warm snout on my palm to look forward to. That dog probably knew the staff better than its owners. Two men dragged our suitcases away from us and exchanged glances when they saw the baby. I couldn't imagine how much they gossiped about the Fox family. There was always a lot to gossip about.

Ben laid down his diaper changing materials while I stood back, slightly terrified about the nastiness we'd uncover in Sophie's diaper.

"This is such a mood killer," I muttered.

I should have been showing off my sexy lingerie to Ben, not diving into a diaper full of baby caca. I didn't want to become a mother like this. I furrowed my nose as I stared at Sophie's diaper. I could handle thinking about university and school, but I'd never planned for a future.

I wanted to write a book or something, not spend the rest of my life raising a kid I never planned on.

"Not a mood killer," Ben said. "Fun. Ready for the surprise?"

"It's poop. Not exactly a great surprise."

"More enthusiasm, Liberty," Ben chastised with a wink.

He grinned and then we peeled back the diaper. The impact of the stench followed immediately.

"AHHHHHHH!"

Ben wrinkled his nose and gagged, dramatically stumbling backward. Sophie made a gurgling noise as Ben teared up and his cheeks turned a brilliant red. I held my nose and clutched my stomach to stop myself from throwing up everywhere.

"It's a bomb! She's a tiny cinnamon-colored *bomb!*" Ben choked out through gags.

"We're sure this isn't your dad's baby too, right?" I whispered. A cough nearly winded me as I doubled over after Ben's lead.

"Unlikely. I think your mother was pregnant long before she met my dad. Think about it. The timing."

Ben was right. No human alive could gestate that fast. Not even my crazy ass mother.

"She's done stranger things," I muttered.

"My guess is this is her mob connection. A mafia baby," Ben said bitterly. "She's certainly got a weapon of mass destruction in her nappy."

"Great. So this baby has two crazy ass parents. She's probably going to kill us in our sleep when she grows up…"

Ben smirked. "Dark mind, Liberty. I like it. But little Sophie couldn't hurt a fly."

I didn't bother pointing out that whatever she'd just released from her butt was about to kill us right now.

"This is seriously the worst smell I've ever experienced," I said, wishing I could wipe my eyes but terrified of cross contamination.

"Her butt is like a nuclear blaster," Ben muttered, "Baby wipe."

I handed him some wipes. We groaned and gagged throughout the entire process. When we had a clean nappy on Sophie, she gurgled enthusiastically and made other strange baby noises.

"Do we have to feed her again?" I whispered.

Ben groaned.

"We need a nanny so both of us can take a shower. I'm sure my nostrils are permanently singed with the fresh scent of baby shit."

"I'm sorry," I whispered.

Ben turned to me, seriously puzzled. "What?"

"This is my fault," I answered, my voice warbling.

Ben pressed his forehead to mine and his ruby lips to my nose.

"Don't say that, Liberty."

"It is," I said, my voice finally cracking. "Even if I'm not a charity case anymore, my life always fucks things up."

"That's not true," Ben insisted, grabbing my shoulders. "This isn't fucked."

"Yes, it is! We're supposed to have *sex!* We're supposed to get *drunk!* We aren't supposed to take care of some dumb baby!"

Ben stopped my lips with his and then whispered, "Shh... my sweet thing. We can still drink. We can still fuck. But we should definitely not have any part of this conversation in front of Sophie. She's not a dumb baby. She's innocent."

We both glanced over at her, arms and legs flailing as she lay on her back in the middle of the bed. He was right. She was innocent. No matter how I tried, I couldn't make myself blame her.

"She's beautiful," Ben whispered, "And she's a part of you. That means I love her already."

"I never wanted to be a mom this young. Look at my mom. She's the worst mother alive. I'm going to be like that! I'm going to screw this all up!"

I thrust my hands against Ben's chest, but I couldn't hit him hard. I just caved against Ben's broad muscles and allowed him to hold me for a moment. He was so strong and so much stronger than me. I didn't know how he could be so calm about all of this. I couldn't become like my mother.

"You won't," Ben insisted, grabbing my cheeks. "Liberty... you aren't like her. You're loving. You care about people. You're so smart that I get smarter just from hanging around you. You are an angel. You're my angel. And you won't be like your mum. I won't let you think so."

He grabbed my hips and kissed my forehead, and then my lips. And then we heard noises downstairs in the chalet. I froze. Barnaby. Yelling. And then his parents yelling after him. Ben picked Sophie off the bed and held her to his chest.

"So... shall we go distract them from Barnaby's latest crime with some trouble of our own?"

"They're going to hate me," I whispered, secretly thinking that there wasn't much of a chance Emma could hate me more than she already did.

"Shh," Ben murmured, "They won't. I won't let them."

We wandered downstairs together. Ben let a loud greeting boom throughout the house. His father stopped yelling at Barnaby, who grinned and flashed Ben a grateful thumbs up.

"What are you holding?" Arthur asked calmly, hands on his hips like he thought this entire situation was some kind of prank.

"Mum. Dad. Eva. Junior. Liberty and I have some news..."

"Dear God," Ben's mum whispered and then she stumbled backward and fainted or pretended to faint. Junior caught her. Eva shrieked.

"I'm an aunty!"

"No!" Ben snarled. "Can you let me finish?"

Ben handed the baby over to me. And then he explained. Dramatically. Ben's mother returned to consciousness. Charlie handed her a vodka soda. Which helped, at least in spirit.

When she'd heard enough, she stormed off. Ben seemed to think this was the best he could expect from her. Arthur patted Ben on the back.

"Good lad. Good lad. Stepping up," Arthur offered. "If you want this to go away… ask."

He wandered after their mother, and the siblings gathered around the piano with martinis. Ben and I took Sophie upstairs and took her to bed. Ben was the one who put her down and got her to sleep. He was a natural at all this stuff. For once, I felt… stupid.

"It's time to see our room now, isn't it?"

"What about Sophie?" I whispered. "Won't we have to feed her during the night?"

I didn't have a clue what she needed. Ben wrapped an arm around me and tried to comfort me. He knew I didn't want to disappoint her. She was ours — at least for now.

"After our shower, I'll get one of the staff to look after her," he whispered. "We have plenty of people trained in childcare and this is exactly why we have staff."

"Are you sure?"

Ben chuckled.

"The Fox staff practically raised me. She'll be fine. We need time to figure this out, anyway. Time *together*."

He pushed hair out of my face, and we kissed. I wrinkled my nose and pulled away.

"I can still smell baby poo," I whispered.

"Shower," Ben murmured, "I need to get *you* into the shower."

I took Ben by the hand and felt my way along the halls to our bedroom. I was too tired to appreciate how beautiful it was. As usual, Ben put every thought into the details he requested of the staff. We had a large canopy bed, a crackling fireplace, and an adorable hot chocolate station near the entrance to our en suite bathroom.

Ben slapped my bottom.

"Ben!"

"Get naked, Libs. I need you once before tomorrow."

"What's tomorrow?!"

"Your first day skiing," he murmured, "Now strip."

The Bunny Slopes

I didn't want to leave Sophie alone with the nanny until I met her. Our meeting went well and Ben's interrogation (and threats) were all taken well. She took Sophie right into her arms and held her close, like she really loved her. Warmth spread through me as I watched them together. I tried to tell myself that I could handle the separation.

"Only a few hours, okay?"

My palms sweat, even if the chalet was freezing. Something was very wrong with the entire concept of skiing. I couldn't fathom Marley, Rhonda, or anyone I knew back home, strapping wooden sticks to their feet and letting those stupid flimsy sticks rocket them down a mountain. The Alps were beautiful in the way I would have been content to admire from a distance.

Not Ben. Not the Fox family. They needed to get deep into the action. Ben's parents left for the Black Diamond slopes early. Charlie joined them — without Theo. They'd patched up their relationship for the time being, but after the enormous fight at Blackmoor, Theo didn't enjoy rubbing their relationship in the family's face. Eva-Marie put her arm around Theo and shook her head in disappointment, whipping her ski goggles around her other arm.

"They're such wankers."

"They're parents. It's their job to protect their young..." Theo said, desperate to be charitable.

"My father cheated on my mum," Eva balked. "He has no right to judge you and who you love."

Arthur Jr. didn't ski. He snowboarded. And that morning he nursed a hangover on the velvet couch. I carried my heavy skis alongside Ben. He tried to hold my hand, but I was already sweating in my outfit. We got to the ski lift, and I glanced up at the top of the mountain and the little cords that allegedly held the lift.

"We're supposed to sit on that all the way up the mountain?"

My voice came out like a squeak, an effect that I definitely didn't intend. Ben put his hand on my back.

"Don't worry."

Don't worry? Was that the best Ben could do? Against my better judgment, I sat on the lift and Ben sat next to me. The chair swayed and my stomach swayed with it. What the hell was I doing? Theo sat on Ben's other side. Eva-Marie waited for the next lift so she could sit next to a cute stranger. Before I could protest, the lift carried me too far off the ground. I squeezed my eyes shut.

Riding the lift already felt like an Olympic sport. Did Ben really expect me to fling my behind down the slopes after this? I squirmed uncomfortably and tried not to hold my breath. I could get through this white boyfriend experience alive if I just calmed down.

"Ready?" He murmured. "We're about to get off."

He took my hand, and I pressed my feet on the ground, my boots landing with a thud. Theo had his skis on already, and he slid ahead past the ropes. There wasn't an enormous crowd. A couple people spoke to each other in German and a few in French. Theo spoke French to a couple, and they let him go ahead. Before we could say goodbye, he slid ahead. He was so smooth. I felt like an awkward foal stumbling forward.

The Swiss skiers stared at us. I was the only black person there and by the time ten or fifteen people stopped to look at me, I realized how obvious it was. I looked at Ben like I wanted him to save me. Or like I wanted to kill him. I somehow wanted both. Ben helped me get my skis on and strapped his skis on.

"Ready?"

"NO!"

"Slide your feet. Come on..."

I drifted, and Ben waited for me, eagerly demonstrating. I gripped my ski poles for dear life as I imitated Ben's movements. Oh God. This was so embarrassing. I felt certain everyone there was staring at me. Did they think I was too awkward to be there? Or too black? None of them smiled. But Europeans never smiled like Americans did. Ben explained how to hold the poles. He didn't notice how awkward I felt. Or looked. I gave him one wild-eyed "save me" expression, and the corners of his lips tugged into a smile.

"You're doing great."

"I'm scared out of my mind!"

"We're on the bunny slopes. They're easy... I promise."

"I'm going to fall!" I squealed.

"Careful..."

He led me to the top of the slopes after a brief lesson. I still thought I'd die if he left my side.

"Want me to go first? That way I can catch you at the bottom."

"Yes," I exhaled.

I had no choice but to ski to the bottom. Despite the terror gripping my chest and my loose grasp on the quick ski lesson Ben gave me. I didn't have a choice. I stuck my poles in and propelled myself forward, bending my body to keep my knees from buckling inward and holding my poles behind me. I wobbled. And screamed. Loud.

I forgot the most important lesson. How to stop. And I was going fast. So fucking fast. I slammed into something solid and firm.

I'm dead, I thought, I'm fucking dead. But the firm surface wrapped its arms around me and kissed my forehead, and my skis clicked against Ben's.

"You're fine," he murmured. "You did it."

I exhaled loudly as his arms clamped around me protectively.

"I'm alive," I whispered. "I'm really alive."

"You did it. Now... we're going back to the top."

"Can I breathe for a sec?"

Ben chuckled and then bent down, rubbing his fingers over my lips and then giving me very warm kisses that made the wintry day ten times better.

Theo and Eva did a few runs on the bunny slopes together. Eva didn't care about getting better at skiing, and Theo only skied for the company. Ben kept adjusting my stance and encouraging me down the slope. He wasn't a poor teacher, but I was a horrible student. I learned fine, but I yelled at Ben the entire way.

When the sun crested high enough in the sky to leave a deep red sunburn on Theo's face, we traveled to the bottom and took our skis off to return to the chalet.

Arthur Jr. still slept on the couch, and he woke with a start when we all traipsed through the door. Charlie caught up with us on the walk home. Their parents went out for lunch with family friends they met on the slopes.

I needed a nap. And maybe a healthy dose of Xanax. Possibly an unhealthy dose. The chalet chef made a delicious coq au vin for our late lunch, along with port and dessert for later. We gathered around the kitchen counter as the chef handed out our places of lunch. Charlie and Theo sat close together, Eva sat between the two couples.

"I got his number, you know," she said, "The Frenchman. I'm going over to his place tonight. His parents have a hotel room."

Ben scoffed.

"You're dating a man who doesn't even own a place here? That's new for you."

"He's dashing and French. I don't care if he's rich or not," Eva said.

We all knew she cared if a man was rich. She probably just wanted a winter fling.

Charlie laughed.

"Yeah. Sure. I believe that."

"Shut up!"

Once we finished lunch, I raced upstairs to relieve the nanny. Sophie. I hated leaving her alone. The feeling didn't come all at once, but the more time I spent with Sophie, the more I bonded to her. She smiled when she saw me, like she recognized my face. Ben came upstairs behind me as I clutched Sophie to my chest.

"Libs. How is our little girl?"

"She survived a morning alone. I'm not sure I did."

"Adele's an exceptional nurse."

Adele smiled and bustled out of the room to allow us privacy. Ben took Sophie from me and she gurgled when she saw him.

"Mummy and daddy are home," Ben whispered.

"Stop it," I whispered back.

"Stop what?"

"We aren't her parents."

"I know that," Ben said, "But right now... we are."

"What if she comes back?"

"Hm?"

"Kerri."

I didn't want to call her my mom anymore. She didn't feel like a mother. She felt like a big fucking problem.

"I won't let her do that to you. Or to Sophie."

Ben stroked Sophie's head. He had this look in his eye. Like this made him happy. Like this was what he wanted. But I didn't want this responsibility. I wanted to be a normal teenager.

"Why don't we take her for a walk in the village this afternoon," Ben suggested.

"There's a village?"

Ben chuckled.

"Of course! We have someone new to buy Christmas presents for. Little Sophie."

He gave her his finger, and she grabbed onto it, smiling.

"Mafia Sophie," I whispered.

Ben kissed her forehead.

"Our Sophie."

"Christmas shopping then. Let's do it."

Baby's First Diamonds

I carried Sophie to the car while Ben carried her baby bag. We watched baby videos in the car as Rolf — their Swiss driver — drove us to the shopping street in the car.

"Do you think we need a baby monitor?" I asked after we got out of the car, "I don't remember ever having one of those..."

Ben shrugged.

"Dunno. I think that's what nannies are for."

We had similar ideas unless it came to nannies. Ben didn't see why we couldn't leave most of the work up to nannies.

"We had nannies, and we turned out great," he insisted stubbornly.

I kept my thoughts to myself about that comment. Carolers sang on the streets in German and French. It was cold, but snow fell everywhere, almost like they'd invented the place to have the right amount of Christmas cheer. The smell of warm cinnamon, eggnog and the sharp, chilly smell of snow filled the air. I could even smell peppermints.

"So… we shop for Sophie, and then we split up and shop for each other. Fair?"

"Totally," I answered, already distracted by a pair of Mr. and Mrs. Claus mimes who gave each other big kisses on the lips.

"We ought to get her something special. She's not even six months. Baby's first diamonds?"

"You want us to get diamonds for an infant?"

"Earrings, so she can't swallow them," Ben answered, like getting diamonds for a baby who could barely hold her head up made all the sense in the world.

"Aren't diamonds a little expensive for a baby?"

Ben shrugged.

"Is it too early for piano lessons?"

I was about to rip into him when I saw the smile spread across his face.

"Sure," I laughed. "A baby grand piano for a baby who can't walk. That makes sense."

"I heard Chanel has a new collection of cloth nappies."

"You realize what nappies are for, right? She's going to shit all over them whether we get them from Walmart or Chanel."

"Walmart?" Ben asked, like he'd never heard the word before.

"Never mind. Maybe not Chanel."

"Okay," Ben muttered, furrowing his brow, "I'd think better if I had a smoke."

"You quit! And you can't smoke around a baby, she'll get lung cancer."

"I won't. But… fuck. I need a cigarette."

"Focus, Ben!"

"What about that!"

He pointed toward a storefront with a name that I loosely translated to Teddy Bear Palace.

"It's adorable! They're so big and pink!"

Ben put his hand on my shoulder, "Let's go in."

We entered the store and a blond sales woman approached Ben and spoke to him in rapid German. He muttered something in stilted French, and she switched to French. Ben stumbled through a few more phrases, and she smirked as she let him speak before answering in English.

"Yes, for your wife and baby, we can find perfect teddy."

Ben turned red.

"Can we get any of them with diamonds?"

The woman raised her eyebrow and then leaned forward. "For you, Monsieur Fox, absolutely. I will call Bernard and you can pick up the bears tomorrow?"

"Thanks. You know my father?"

"Ah, yes. He is in Switzerland many many times a year."

Ben nodded, and we placed our order before heading out into the street.

"I didn't know your dad spent so much time in Switzerland."

"Neither did I," Ben answered, shrugging. "Let's get her more presents."

I assumed we'd get Sophie one or two gifts. She couldn't speak and I remembered little about being a baby, but I could — with a measure of certainty — feel assured Sophie wouldn't remember this. We ordered her three more stuffed animals from a different store before I caved and let Ben get her a pair of diamond earrings. He'd give them to her properly once she was older, but he insisted on putting them under the tree. I got her cute outfits, winter socks, a hat, a little reindeer costume for the inevitable Fox Christmas party.

This year, they'd have one in Switzerland and we'd all fly back to Scotland for boxing day and have another party then. I half-jokingly wondered whether we should get caffeine pills to survive the holiday season. Ben seemed eager. Rolf drove two cars full of presents back to the chalet so the nanny could wrap them. We changed Sophie at a changing station and fed her from her bottle, hoping we could spend a few more hours shopping, but Sophie had enough. She wailed, and Ben took her from me, cradling her to his chest. She enjoyed falling asleep against his chest better than mine. Maybe I reminded her of Kerri, I thought glumly. It was silly, but a part of me thought Sophie didn't like me as much because I reminded her of my mom.

Our mom.

"We ought to take her home," Ben whispered, once he got her to half-sleep against his chest. I nodded, and we called Rolf to get us home. We always had tomorrow to shop.

At home, Adele gladly took Sophie from us to put her to bed, allowing us a moment to step into the kitchen and wolf down some food. Ben poured me a massive glass of red wine.

"What's that for?"

"You look glum."

"I'm not."

"Don't lie to me, Liberty Jones," he murmured.

I relented, although I didn't want the wine.

"What if she doesn't like me?"

"Who?"

"Sophie."

"She's a baby. She likes milky tits and naps."

"In case you haven't noticed, I don't have milky tits. And please, never use that phrase again."

Ben borrowed a sip from my wine, and I had some after he did. Fine. Maybe I wanted the wine.

"She falls asleep more easily on your chest."

"You fall asleep easily on my chest. She knows who her daddy is."

"We aren't her parents, though," I whispered.

"Not yet."

"We snuck an illegal baby into Switzerland, fine. But that won't work forever. What about pre-school and kindergarten?"

"I'll talk to my dad. He sorts stuff like this all the time. Okay?"

"Fine."

"And Sophie doesn't hate you. She looks like you. Except in caramel."

"Ben!"

"Sorry, that's what they refer to as fetishization."

Ben could be so confusing. "What the hell are you talking about?"

"I'm learning about racial sensitivity," he answered with a cocky grin, 'borrowing' more of my wine.

He wrapped his arms around me from behind and inhaled deeply. I didn't have time to question where exactly he was learning this racial sensitivity from.

"Mm," he murmured, "You smell like snow."

I giggled and leaned into him.

"You smell like boy… and baby."

"Hm," Ben whispered, "I'd rather smell like you."

"I'd rather smell like soap."

Ben leaned forward and then I felt it, straining through his trousers, hard and urgent.

"Upstairs," he murmured.

Yeah, upstairs sounded nice. But kissing him down here was nicer. I raked my fingers through his long brown hair. It was always dark in the winter as his skin lost its rugby glow. I raked my fingers through his deep stubble and Ben groaned.

"You are warm," he whispered between kisses.

"So are you."

"I've got you, Jones," he whispered. "I won't let you down with her. I promise."

We kissed more, and Ben's hardness thrust more urgently from his trousers. He growled as he pressed his hips forward into me. "I need you upstairs. Now. I can't wait any longer."

Impatient In The Bedroom

Ben couldn't wait to get me to our room. Once we left Sophie, he pushed me up against the wall and kissed me. I allowed him to set the pace, first slowly pecking my lips and then roughly parting them with his lips and pressing his tongue into my mouth. His hands rushed to my hips, and he whispered, "Are you cold, Libs?"

I was. But I was getting warmer with his mouth on mine and with his lips fervently working mine apart. His hands squeezed my hips, and they ran over my waist, to my hips, and over my butt. I wanted him to do more. I ran my fingers over his cheeks and pressed my fingertips to a bit of hair that grew on his chin.

Ben smirked. His eyes were so green. And his hair had a couple blond streaks from skiing.

"Are you going to take my skiing again?" I whispered.

"How the hell are you thinking about skiing right now?"

I giggled, and Ben kissed my neck. I put my hands against him finally. He was warm. So warm. I raked my fingers through his hair and pushed my lips against mine. It's so much harder to heat large houses.

I grabbed onto his torso. I never wanted to stop touching him. I loved touching Ben's body. It helped that right after rugby season, his body was perfect. Every inch of him burned with fire. I pressed my hand beneath his shirt and squeezed my thighs together when I touched the first bulge of his abs. Ben let me touch him. He let me run my hands over each of his abs and touch the smooth sides of his torso.

"Come," he murmured, "I want you in bed."

His lips were dark berry pink from so much kissing. Ben snaked his fingers through mine. His index finger stroked my palm, and he pushed the bedroom door open. The housekeeper lit the fireplace for us earlier, so our bedroom was nice and toasty. Ben pressed me against the door, and my hands rushed beneath his shirt again. Warm, but then burning once I pressed against his abs. I slipped my hand down his pants and the enormous fleshy heat filled my hand. Ben groaned.

"Impatient, are we?" he murmured as I grasped his growing shaft.

I pressed one hand against his chest, pushing Ben away so he couldn't lunge for me and kiss me.

"I can be patient," I whispered.

Ben chuckled as I leaned forward and gave him the slightest teasing peck.

I ran my fingers down the length of his shaft until I got to the head and flicked my index finger over the tip. Ben bit down on his lower lip again and then grabbed my cheeks to kiss me. I kept my hands in his pants, playing with everything down there, getting him hard and working myself up.

He was hot. Always incredibly hot. And it was torture to wait for him.

"Clothes off," Ben murmured, pressing his lips into my neck. His straight nose tickled my neck. The tip of his nose was so cold it made me giggle when it touched my neck.

Ben helped with my sweater, running his tongue over my exposed collarbone once he worked the sweater off.

"Still cold?" He murmured.

He grabbed the small of my back and sucked the top of my breasts exposed through my bra, pulling my boobs out and running his tongue over my nipples. I moaned. Ben's tongue was the perfect temperature, and he sent waves of warmth surging through me. He led me into bed and worked my pants off so fast I couldn't tell how he did it. Ben hiked my legs up and kissed my stomach, trailing kisses to my panties.

He ran his hand over my underwear.

"Wet," he whispered, "So wet."

He peeled my panties off and spread my thighs open for his tongue. I let him push his tongue between my lips, sliding along the length and wrapping the flattened tongue around my soft pearl until I came. Loudly. Ben nibbled my outer lips and French kissed my pussy before slipping his tongue inside me again.

I moaned as his tongue went deeper inside me. Ben gripped my thighs and licked every inch of me until I was hot and dripping and climaxed so many times I lost track of how many times. How many times didn't matter. All that mattered to me was how good his tongue felt against my entrance and how badly I wanted that enormous trunk between his thighs, between mine.

I pulled Ben close to me and grabbed his cheeks, holding him in my hands as he worked his way out of his pants. Ben's thighs and ass were as firm as the rest of his body. I put my hand on his smooth pale butt and drew him in. Ben smiled at me as he pressed the tip of his head against my entrance.

"You'll never know how good it feels to be like this," Ben whispered. "You're dripping."

I never answered him. He pressed the head of it between my legs, and I moaned as he buried the length inside me. His first thrust was quick and urgent. We both needed this. We both wanted this. Ben pounded into me until I came and then rolled onto his back and I got on top. I moved my hips as we both moaned and came together.

Ben held me against him, naked, with his cock buried inside me until he rolled me on my side. He pulled my naked body under the blankets and drew me next to him. We both needed this — sweet release, the warmth of each other's bodies and togetherness. We hadn't had it in so long. We'd suddenly become parents, and we hardly talked about a plan. We didn't have one. And now we had sex. I didn't want to talk about a plan. I just wanted to be with Ben.

I could at least see Ben's side about one thing. I was glad we had nannies and the full Fox staff to help us. I didn't know how I'd survive this otherwise. Ben kissed my earlobe and murmured, "You're thinking so loud."

"I am not..."

"Go to sleep, Liberty. Tomorrow we'll hit the slopes again."

My phone must have been ringing as we fell asleep, but I didn't see the missed call until morning.

Accused of Theft

Ben and I hovered over the phone.

"I know it's her."

All my fears rushed into me at once. She was coming. I was sure of it, and I was sure that Sophie would disappear just like that. As my stomach twisted, Ben moved his torso around mine. He pulled hair away from my face and kissed my cheek reassuringly.

"It's an unknown number," Ben said reasonably. "You can't be sure."

"It's Kerri. She's going to come and take Sophie away from us."

Ben rested his palm on my shoulder.

"We won't let her, okay?"

"Why aren't you more scared?"

"We have nothing to fear."

"Speak for yourself! She gave Sophie to us like she was nothing. What if she sells her?"

Ben squeezed my shoulder.

"I promise. I won't let that happen. Trust me?"

"Yes."

"Now, let's have some time with Sophie so we can hit the slopes."

"I'm going to ski to my death today. I know it."

"You'll get better. Promise."

"It scares the crap out of me."

"And then makes you get all horny when we're home."

"Ben!"

He laughed and kissed my shoulder.

"Hurry. I need to see Sophie."

I followed him out of the room, and we picked Sophie up. I probably imagined the look of confusion on her face. Babies all look confused at that age. Ben couldn't wait to hold her, and we changed her and fed her until Adele came in to take over nanny duties so we could get ready for the slopes. Après-ski Ben had to go pick up the custom gifts in the village, and we'd finally get gifts for each other.

Kerri's phone call unnerved me. I was quiet through breakfast and Ben noticed, even if he didn't mention how quiet I was.

I still thought the ski lift was scary, but Ben held my hand on the way up. Eva-Marie and Charlie were too hungover to join us, so it was just Arthur Jr, who split off early to the Triple Black Diamond, and Theo joined us on the bunny slopes. I could hardly remember how to hold my poles, and I swore the mountain looked bigger this time.

"I'm going to die," I whispered.

Ben skied to the bottom of the slopes, but Theo stood behind me.

"Want me to push you?" Theo offered.

"Why would I want that!?"

"It's how I learned to swim. My dad pushed me off the yacht in Greece and… well, I learned eventually."

"That story isn't as heartwarming as you think," I muttered.

Theo grinned, and then I felt his large hand on my back and I screamed as I went sailing down the hill.

"I wasn't ready, you monster!!!"

I couldn't balance myself at first and I already predicted breaking both my legs and possibly my neck. Before I hit the bottom, I found my way, and I even turned my skis as I reached the bottom of the hill to avoid smacking into Ben and creating an entanglement of limbs.

I gasped and pulled off my goggles.

"I did it!"

Theo skied down the hill after me and laughed.

"Your scream!"

I pushed Theo, and he fell back into the snow. Ben threw a wad of snow at his head.

"Hands off my girlfriend next time."

Theo laughed and then sputtered as snow melted in his mouth.

"You two are both equally horrid!" Theo complained.

Ben stuck a hand out to help him up, and I grabbed his other hand.

"Push me again and I will kill you," I threatened.

We grabbed the lift back up and sailed down the mountain again, this time skiing side by side. Ben could make himself go faster than the two of us, but at least I wasn't completely convinced I'd die.

"She learns quick," Ben told Theo, and he nodded. I was happy to at least not make a damn fool of myself on the slopes. After Theo's nose turned red, we met up with Arthur Jr. and had potato leek soup and red wine at the lodge before returning to the chalet to change for shopping in the village.

Ben and I hurried to Sophie once we had normal warm clothes on. Adele tickled her tummy on her floor playpen and shook little mobiles over her. We took over, tickling and playing with Sophie, until she cried and demanded some sleep. Adele put her to bed and Rolf drove us to the village. I faced an impossible task here. Figuring out what the hell to get for Ben Fox. He still had my Christmas gift from last year. But I knew I could do even better than that.

Switzerland had some of the best chocolate in the world, but Ben hardly ate sweets. He wore little jewelry. Maybe cufflinks at formal events. And he liked clothes.

I walked into a men's bespoke clothing stores and a tall Swiss man cleared his throat dramatically before storming over to me.

"EXCUSEZ MOI!" he yelled.

"Hi, sorry I don't speak French."

He scowled.

"Were you stealing that sweater?"

I folded my arms, my mouth hanging open. Geez. Usually when people followed you around a store like being black made you instantly suspicious, they at least tried to hide it. I didn't even have Ben here as a crutch.

"Um, no. I was touching it because I want to buy a birthday gift for my boyfriend," I snapped.

Maybe Kerri's missed phone call put me on edge, but I wasn't in the mood for bullshit.

"Can you afford anything in this store, mademoiselle?"

"Actually, I can. How much is that sweater? In a large?"

"It is €800."

"Great. Do you have one in navy?"

"Oui."

"Do you have it in olive?"

Olive would go nicely with Ben's eyes. He looked amazing in green. I imagined lifting the sweater and touching his warm abs beneath them. Perfect.

"Oui."

"And what about neck ties?"

I ended up spending €4,000. Fuck. I felt stupid as the guy packed up the shopping bags, but I was on fire with anger. Sometimes, you have these moments in public and you let it go. Sometimes you think, "Oh, I got time today."

"Thanks," I said once he finished, "And it's pretty racist to assume someone can't afford something because they're black. I wasn't stealing anything. You knew that. You just wanted to make me feel unwelcome here."

He blanched, and his eyes widened.

"Mademoiselle," he replied stiffly, "That is not what I meant."

"I don't care what you meant. The point is, I could afford all of this."

I grabbed the bag and stormed out before waiting for a response. Well. Now that I had more gifts than I'd ever bought for someone in my life, I'd have to get a present that I didn't buy just to prove a point. I felt a little stupid, but someone has to tell those people off. No regrets. At least I wasn't at a restaurant where he could spit in my food.

I walked into another store with a weird French name that had glass ornaments in the window and froze. Oh, no… What the hell were they doing here? I tried to run out before they saw me, but I was too late.

* * *

A Fight In The Chalet

Millie grabbed Hope's arm, and they turned to sneer at me. Hope folded her arms as I waved and tried to walk past out of the store. Millie blocked me.

"Where are you going?"

"I'm in town for the holiday."

"She didn't ask that," Hope snapped.

"We asked where you were going," Millie added.

"Ben. I'm heading to see Ben."

"I'm sorry. Not like you care," Hope sneered.

Was that supposed to be an apology?

"The least you could say is apology accepted," Millie finished.

Since when were they that close?

Barnaby walked into the store. Where the hell had he been all day? He never came skiing with us, and I'd hardly seen him. He didn't get along with his parents, so I figured Barnaby lay low in some hidden wing of the enormous chalet.

"Liberty. Hope?"

Barnaby put his arm around my shoulder.

"Millie," he continued, recognition settling in, "How are you two holding up?"

He directed the question at the sisters. They all had goggles tans deeper than Ben's from hours on the slopes. I bet they'd been skiing since they were kids. Millie slunk away as Arnie asked his question, but Hope stood her ground. She wasn't afraid of Barnaby. His eyes sparkled with a well-rested luster as he waited for Hope's response.

"I was apologizing to Libby."

"It wasn't much of an apology."

Now that Arnie was here, I felt she wouldn't cause a scene. Ben could have mentioned that he vacationed in the same ski town as Hope and Millie, but maybe he didn't know.

"What do you want me to say? I tried to get them to chill. You got what you wanted, anyway. Everyone feels sorry for you."

"I didn't want that," I argued.

When would I learn to stop getting into stupid arguments with stupid people? I folded my arms and Arnie removed his arm from my shoulder to stuff his hands in his pockets.

"Careful, Hope. My brother may not be here, but I am. Liberty is like a sister to me."

Since when? I guess we'd been getting along. And we still waited for our results on class rank, so we weren't at each other's throats. I knew I hadn't lost my rank to Arnie, but the hope that he'd defeat me kept him away from sullen tantrums. Plus, we were lab partners.

I wanted to ask how the heck he found me.

"Whatever. If she doesn't want to hear sorry, that's not my problem."

Hope slunk away. She would have caused a scene if Arnie hadn't been there. I was sure of that now. I relaxed and Arnie elbowed me.

"What the hell are they doing here?"

"What are you doing here?"

"Ben sent me to find you. He didn't want to spoil his Christmas surprise."

"Is the car around?"

"Yup."

Arnie lifted the bags out of my hand without asking and tucked them into the trunk. Rolf took us to meet Ben for a mid-afternoon meal. Croissants, hot chocolate and red wine. Ben ordered everything before we got there and his twin brother sat next to him. They were looking more alike, but Arnie was still gaunt compared to his brother. They could pass as each other if they caught me by surprise or if I wasn't looking carefully enough.

Arnie didn't mention the encounter with Hope or Millie, so I figured he didn't want to bring it up and I could tell Ben later.

After we ate, I needed to finish shopping. Ben seemed suspicious.

"I hope you aren't going overboard."

"I don't know if I'm going overboard!"

How could I know? He was the one who knew what overboard was. I did not understand how much money I could get away with spending. From what I last heard from Leonora, everything in my account right now was mine. The accountants would let me know if I fucked everything up. It didn't sound like a perfect system, but I couldn't complain about having more money than I ever expected to see in my entire life.

Daddy would have wanted me to be grateful. And Niecy? She would have been so grown up by now. I would have been thinking about buying her a car or putting money away for her college expenses. So utterly responsible. Kerri would have probably bought herself a butt to rival Kim Kardashian's and a new car. I couldn't guess what else she'd spend her money on, but I could guess she wouldn't spend it on her kids.

I bought more Christmas gifts for Ben, with Arnie's unsolicited advice carrying me through the entire experience. His advice, although unsolicited, at least wasn't useless. He was genuinely trying to be useful, and I figured I ought to be grateful for that. Arnie could be worse. *So* much worse. He had been worse.

"So," Arnie said as we walked back to the car together, him carrying half my bags, "I'm looking for a new girlfriend."

I groaned.

"Tell me you aren't going back to Hope."

"I'm not," he answered, sounding wounded, "Do you think so low of me, Miss Jones."

"Eugenie was a nice girlfriend."

"You sound like my mother."

"Your mother knows about Eugenie?"

"No. She still isn't talking to me."

"Oh."

"It's my fault. I continue to pay for the sins of my past."

"Everyone's favorite sociopath," I muttered.

If Arnie heard me, he didn't acknowledge the comment. Ben waited up for us at the chalet and when we got back, he sat in the living room with Sophie on his lap. Rolf carried the Christmas gifts upstairs to one of the guest rooms so I could wrap them later. Eva-Marie sat at the piano, struggling through a riff on God Rest Ye Merry Gentlemen.

Charlie sat on the couch criticizing her while Arthur Junior leaned against another couch clutching a full bottle of whiskey. Ben's mum and dad sat on another sofa, staring in the fire, half paying attention to their children. Once I sat next to Ben and Arnie edged his way onto the piano seat next to Eva Marie, I noticed how somber they all were.

"It's not the same without her," Arthur Junior mumbled.

Everyone heard him, but they all pretended not to, except for their stiffened backs.

"It's impossible without her," Eva whispered, running her fingers across a scale and sighing wistfully.

Arabella. I wistfully held onto a lock of Ben's hair, but he didn't acknowledge any sadness publicly. He just bounced Sophie and let his lips relax into a gentle smile. It would have been a bigger one if he weren't thinking about his sister.

"Little Sophie..." he whispered, "We won't let you go..."

I yearned to hold her and soon got my wish. Ben handed her over to me and sprung for a bottle of Scotch from the kitchen.

Ben's mother spoke softly, "I hope you boys don't bring home disappointing grades from Rapetti, what, with all the trouble you normally get up to."

Ben bit his lip. His grades would be worse than Arnie's but better than he normally did. I thought that was worth celebrating, but then I remembered that the Fox parents could be cruelly critical.

"Liberty?" Arthur Fox demanded, "What about your grades?"

"They're excellent. Despite everything."

"Hm. Good. Right. Benjamin? Scotch for your father."

Ben poured his father a glass and handed it to him.

"Good lad."

"So. What do you plan on doing with a baby while you complete college?"

Mrs. Fox wanted to sound patient. I knew her well enough at this point to understand that. But she couldn't help sneering. I bit my lip. This was my fault. Kerri was my fault. And because of that, so was Sophie. And we hadn't thought about what we'd do with her. I hadn't.

"They won't let you have an infant in the dorms. Rapetti is not the sort of institution that encourages teenagers to become mothers. Or fathers."

"Leave it, darling," Mr. Fox murmured.

She sniffed.

"Leave it? My son now has the responsibility of a bastard when he ought to think about Oxford. I will not leave it. What am I supposed to tell my friends at the Christmas party? We can't bloody well tell them the truth."

"They could learn to mind their fucking business," Ben snapped.

Oh boy...

The piano stopped. Everyone stared at Ben. He had that cold and all too familiar expression on his face.

"I'm sick of it. And if you want to blame this on Liberty, you can all get fucked straight to hell. This isn't her fault, and she's handling it better than any of you lot would. So worry about champagne and the dinner menu, but leave my girlfriend out of this."

"You ought to speak to your mother with more respect," Arthur grumbled half-heartedly.

"Were you respecting her when you cheated on her?"

"Benji!" Eva-Marie gasped, "Relax!"

"I'll relax when everyone else does."

I squirmed uncomfortably. I always hated it when Ben went full-white-boy on his parents. Kerri had to push me to the brink before I talked to her like that.

"My apologies, Ben."

His mother rose and stomped to the kitchen.

"You've upset her," his father said gruffly.

"And?"

"You ought to respect your mother."

"I could say the same to you."

"Don't spoil a nice evening, Benji," Eva chided.

She ran her fingers over the ivories, and Arnie followed her lead, pressing his fingers into the black keys.

"We can play something together," Arnie suggested, "What do you think?"

"Can you still play?"

"Poorly," Arnie admitted, hunching over the piano next to his straight-backed sister.

They hammered out what was mostly noise on the keyboard until Charlie grumbled.

"Can you two shut up and play something that doesn't sound like cats fucking?"

"What do you know about cats fucking?" Eva snapped.

"We need more drinks."

I held Sophie as Ben poured another round of drinks and Eva obediently plucked out Joy to the World on the piano.

"This tastes right," she murmured, sipping the Scotch.

Ben put his arm around me and he smelled deliciously of Scotch. I wanted to bury myself in his warmth and simmer there. He kissed my cheek.

"We ought to put her to sleep."

Sophie stared at him wide-eyed. He leaned in and flicked her nose with his thumb. She made a gurgling sound and then kicked her legs out. I lifted her to take her upstairs and Ben followed. Once we set her in bed, we put on her lullaby mobile and called Adele in to monitor her as she fell asleep. Once we left her nursery, Ben sighed and took my hand.

"Sorry for the mess downstairs."

"It's fine. I get why your parents feel upset. I didn't plan on becoming a mother. And your mom has a point. What about after the holiday? We have one more semester left, but we can't exactly bring a kid on campus."

"No. We can't. And you can't handle this alone. You have to study for A levels."

"So do you!"

Ben snickered, "I'll get the same shitty grades whether I study or not. You're the one competing with Arnie for first."

"I'm winning."

"Good," Ben murmured, leaning forward to kiss my head, "Keep winning. I'll speak to my father. It's time we get Sophie's paperwork sorted."

"Sophie Jones."

"No," Ben said, "Sophie Fox. And it's about time you change your last name too."

"Legally?"

"Yes," Ben said, smiling finally, "But not only legally. We ought to get married. We're already promised. And I want to make sure nothing comes between us and that promise."

He kissed my hand.

"That's the whiskey talking," I teased.

He kept his lips fixed to my hand and shook his head.

"No," he murmured, "It isn't. I love you."

"What if I don't want to change my last name?"

"You don't?"

I bit my lower lip. Okay, I wanted to change my name for a long time. It was too easy for anyone in America (or England) to Google me and find out what happened to my dad and sister. It scared me to know how easy it was to find information about my life. Getting away from the media by coming to England helped, but I wanted freedom from all of it. I didn't have to go back to America with my tail tucked between my legs anymore. I'd won plenty of money and I had Ben.

I could... move on. I'd never stop thinking about my dad or Niecy. They'd always mean the world to me. But I didn't have to keep allowing my past to define me. I exhaled.

"Yes," I conceded, "I want to change it. Desperately."

"It's settled then. We're getting married."

I gasped.

"This was your proposal!?"

Ben turned a deep shade of red and mumbled, "Okay. You're right. That was definitely the whiskey talking. I meant to plan this way better but... if I'd made it a complete surprise, maybe you would have said no."

"I shouldn't complain," I mumbled, feeling suddenly conscious of how ungrateful I sounded.

I wanted to marry him, and Ben already gave me a pretty ring. It could be my engagement ring, even if I wore it all the time since we got back together and it wasn't new. The principle was the same.

Theo stumbled out into the hallway, yawning.

"Hey. You two. What are you up to?"

"We put Sophie to bed."

"Sophie..." Theo murmured, "I have an idea about that. Why don't you make her middle name, Theodora? After me."

Ben's lip curled in disgust.

"That is a *horrid* name."

"That was my great-gran's name, you twat."

Ben didn't seem embarrassed.

"It's not a bad name. Ben's drunk," I said, glaring at Ben. He could stand to be a little nicer to Theo.

"Where's Charlie?"

"On the couch. Drunk."

"Perfect. You two want to share a spliff? I've got some primo Swiss weed. I heard it's infused with chocolate."

We declined Theo's offer but followed him downstairs. I was giddy. Ben and I would get married. We'd do it. I didn't know when, but I knew that I wanted it to happen. And I almost couldn't believe that he wanted to marry me. I wanted to pinch myself. And then I wanted to celebrate. He didn't announce it when he went downstairs, so I said nothing. But I smiled to myself the rest of the night. I couldn't help it.

Soon, I'd be Mrs. Liberty Fox.

bit.ly/benandlibby5

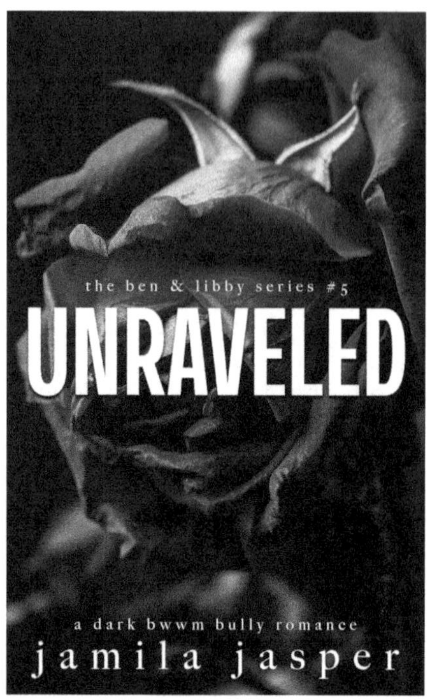
the ben & libby series #5
UNRAVELED
a dark bwwm bully romance
jamila jasper

Extremely Important Links

ALL BOOKS BY JAMILA JASPER
https://linktr.ee/JamilaJasper
SIGN UP FOR EMAIL UPDATES
Bit.ly/jamilajasperromance
SOCIAL MEDIA LINKS
https://www.jamilajasperromance.com/
GET MERCH
https://www.redbubble.com/people/jamilajasper/shop
GET FREEBIE (VIA TEXT)
https://slkt.io/qMk8
READ SERIAL (NEW CHAPTERS WEEKLY)
www.patreon.com/jamilajasper

JAMILA JASPER

Diverse Romance For Black Women

About Jamila Jasper

The hotter and darker the romance, the better.

That's the Jamila Jasper promise.

If you enjoy sizzling multicultural romance stories that dare to *go there* you'll enjoy any Jamila Jasper title you pick up.

Open-minded readers who appreciate **shamelessly sexy romance novels** featuring black women of all shapes and sizes paired with smokin' hot white men are welcome.

Sign up for her e-mail list here to receive one of these FREE hot stories, exclusive offers and an update of Jamila's publication schedule:
bit.ly/jamilajasperromance

Get text message updates on new books:
https://slkt.io/gxzM

Extremely Important Links

ALL BOOKS BY JAMILA JASPER

https://linktr.ee/JamilaJasper

SIGN UP FOR EMAIL UPDATES

Bit.ly/jamilajasperromance

SOCIAL MEDIA LINKS

https://www.jamilajasperromance.com/

GET MERCH

https://www.redbubble.com/people/jamilajasper/shop

GET FREEBIE (VIA TEXT)

https://slkt.io/qMk8

READ SERIAL (NEW CHAPTERS WEEKLY)

www.patreon.com/jamilajasper

JAMILA JASPER

Diverse Romance For Black Women

More Jamila Jasper Romance

Patreon

13 SEASONS OF SERIAL CHAPTERS

NEW preview chapters published WEEKLY on my Patreon.

Read all 6 seasons of *Unfuckable* (Ben & Libby's story)...

UNFUCKABLE

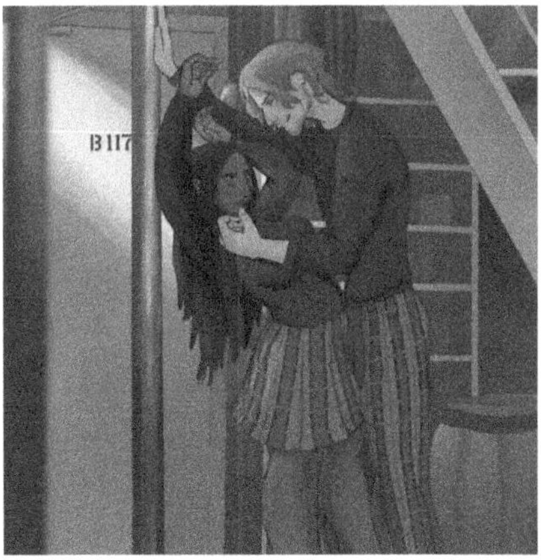

For a small monthly fee, you get exclusive access to over 375 chapters of my first completed bwwm dark and spicy serial romance, as well as the spin-off serial…

DESPICABLE

The second serial, despicable has 300 chapters available for all Patreon subscribers to access instantly and… we officially have a **third completed spin-off bwwm romance series.**

And yes you get access to all of this at the $5/month tier with more benefits at more pricey tiers.

The third serial is about Clover + Thomas. Thomas has a shocking connection to a character in the second serial and Clover is an all-new African American female lead.

POWERLESS

This series has three *very long* "seasons" of chapters, the length of five full-length novels all-together.

You will probably have over three months of binge-reading before catching up to current content, making this one of the most 'bang for your buck' author Patreon subscriptions out there.

Don't take my word for it.
Check the post history:
www.patreon.com/jamilajasper

PATREON HAS MORE THAN THE ONGOING SERIAL...

INSTANT ACCESS

- NEW merchandise tiers with **t-shirts, totes, mugs,** stickers and MORE!
- **FREE paperback** with all new tiers

- <u>**FREE short story audiobooks**</u> and audiobook samples when they're ready
- #FirstDraftLeaks of Prologues and first chapters **weeks** before I hit publish
- Behind the scenes notes
- Polls and story contribution
- Comments & LIVELY community discussion with likeminded interracial romance readers.

LEARN MORE ABOUT SUPPORTING A DIVERSE ROMANCE AUTHOR

www.patreon.com/jamilajasper

Thank You Kindly

Thank you to all my readers, new and old for your support with this new year.

I look forward to making 2023 an INCREDIBLE year for interracial romance novels. I want to thank you all for joining along on the journey.

www.patreon.com/jamilajasper

Thank you to my most supportive readers — my Patreon subscribers!:

Jessica G.

Danielle

Yola

Joslin

Alexciz

Stacia

Ayanna

Asia

Hailey

Kaya

Nikki

Naomi O.

Jessica J

Chakiya

Noelle

kourtnee

Martha

Nikki Valentina

xjkpop

Valeria

BlkBae

SweetS

Msteeq

Rhonda

Darrah

Killa

Shavon

Misty

India

Kassandra

Imani

Nala

Chantell

Benvinda

Roger

Lexi B

Zapphire

Vbrooks

Tasha G

Kiera

Valencia

Stacy

YANITZA

Texansgurl76

Emma

Tinette

Jenny

Mariah

Nale

Tanisha

Trenita

Shelle

dulcemaria413

Shanice

Letarsha

Tania

Neeka

Julia

Linda

Lisa

Jiannie

Jillian

Tameka

Asia

Scarlette

Olwyn

R W

Fayefaefee

Brianna

Tiffany

Katie

Diamond

Kera

Tia

Love Reading

Dominique

Sheria

Jennifer

Georgette

Monique

Wendolyn

King Turtle22

Jessica

Nic M.

JustChill

DJC

Atira

TheeLastHokage

Yvonne

Chrissy

Janelle

Rian

LaRonda

LaRonda

Deanna

dlawson382

Jasmine

Haley

Belinda

Sercee

Yvonne

Jadelock

Farah

Tamiya

Quin

J.Payton

Geek Girl

Ashley

Rubi

Pilar

Sandra

Jurnee

Anni

Shannet

Joneesa

GlitzyHydra

Amanda

Barbara

Brianna

Jamica

Lyons

MARY ANN

Marketia

SarahD

LoverofHawaiiHearts

ceblue

Yolanda

MonaGirl Lewis

Dianna

Mary

amna

Nysha

fayola

Ty

Abria

Shyra

Andi-Mariee

Jamila

Naee's World

KEISHA

Jennett

Fredericka

Candece

Chante

Pholuv

Lydia A

Sabrina

JM

Jackie

Mo

Natrilly83

Ashaunte

Tolu

Margaret

Wendolyn

Lori

Dionne

ZLB

Kristina

Nicol

ELBERT

A. Harris

Jesi

Brenda

Desiree

Angela

Frances

LaShan

Only1ToniD

Debbie T.

Tiffanie

April L

shawnte

Kay

Lisema

Yvonne F

Natasha

Colleen

Julia

Amy

Jacklyn

Shyan R

Kiana B

Pearl

Javonda

Sheron

Maxine

Dash

Alicia

margaret

Love2Read

Juliette

Monica

Sandhya

MaryC

Trinity

Brittany

June

Ashleigh

Nene

Nene

Deborah

Nikki M

Dee

TyKira

Kimmey

Laytoya

Shel W

Arlene

Judith

Mary

Shanida

Rachel

Damzel

Ahnjala

Kenya

momo

BJ

Akeshia

Melissa

Tiffany

sherbear

Nini J

Curtresa

REGGIE A.

Ashley

Mia

Tink138110

Phia

Sharon

Charlotte

Assiatu C

Regina

Romanda

Catherine

Gaynor

BF

Perpetua

Tasha G

Henri Ann

sara

skkent

Rosalyn

Danielle

Deborah J

Kirsten

ANA

Taylor R.

Charlene

Louanna

Michelle

Tamika

Lauren

RoHyde

Natasha

Shekynah

Cassie

AnnaBooms

Keitheena

Nick R

Gennifer M

Rayna

Anton

Jaleda

Kimvodkna

JaTonn

Jazmine

Anoushka

Raynischa

Audrey

Valeria

Courtney

Donna

Patrisha

Jenetha

LaKisha J.

Ayana

Taylor

Christy

Monica

FreyaJo

GRACE

Kisha

Christine

Alexandra

Amber

Natasha

Stephanie

LaKisha

kristylove7

Cynthea

DENICE

Latoya

monifacd .

Doneishia

Mariah

Gerry

Yolanda T

Yolanda P

Susan D

Phyllis H

Alisa K

Daveena K

Desiree S

Kimberly B

Robin B

Gary S

Stephanie MG

Georgette A

Kathy

Marty

JanetDaniels

Megan

Shelle

Delores

Janet

Lydia

Phyllis

Freda

Charlott R

Join the Patreon Community.